A NOVEL

Violet and the Veterox

The Veterox

A. Crouch

ROSAVELLE PRESS/ COLORADO SPRINGS

A. Crouch/Rosavelle Press
Colorado Springs, Colorado
www.rosavellepress.com

Publisher's Note: This is a work of fiction. Names, characters, places, and incidents are a product of the author's imagination. Locales and public names are sometimes used for atmospheric purposes. Any resemblance to actual people, living or dead, or to businesses, companies, events, institutions, or locales is completely coincidental.

Cover Design by Gail Dishman
Book Layout © 2014 BookDesignTemplates.com

Violet and the Veterox/ A. Crouch -- 1st ed.
ISBN 978-0-9904067-0-9
Library of Congress Control Number: 2014915061
(Rosavelle Press) (Colorado Springs, Colorado)

Be Kind. Rewind. Repeat.

Happiness. Give a lot and expect nothing. Many people have done that for me, and I'm endlessly grateful. My husband, my three girls, my mother and her husband, my sister, my grandma Ellen, my good friend Gail, Pat and Tom, my dad and Deanna, and countless other family, friends, and random strangers. I know how lucky I am, and I'm thankful more than words can convey.

Contents

Prologue 1

One 3

Two 9

Three 17

Four 27

Five..31

Six 43

Seven 51

Eight...69

Nine...103

Ten 111

Eleven..119

Twelve..125

Thirteen 135

Fourteen 141

Fifteen 145

Sixteen...149

Seventeen 173

Eighteen 189

Nineteen 205

Twenty 231

Twenty-one 249

Twenty-two 259

{P}

Prologue

My mother looked beautiful. The bright red dress she wore draped gracefully over her body, highlighting her pale white skin, dark chestnut-colored hair, and deep sapphire-blue eyes. Some have said the resemblance between my mom and me is irrefutable. Normally I wouldn't agree, but looking at this particular photograph, I couldn't deny we did look similar. I'd certainly inherited her almost-translucent pale skin and dark blue eyes.

Next to my mother, Violet, stood a man in a dark gray suit and black tie. His name was Ethan Crailene. He smiled brightly, and his eyes, a shade of cobalt blue, seemed to sparkle as he posed for a picture with my mother. They leaned in toward each other, just as one might expect from two friends. The camera captured the excitement present in the room. People in the background, dressed in similarly exquisite gowns and suits, smiled cheerfully.

Twenty seconds after the picture was taken, one of them no longer existed. A bomb exploded. The tables close by, ornately decorated with white-and-yellow dishes, were thrust in every direction. The

1

crystal wineglasses, broken into pieces by the blast, became shrapnel, and one piece lodged itself into my mother's head. By the time my father reached her, it was too late. Knowing her time was coming to an end, she spoke her final words. "Please tell everyone I love them." Polite to the very end.

My own world was about to combust just as spectacularly. The walls around me would fracture into tiny fragments and it would feel as if a few pieces had become imbedded in my brain. Unlike my mother, I would survive, but the currency exchanged for my life would be in blood, and it would require far more than existed in my body.

{1}

One

I didn't have many years with my mother. She was a Neonatologist and Perinatologist at a large hospital in Chicago. Her job was to care for babies and pregnant women, those in the most critical condition. From what I did remember of her and what my father had told me, she was a very kind and gentle person. On rare occasions she was known to be fiery and passionate. Her personality sat in juxtaposition to my own. I was passionate, and I was kind, but I wasn't known for being gentle.

Her busy schedule didn't allow for much time with me, but I did remember her calm voice and the methodical way she brushed my long brown hair after baths. On the nights that she could make it home from the hospital, she would read me a bedtime story. As time passed by, it became harder and harder for me to recall memories of her. It felt as if a little piece of her slipped away each year.

The man in the picture, Dr. Ethan Crailene, and my mom were good friends. They met back in college while studying for biomedical degrees. Their friendship continued through the course of medical

3

school, but once they selected specialties to pursue, the path for them parted ways. Dr. Crailene went into epidemiology and neuroscience, the study of viruses and the brain, while my mom wandered into the neonatology and perinatology fields. They wouldn't meet up again until the plague was in full swing.

My father, Xander, met my mother while they were both volunteering at a free clinic in Chicago, Illinois. My dad was a high school science teacher, but he had always had a passion for medicine. If he could've chosen a career all over again, I was sure that he would have become a doctor. In a fateful twist, both my parents ended up at the same clinic.

My mom was fond of helping those with the most need, which usually meant the people who were on the lower economic end. Thus, although she had crazy hours at the children's hospital in Chicago, she made an effort to spend a few hours every day volunteering. My dad, who was volunteering as a medical assistant at the time, claims he fell for her almost immediately.

He told the story like only a few days had passed. "Your mom would walk into the clinic after a long shift at the hospital, still dressed impeccably, often in a black pencil skirt and a white button-down blouse. Her long, dark hair was normally curled and styled neatly. On certain days, her hair would be messily thrown up into a ponytail, which was usually the only giveaway that she'd had a stressful day. But even on those days, she would patiently and happily go from room to room, taking ample time with each person she was seeing.

"I knew after a few weeks that I wanted her. I spent the next six months trying to get a date with her, and, somehow, I did. I guess she liked my quirky sense of humor and charming good looks, because six months later, she married me."

4

The euphoria was cut short. Not because my parents weren't crazy about each other, but because something life changing was about to happen—the plague.

In the past few days, I had become keenly aware of the many aspects of the plague. My history class required me to write a lengthy paper on the topic, and I had absorbed as much information as I possibly could in the short amount of time given. I was confident that I knew the science behind the virus. The story had already begun to roll out of my brain in perfect order:

The virus that would become responsible for the global pandemic was a rare type of influenza called Z3C7. Retrospect told us that the virus had probably been in existence for a long time. It circulated silently among chickens and other bird populations for several years before it was discovered. There were no outward signs that Z3C7 was attacking the animals' immune systems. Bubbling under the surface, it was about to explode.

The first cases of Z3C7 were reported in a rural area of China sometime in early April of that year. Patient zero, a twenty-year-old female, had recently been working in the poultry markets. Her symptoms were terrifying and eerily similar to another famous pandemic.

In 1918, the Spanish flu killed fifty to a hundred million people worldwide and was known for being a quick and brutal killer. Back in China, patient zero became ill with a high fever, cough, bone-shaking chills, and shortness of breath. It rapidly progressed to pneumonia. In what ended up being a hallmark of the virus, her lips turned blue. When her blood was so overrun with infection, her organs shut down, ending her life.

Soon several more cases popped up with a similar result—death. Z3C7 was killing at an astonishing rate of 60 percent or six out of every ten people. If there was a silver lining to the virus, it was that it hadn't yet successfully jumped from human to human. It couldn't spread beyond those in direct contact with the infected chickens.

Many viruses have the ability to pass via animals. They are termed zoonotic diseases and were, and continue to be, fairly common. West Nile, rabies, and viral hemorrhagic fevers like Ebola are all good examples. However, most viruses have a hard time making the necessary mutations to become easily transmissible person-to-person. It's a tough jump that usually takes decades.

Leading experts at the World Health Organization were confident that if the virus was able to mutate and spread person-to-person, it was years and years away from doing so.

Despite the assertions of the World Health Organization, Dr. Ethan Crailene was hesitant to trust this opinion. As a leading epidemiologist, he understood the novelty of the virus and how severe of a problem it had the potential to become.

With normal strains of influenza, like the seasonal flu, a vaccine can be created. A vaccine works by creating an immune response in the body so that when one comes down with the actual virus, the body already recognizes the virus and understands how to respond.

Imagine trying to put out a fire. If you'd been educated in firefighting, you would know the technique to quickly and efficiently put out the flames. If you weren't trained in firefighting, you might try several ways to extinguish the fire, because you wouldn't know what to do. You'd scramble. That's how your body reacts when it contracts a new virus. A vaccine renders you the fire fighter.

Since Z3C7 was unique, no vaccine had ever been developed for that specific strain. Many expert epidemiologists weren't even confident that a vaccine of the conventional type would work against it.

Most troubling was the way the human immune system seemed to respond to the virus.

The virus wasn't just affecting the elderly or small children, like most strains of influenza did. Similar to the Spanish flu of 1918, the virus viciously attacked young, healthy, and robust immune systems.

Instead of mounting a normal immune response, Z3C7 caused the body to overreact. One of two things occurred. Either the patient would die from a cytokine storm, essentially causing the person to drown from a severe fluid buildup in the lungs, or they would succumb to bacterial pneumonia and sepsis, an infection that swiftly doomed the victim to death.

Hindsight, as always, is twenty-twenty. The virus should have been taken more seriously, but at a time when the world was in the middle of a financial crises and amidst false proclamations of other "pandemic" viruses in the years prior, there was little support to fund a multimillion-dollar endeavor to protect the population from a threat that was not yet even viable.

Later, Dr. Crailene would go on to say that he, "just felt that something wasn't right, and he couldn't seem to push that feeling away." Whether it was luck or an actual premonition of sorts, he would turn out to be right in the worst possible way. He began working on what would become an all-consuming passion to create a vaccine. He had an idea, albeit a nonconventional one, and it would work.

I stopped typing and glanced at the clock. It was two thirty in the morning, and I was tired. I knew I shouldn't have procrastinated so long. I'd known about the assignment in my world-history class for months. Truthfully, I was very good at "winging it" as they say. The rush of pressure enthralled me. I was good in tight situations, and knowing that always pushed me to wait until the last possible moment to finish things. That was essentially the reason I'd delayed writing the paper. Prior to the research I'd done in the past few days, I hadn't even had much interest in Z3C7. I now found myself fully engrossed in the story.

{2}

Two

"Wake up, it's me, Big Bird, and it's time to get up. Open your little eyes now; don't roll over and go back to sleep. Come on now...one foot out of bed and now the other. OK, have a nice day, and don't forget to wind the clock."

It was already 10:07 a.m. My circa 1969 Big Bird alarm clock never failed me. Even in my grumpiest of moods, I couldn't help but laugh or at least smile when I heard it. I knew it was a little strange that a twenty-year-old still used a Big Bird alarm clock. I thought it was even stranger to use a normal alarm clock that loudly and obnoxiously beeped, abruptly waking one up.

I slipped my feet out from under the covers and onto the dark, smooth wood floors. The light was slowly peeking around the curtains. I said softly, "Open," and the curtains slid apart, letting in the beautiful spring sunshine.

We lived in a gorgeous, old house in the heart of Lincoln, Nebraska. Nicknamed "The Twenties," it was an impeccable example of the Roaring Twenties' architecture. The house, with its iconic gray stone pillars and orange tile roof, was set in the middle of a sprawling green lawn sprinkled with oak trees.

The house had been modernized, mostly by my dad. Naturally, being a science teacher, he had an interest, or rather passion, for technology. The voice-commanded curtains were only the tip of the iceberg in this house. Admittedly though, I had grown fond of the curtains, despite how outrageous they were.

All five bedrooms were painted in a range of colors, representing the wide range of personalities in our family. Mine was a bold cherry red.

I had vague memories of living in Chicago, but I was only five years old when we had to uproot ourselves and leave in the wake of my mom's death. The main difference between Chicago and Lincoln was the decrease in population and buildings. Chicago had many tall skyscrapers; Lincoln had but a few.

In Nebraska, the land was so flat that you could see for miles and miles. The sunsets were breathtaking and full of color. Pink and yellow and orange contrasted starkly against the brilliant blue sky and white puffy clouds. It was hard to beat the feeling of openness and freedom that the prairie sky amplified.

I assumed that my mom had a pretty substantial life-insurance policy, because we'd never been poor. I highly doubted the salary of a science teacher afforded voice-activated curtains.

I quickly stepped into the shower and was back out in five minutes. I walked to my closet and chose an emerald-green strapless dress, a white cardigan, and a pair of matching white high heels. Luckily, it was Sunday, because by the time I finished pulling my hair up and did my makeup, it was ten thirty—well past the time I normally had to be at school.

I wandered through the hallway and down the two flights of stairs.

I had the pleasure of living on the third floor of the house. Unfortunately, elevators weren't in the budget.

I could hear Isaac and Rosa bantering in the kitchen. As usual, they were "discussing" what would be on the menu for lunch. Isaac had a penchant for the more nutritious meal choices. He'd choose a bowl of vegetables over a hamburger any day. Rosa was obsessed with gourmet cooking. You could see where the conflict arose. One would think that twins might be a bit more alike. The many years that they'd spent apart were evident in their opposite personalities and viewpoints.

Today Rosa was wearing a white pencil skirt and a beautiful yellow blouse that really brought out the pale-blue color of her eyes. A small black belt was cinched at her waist. The red lipstick she always wore was impeccably applied. Her light blond hair was messily pulled back and pinned in a 1950s-ish style.

With Isaac, it was pretty easy to predict what he would be wearing. A dark gray suit, a white or navy-blue collared shirt, and a slim navy-blue or orange tie. On this day, he'd went with a white shirt and navy tie. His dark brown hair was styled so that it stood up a bit in the front, but, as usual, it was his eyes that took center stage. They were a vibrant shade of emerald green. I'd always found him very attractive.

The truth be told, I had a little bit of a crush on Isaac. I knew that it sounded juvenile and immature, a sentiment that I normally went out of my way to avoid. Still, I couldn't deny the attraction. I was pulled to him. It probably also sounded absurdly incestuous as well, but I had never thought of Isaac as a sibling.

Both Rosa and Isaac were adopted after the plague ended. Their parents died during the pandemic just a few weeks after they were born. I couldn't recall any memories of the years Isaac lived with us, as I was barely five when he left to go live with a relative. He didn't return until I was seventeen and he was twenty-two. Nearly four years later, we were still trying to figure out how to maneuver around each other.

Isaac was reserved, calm, and a little bit mischievous. I had always envied him for being the rule breaker that I was not. He had a cunning ability to speak the truth while at the same time stunning you with his charisma. It cut the sting of his honesty well. We were friends, or rather friendly, but he had always tried to keep me at arm's length. I knew that it was an intentional action, because, despite a great effort, his eyes always seemed to convey his thoughts much better than his mouth. Maybe the mystery was what kept me intrigued.

Rosa, on the other hand, I considered my sister and one of my best friends. She was thoughtful, patient, and unabashedly kind. She spoke carefully and with great thought. It was a bit like she was an eighty-year-old in a twenty-six-year-old's body. I loved the way she brought perspective to any situation.

Many times Rosa acted like a surrogate parent—a strict one. In my entire career as a student, I was only allowed to stay home due to illness a handful of times. My dad took her opinion as truth. If Rosa said that I wasn't sick, he believed her. It was undoubtedly annoying, but I could see the great service she'd done by not letting me get away with the things other kids did. I likely owed my mathematical ability to her strict authoritarian style.

I descended the final few steps and finally reached the kitchen.

"Hey, you two, what's for lunch?" I asked, smiling.

"Good morning, Evangeline," Rosa said, obviously ignoring my question.

"I think that's still up for debate," Isaac said, flashing a smile. "Evie, how is your paper coming along? I noticed the lights in your room were still on when I went downstairs to grab a glass of water at one o'clock. Waiting until the last minute again, are you?" he said, knowing that it would be a subject of contention between Rosa and me.

Only Isaac called me Evie. I didn't make up the nickname. Most people called me Evangeline. One day, out of the blue, he started calling me Evie. It annoyed me at first, which was probably what he was intending to do. I just let it go, thinking maybe he would forget about it. Unfortunately, he did not.

I turned toward Isaac. "That's true. I was working on my paper." I paused. "And I don't think you were just grabbing a glass of water…I heard the front door close," I said.

I knew this would get him into trouble with Rosa. She had a type-A personality and was a worrier as well.

"Isaac, I told you that you need to at least let me know when you're going out," she said. "I don't care that you're leaving, but I should at least know when you're gone in case something happens to you."

Isaac glared back. He didn't bother to respond and walked out of the kitchen and onto the porch.

"I'm serious, Isaac. You could wind up in a compromising position, and I wouldn't be able to help you at all," she yelled after him. She rolled her eyes.

Something made me feel like there was a deeper meaning to this conversation that I was missing.

Rosa turned back to me and changed the subject. "How many pages do you have written for your paper?"

I knew this conversation was about to turn into a lecture.

"About three or four," I said, trying to sound confident.

"It sounds like you have a long way to go," she replied, the admonishment clear in her tone of voice.

"Have you considered talking with Dad about the plague?" she asked. "You know, he has some very interesting firsthand knowledge. Dad and Mom were pretty heavily involved in the entire ordeal, working and volunteering for the hospitals in Chicago."

I'd never considered that angle. It was easy for me to forget that my dad had ever lived through Z3C7, because he never spoke of it, at least not around me.

"Do you think he would be willing to talk about it?" I asked. "I've never heard him utter a word about the plague. I assumed it was due to the memories of Mom associated with it," I said.

"I think you might be surprised. I have a hunch he would probably be open to talking about it. Ask him. It can't hurt, right?" she said.

I knew that last part was a rhetorical question. She seemed fairly confident he'd be willing to talk.

"Okay, I'll ask him. Where is he anyway?" I asked.

"I think he's on the porch with Isaac," she replied.

While it might sound peculiar for a daughter to say this, my dad was a handsome guy. I could see why women found him attractive. At almost six feet tall, he towered over me.

In some cruel twist of fate, I ended up barely over five feet four. For years, I had held out hope that I would suddenly hit a growth spurt. I'd convinced myself that it was a matter of time. After all, both of my parents were fairly tall. Alas, at twenty years old, I knew my chances of shooting up five inches were close to zero.

My dad's eyes were a combination of blue and green. Actually, his left eye was a bit greener than his right. Thick black hair covered his head which was trimmed short and always styled neatly.

I walked out onto the porch. It could be considered a porch only in the most literal sense, as it was really more of a veranda, a more pretentious version of a porch. It was enclosed in wall-to-wall windows, which slid completely open so that in the summer, spring, and fall one could enjoy the outdoors. In colder seasons or on the scorching days of summer in Nebraska, the doors would close to keep the ghastly weather out. Still, even in the winter it was fun to go out and sit on the warm veranda, looking out upon the snow-covered oak trees and watching as the grass became ensconced in snowflakes.

Today my dad was dressed casually in dark blue jeans and a red polo shirt, but normally he wore gray pants, a button-down shirt, and a tie for work. As I took a step closer to him, my mind raced. A knot formed in my throat.

"Hey, Dad, I was wondering if I could ask you something."

"Sure, what's on your mind?" he replied.

"Well, let me first say I'm a little nervous about asking you this question, because I don't know how you will feel, but I'm writing a paper about the plague for a world-history assignment, and I was wondering if you could tell me about it."

"Of course," he said and then paused. "But I have to warn you the things I witnessed during that time were very dark. It was a sad and extremely chaotic time. It won't be a conversation full of pleasantries."

Isaac chimed in, "Evie, are you sure you want to know? Once you start down that road, you may not be able to forget the things you find out."

He made this statement like he was speaking from experience. Part of me wanted to heed my dad's and Isaac's warnings, but a larger part of me was insanely curious.

"Yes, I can handle it," I said, not quite sure if that was the truth.

{3}

Three

Isaac appeared uneasy, a very uncharacteristic emotion for him. He glanced over at me with a look I couldn't quite decipher.

My dad began, "Evangeline, the world was a very different place prior to the plague. The population was booming. Chicago, in comparison to today, was a chaotic madhouse. Your mother and I lived in a three-bedroom condo on the thirty-third floor of a high-rise building called Hightower. Even on a neonatologist's salary and my less substantial contribution as a high-school science teacher, the three-bedroom condo was at the higher end of what we could afford. Space was *that* coveted and costly. We were married on April twenty-third," he said.

I should probably have known that date, but I didn't. I couldn't even remember what my parents were like together. A photo of their wedding day hung on the wall of our entryway. It always made me feel happy, and I could imagine, for a moment, the bliss that they must have felt during that time in their lives. I loved that picture.

"In May, your mother heard about the Z3C7 virus appearing in remote areas of China. I remember her telling me about the terrifying symptoms and the concern over whether or not the virus would be an issue. She said a friend of hers at the World Health Organization had witnessed the disease firsthand and was quite concerned. Of course, she was speaking of Dr. Crailene. Ethan, as she referred to him, thought the WHO's conclusion that the virus was several mutations away from being of any concern to humans was risky and irresponsible.

"Although she held him in high regard, I don't think she took him seriously. Obviously, nobody else did either. The spring turned into summer, and the number of patients with Z3C7 dwindled, as usually occurs in the warmer months of the year. It wasn't until October that the numbers started to climb and at an astonishingly fast rate. We didn't know it then, but the virus had mutated. It was spreading from human to human—"

I interrupted him. "How did you not know that it was contagious? It doesn't seem logical that the media didn't catch onto it right away. I would think that sort of news would be available almost instantly," I said.

He looked off in the distance for a moment and then continued:

"Yes, that's what we all thought as well. What we didn't count on was how the governments around the world were secretly responding. We were all lulled into thinking that we had a good handle on the information we were receiving. It couldn't have been further from the truth, as we all learned in retrospect. In the post-pandemic trials, a lot of information came to light. China, first and foremost, kept the number of deaths from Z3C7 hidden for almost fourteen days. The Chinese national news was reporting that due to cooler weather, the virus had reemerged in the poultry population and was causing a few new cases.

Of course, there were rumors, blogs and such, but most people just dismissed them as extremist. China had the ability to conceal a lot of information with the strong censorship it had over the country. It wasn't a hard thing to pull off. However, the CIA figured out what was going on rather quickly. It just goes to show we have no idea how much the government actually knows.

Within the first forty-eight hours, a select few intelligence officers and upper officials, like the president, had a good idea of the disastrous consequences that were to come. In a rather cunning move, or possibly a most grave mistake, they took action. Secretly, they began to censor what was being reported to the news organizations in the United States.

The most sweeping change, however, occurred in the customs department of the United States. An invisible screen at every single customs checkpoint was put in place. I still can't wrap my mind around how fast it was done. Every person coming into the United States was checked without ever being aware. The screen detected the breath of each person as they passed through, instantaneously flagging them in the computer system if they were positive for the virus and informing the agent to detain the passenger. The agent would escort these people away, tell them they needed to be detained for further inspection, and put them in a holding camp.

You would be surprised at how well this system worked, but it was inherently a flawed system and only intended as a temporary solution to the problem. The United States was trying to buy a little bit more time in order to place the real infrastructure that would deal with the inevitable pandemic. They covertly pulled in most of the military to keep order in the United States. The longer they could hold off fear in the American people, the better chance they had of coming out on top.

Fear is the most savage player in a pandemic. Neighbors turn on neighbors. The chaos that ensues has the ability to bring down an entire population before the virus even strikes. That's what the United States was trying to avoid. It was a logical move, but in a fateful twist, their master plan was actually the Achilles's heel.

Once it was discovered that our own government was concealing the truth about a very, very deadly virus, people started to riot. Nobody trusted the news. Nobody knew who to trust. Fear ran rampant. Your mom and I thought fear had the potential to be deadlier than the actual virus. Unfortunately, we were wrong, as the fatal rampage of the virus would be much, much, worse.

That was at the end of October, and by November second, the first documented case of Z3C7 appeared in New York City. When I say "documented," I mean that it was acknowledged on November second, but the case actually occurred in late October. It turned out that the invisible screens hadn't worked as well as hoped. A few hours after the screening devices were set up in the airports, a five-year-old girl named Neva arrived at JFK airport in New York City. She turned out to be a carrier of the virus and never came down with symptoms. She had the ability to spread the virus to thousands of people. She'd been on three different planes full of hundreds of passengers and hopped through four of the busiest airports in the world. Here in the United States, she was the first of many to carry the virus over the border. Some would be symptomatic, but others, like Neva, were just carriers."

"How many carriers were there total?" I asked.

My dad thought a moment and then answered, "I don't think those numbers were ever released. It was enough to infect multiple cities pretty fast, all without notice. Actually, nobody found out about the girl, Neva, until a few days later, when several of her relatives fell ill with Z3C7. By then it was far too late. All of the planning by the government would soon be heavily tested.

When your mother saw her first case of Z3C7, she was still working in the NICU. A woman had come into the hospital, pregnant and early in her third trimester. She was extremely sick. Within a few minutes, Violet was positive that she had Z3C7. They couldn't do much for the mother. They quarantined her, kept her hydrated, and continuously monitored the baby's vitals. She worsened, as pneumonia overwhelmed her body. Her water broke, and she went into labor. Then her oxygen levels dropped, and she had to be put on a mechanical ventilator. Within hours, she was septic.

Your mom had to make the decision to deliver the baby via C-section, virtually guaranteeing the death of the mother. She didn't have a choice. The pregnant woman probably wouldn't have survived very long, given how fast she was deteriorating, but even the smallest chance that she could have recovered upset your mom.

As predicted, the baby's mother didn't survive the surgery. Her body started to arrest within minutes of the first incision. The baby, a four-pound little girl, was delivered limp and blue, but within a few seconds the NICU team was able to resuscitate her. Despite significant odds against her survival, she made it. I remember your mother celebrating that night, basking in the glow of hope. There was still optimism that this virus wouldn't be as bad as predicted.

The next day she arrived at the hospital to do rounds. The baby was still alive and slowly but definitively progressing. Excited to share the news, she turned and asked the nurse where the rest of the baby's family was.

"I'm sorry to be the one to tell you, Violet. We just found out that there isn't any family left. They were all found dead this morning, at the home of the mother," the nurse explained.

Your mom told me she just stood there, stunned, as the realization washed over her that this little baby girl that she'd worked so hard to save would have no home. Then it hit her. She asked the nurse, "They all died of the virus, didn't they?"

"Yes, that's how it appears."

My dad looked down, and I could see the glimmer of sadness in his eyes.

"As stomach wrenching as that story is, Evangeline, it got worse. As it turned out the little baby girl, still unnamed, would struggle to find any parent at all. Not because nobody wanted her, but because there was nobody left to want her."

The sentence hung in the air for a minute before I realized what he was saying.

"Do you know what happened to the baby?" I asked, trying to deflect the sadness that I was feeling.

"No, I don't," he replied. "Your mother was pulled off of the case and asked to help deal with the more immediate needs of the camps. It was probably for the best, because I don't think it ended well for the little girl."

"Were some areas of the country more severely affected by the virus than others?"

"Yes, the major cities, like New York, DC, Chicago, Seattle, LA, Miami, and Minneapolis. As you might guess, anywhere with a high population was a hot spot. These were areas with international airports, colleges, and extensive public-transport systems. One of the rules in a pandemic is social isolation. That was impossible in those cities, especially the major international hubs. During the initial wave, that's where you saw the boom. As I told you, the first case was in New York, but it was probably just by a matter of hours. The United States, in comparison to the world's most populous countries, did fairly well."

"India and China?" I said.

"Yes, they were two of the hardest hit. As third-world countries, the sanitary conditions in those places were poor, and access to medical care was very limited. They were great breeding grounds for Z3C7. Any country bordering China was in a precarious zone. India, having surpassed China as the most populous country in the world and bordering China on its northeast side, served as a critical link for the virus to spread. We were heavily reliant on those two countries for our supplies and products. It was a very bad position for us to be in," he said.

"How did it spread? Through the world, I mean."

"As you know, it originated in China. It spread into India quite fast. It was really just a matter of hours before it passed into multiple countries from there. There were several major international airport hubs in India and China. Mumbai, Hong Kong, Singapore, Beijing, Shanghai, every one of those airports were taking passengers all over the world to London, Frankfurt, Tokyo, New York City, Atlanta, and Paris. It just devastated those cities. London was particularly affected.

"Back in the United States, everything went into lockdown. Utility workers were sequestered in buildings to ensure vital infrastructures could remain up and running, at least for a period of time."

"How long were they able to keep the electricity, gas, and water running?" I asked.

"It varied by state. Some managed to keep the utilities going for months, others just a few weeks. The government focused its attention on keeping hospitals up and running. They didn't really have control over much else, other than the military," he said.

"What state fared the worst?"

"Florida. It was an absolute mess. Miami and Fort Lauderdale, specifically, which were located in the lower part of the Florida peninsula, had over six million people. There was only one way to get out—to go north. The Everglades bordered everything west, so walking wasn't really feasible. Massive gridlock ensued. Some people, rather ironically, tried to boat to Cuba," he replied.

"What did the government do?" I asked.

"Not much for Florida, I'm afraid. The Center for Disease Control advised citizens to stay home. The government deployed all remaining military to the major cities in the United States. They provided basic supplies and enforced the federal curfew of ten in the evening. Drones actually proved to be a very helpful tool during the pandemic, allowing the government to monitor cities remotely, thus freeing up military and police personnel to assist civilians to a greater degree.

"Your mother and I decided to volunteer most of our time at the hospitals around town. After all, I had no job because of the lockdown, and we had no family at that time to worry about."

He paused. I could tell he was struggling to find words to explain the circumstances of twenty-five years ago. I couldn't really imagine how hard it was to convey the desperation of the world back then, but I could feel it in the way he looked.

"The hospitals were overflowing with patients," he began, "and the government had set up camps all around the city to house the sick.

"As I mentioned, your mom was assigned to one of the camps that was set up in an old school on the lower east side of Chicago. Violet, as the overseeing doctor of the makeshift hospital, was in charge of the pediatric patients, who were treated in a separate place from the adults, much like children's hospitals do today. I volunteered with her there, which we named *Espoir*," he said.

I knew from a French class I'd taken several years ago that espoir meant hope in English.

Rosa's voice rang out from inside the house, interrupting us. "Hey all, it's lunchtime. Shall we take a break and eat something?"

I was fully engrossed in the story and didn't really want to break for lunch. The last hours had flown by.

"Yeah, I suppose we should grab something for lunch," my dad replied. "Did you have something in mind, Rosa?" he asked.

"I was thinking tomato soup and grilled cheese," she answered.

It was my favorite meal. If anything could convince me to take a break, it was tomato soup.

"Sounds great," my dad said. It was his favorite meal too.

{4}

Four

Rosa never made just any grilled cheese and tomato soup. Her obsession with gourmet cooking always led to opulent dishes. One could be assured the tomatoes were probably from our garden, grown organically. The grilled cheese usually consisted of sourdough bread, some exotic cheeses, like Gruyère, Emmentaler, and fontina, plus black truffles thrown in for good measure. Albeit pretentious, I'd rarely had a meal of hers that I didn't like.

Isaac grabbed a white ceramic bowl of tomato soup and a sandwich. He sat down across the table and glanced at me, not meeting my eyes, and then took a bite of his grilled cheese. Normally he was so arrogant and witty. I'd never seen him so quiet.

Rosa interrupted my train of thought, almost as if on cue.

"To me, the most striking reminder of the plague was the size of my graduating class. Just thirty people were in my secondary high-school class, drawn from the entire district of Lancaster County. Prior to the plague, the numbers were closer to six hundred. The two classes ahead of us were even sparser. Not many babies survived the plague.

Even three years after it ended, the population was barely growing."

"Yeah, that's true," my dad agreed. "I remember when they started hiring teachers again. There were still a fair amount of elementary-school kids but very few middle- or high-school students. The amount of babies born drastically increased about five or so years after the plague ended. People finally started the ascent to normalcy."

After we finished lunch, Rosa took our dishes and my dad continued on with the story:

"Camp Espoir was a remarkable example of your mother's abilities. She was tireless. She worked nonstop. I worked nonstop. We slept only a few hours each night. As the directing physician, she was in charge of virtually all of the patient care. I was her assistant and in charge of the tangible aspects of the camp, making sure the logistical needs were being met.

The amount of what we could do for the patients was small, but in comparison to many other countries, we were faring much better. Our rate of death was slightly lower in the beginning, as you might expect in a first-world country. We had antibiotics to help treat the secondary infections, the ones from bacteria that caused pneumonia and septicemia, but we didn't have enough. They ran out fairly quickly. We were a priority camp, since we had pediatric patients, so I can only imagine the shortages in a normal camp. We were forced into focusing on comfort care, like providing food, water, and pain management, rather than life-saving interventions. The majority of our pediatric patients were in the nine-year-plus range, but we always had a few babies and younger children as well.

Violet wanted to make the camp as homey as possible. She would spend the time that she wasn't working or sleeping painting the school. I think it was relaxing for her. It provided normalcy amid the chaotic confines of the old school. Soon many of the rooms were painted an aqua-blue color, and the playroom was a bright and cheery yellow.

Let me say finding paint during that time was a task. Everything around the city was shut down. I managed to get several buckets from a local department store. They remained open during the pandemic, and, needless to say, paint wasn't in high demand. We would give the owners our ration of food and water as trade for the paint. We bartered in a similar fashion for some toys and basic play equipment for the kids.

One night your mom and I were talking about the pets that were being abandoned en masse in the city. We were animal lovers. We thought, why not bring some into Camp Espoir? It's well documented that animal therapy can be exceptionally helpful, especially with kids. It served several purposes, giving the pets a home and providing the love both the patients and animals desperately needed.

It was wonderful…well besides the fact that I added yet another duty to my eighty-hour-a-week volunteer job, making sure all of the pets were fed and their bodily functions were cared for. I had to clean up all of the poop and pee, but it was worth it. The place felt less like a destitute, gloomy camp. We felt good about what we were doing. For the sickest kids, the ones who wouldn't make it, which, sadly, were the majority that we treated, having a beloved animal come by to visit or lay with them in bed helped to ease their suffering a bit.

In my case, it was a little bittersweet. Although the dogs and cats had a new home and seemed happy, we didn't always have enough food for them. Some days, I was more stressed out about the animals than the patients. I would sneak out at night, under the cover of darkness because of the curfew, and scavenge for food several times a week. Most of the time I could find enough to feed them. Some did start to starve, and when I saw that happening, I euthanized them. That was really hard. Some of the former veterinarians in the community would come in to help out, and they provided whatever drugs they had. I was extremely grateful, because the alternative to medical euthanasia was much worse.

It was such a dark period of time. Death was all around, and the atmosphere was burdening. It was impossible to be positive and selfless all the time. Our goal was to provide a happy environment, but under such duress, breakdowns were an inevitable part of life.

I remember one particular day, twelve kids, all from the same neighborhood, died. I walked back to the tiny, little room that your mom and I shared and punched three holes in the wall. I was so mad and so sad.

Your mother spent a lot of hours crying in that ivory-colored room. We became really good at working through our grief there then emerging to face another hour. We had to allow ourselves that time, or else I'm certain that we'd have gone insane. I mean, the sheer fucking fact that we somehow survived an entire two months of Z3C7 was enough to make us think we had some purpose or, at least, someone had a purpose for us.

I had never heard my dad say the word "fucking" before.

"All right, I think that's probably enough for the day," he said. He sounded upset, but his demeanor abruptly changed. "Let's continue this conversation tomorrow night. Don't worry; it's all roses from here on out," he said, laughing.

I knew that he was pretending to be in a better mood for my sake.

{5}

Five

I said good night to everyone and then wandered back up to my room by myself. My mind hummed with thoughts. The story about the newborn that my mom had saved made me particularly sad. I walked over to my computer and pressed the button to turn it on. My dad couldn't answer all of my questions, but the Internet could prove to be an adequate substitute. I knew that it was just a matter of searching a few simple words.

While I waited for my computer to turn on, I walked over to my closet and grabbed a T-shirt and a pair of navy athletic pants. I quickly changed and went back into my bedroom. It was so hot. As a result of being on the third floor of an old house, the hot and humid air from the outside often became trapped inside of my room. Normally I opened my windows at night to combat the heat. I liked sleeping with my windows open whenever the weather allowed. The noise of the street below lulled me to sleep.

I walked over to the center window and pulled it up as high as it would go. A gust of wind blew through the room, knocking over a glass vase full of tulips that I had gathered the day before. The vase made a crashing sound as it rolled off the table and onto the floor, breaking into pieces. The shards of glass scattered out in every direction. I sighed.

Suddenly I heard a voice at the door.

"Evangeline?" It was Isaac.

"Yes?" I replied, but he had already barged into my room.

"Are you all right?" he asked. His eyes darted around the room, looking for the source of the noise.

I pointed to the broken glass. "The wind knocked it over," I said.

He looked relieved.

"How did you get here so fast?" I asked.

"I was just coming up from downstairs. Let me help you clean it up," he said.

I walked over to the bathroom and grabbed the trash bin. Isaac was already gathering up the pieces when I returned. I squatted down on my tiptoes, trying to avoid anything other than the front of my feet touching the ground.

Isaac handed me the larger pieces of glass to throw away. He looked over at me and glanced down at my chest then quickly back up to my face.

"I saw that. Were you staring at my breasts?" I asked, smiling.

"I was just making sure no shards had landed on your shirt," he replied, smiling back. His eyes sparkled.

I shook my head.

"I don't think I've ever seen you in pants and a T-shirt," he said, sort of changing the subject.

"And what do you think? Am I just as stunning?" I said, sarcastically.

"You are always stunning, Evie, but I prefer you in a dress. The tight kind," he replied.

My face felt hot. I bit my lip and shifted the weight of my body from the tips of my toes to the soles of my feet. I overcompensated, and I suddenly started to fall backward.

Isaac grabbed my arm tightly, pulling me upright until I was stable. He released me.

"I should go. I will see you tomorrow," he said. He walked out the door and closed it behind him before I had the chance to reply.

I didn't realize that I had been holding my breath until he was gone. Slowly, I let the air out of my lungs and finished cleaning up the glass. I struggled to find the logic in what had just transpired between us, but chemistry between two people could never be logically explained. Yes, scientifically, the hormones of testosterone, estrogen, dopamine, adrenaline, and serotonin were behind it, but the magnetism that pulled two people together…with some people it was there, but with many it was not. I tried to make the thoughts disappear from my mind and focused back on Z3C7.

I walked back over to my computer and started typing. I wondered what kind of resources were available to help prepare for a pandemic. Surely the government had a checklist or guidelines. They did.

A list of items appeared on the first page that I pulled up, entitled, "Emergency Survival Kit for Pandemic Flu." Ten items with descriptions were shown:

1. Emergency radio with additional batteries
2. Flashlight and backup batteries
3. Canned goods—two-week supply
4. Prescription Medication—two-week supply
5. Formula and other infant necessities
6. Garbage bags
7. Water—six week supply (1 gallon per person per day)

8. Credit Cards, passports, and important documents
9. Bleach or similar cleaning agent—for disinfecting use a half cup of bleach per gallon of water. For drinking use eight drops of bleach per gallon of water
10. First-Aid Kit (should include fever-reducing medicine, like Tylenol, and antidiarrheal)

I looked through a few more websites, which all contained the same information on what to do in the event of a pandemic or other emergency situation. There were guidelines for community organizations, schools, governments, and workplaces. I perused all the information provided and decided to turn my search elsewhere. What happened to Camp Espoir, and were there records of it?

I searched for "Camp Espoir," and right away an article entitled, "Camp Espoir, There Is Hope" popped up. It was by a reporter named Astrid Seldon . It read:

Dr. Violet Rolieux and her husband, Xander Rolieux, attempted the impossible. They tried to put a dent in the 60 percent mortality rate that Z3C7 carried. They succeeded, lowering the death rate by 2 percent with their unconventional approach to treating the patients.

Dr. Rolieux, or Violet, as she preferred, explained, "Our focus is to create a happy, loving environment for our littlest patients. Whether or not these kids survive, it's our priority to make this a happy and peaceful place for them. Living through Z3C7 will be enough of a struggle on its own. I don't want Camp Espoir to contribute to that. We want them to leave here and be hopeful of a new tomorrow, whether that day actually comes tomorrow or in a year. Positivity and kindness are infectious. That's what we want these kids to take away."

As I walked through the camp, a dog, whom I later learned was Violet and her husband's beloved black lab, Lila, came to greet me. I walked down the cheery yellow hallways toward the patient rooms. Some of rooms were painted in a bright blue and a few others in bright pink.

Dr. Rolieux explained, "We've had a few little girls request pink, which, of course, we couldn't say no to." A smile appeared on her face. She continued, "My husband and I really try to make the camp feel as close to home as possible. Parents are allowed, at their own risk, to stay with their children or meet in specially designated areas. The precedent among other camps is to keep visitors, including parents or relatives, away. I don't feel that's a good decision, and we don't adhere to those guidelines."

As we walked toward the playroom, I heard jazz music. I looked at Dr. Rolieux, who was dressed in a navy-blue pencil skirt, a fitted white shirt, and black high-heeled shoes with the trademark red soles of a well-known designer.

"Do you always dress this impeccably in the middle of a pandemic?" I asked.

She laughed heartily, "You know, I used to dress like this every day prior to the pandemic. This is the outfit I wore the day I arrived. I haven't been back to our condo since then. It's not a particularly practical outfit to launder when you encounter what I do every day. So in answer to your question, no, most of the time you will catch me in scrubs, looking a bit more disheveled. This outfit makes me feel normal, and I'll take any opportunity I can to feel that way again, if only for a few minutes."

The article ended, and at the conclusion there was a note:

"See also: The controversial Veterox vaccine trials took place a few weeks after this article was published. More information on the Veterox vaccine trials can be found here.

The link led to another article:

When Z3C7 became a pandemic, the Center for Disease Control (CDC) and the World Health Organization were left completely unprepared. Although many organizations had started working on a conventional vaccine for Z3C7, most epidemiologists had come to the conclusion that with the complexity of the virus, it would take over a year, possibly longer, to create.

The population was facing a steep descent, with the virus killing six out of every ten people it infected. It was spreading swiftly across continents. Experts knew a vaccine available in a year would be too late. Half of the world's population would likely be dead. The world focused its attention on a doctor who claimed he had a cure for the virus, Dr. Ethan L. Crailene.

Dr. Crailene had been working on the Veterox vaccine with funding from his own personal accounts for several months prior to the outbreak. He was on the ground as one of the first eyewitnesses to Z3C7 when it took hold in China and had studied the virus at long length. In an interview when the cure was first announced, he spoke about the novelty of the virus and how he went about creating the injectable medication.

"I had to think outside of the box. Instead of a vaccine, which would only prevent the disease and takes a good six months to manufacture, I needed to create something that would fight the virus while it was attacking the body. Simply put, I needed to change the way our immune system worked against the virus. That is what I set out to do, and I'm so thrilled to report that I succeeded."

I scrolled through another article and yet another. I couldn't seem to find any information on what the actual Veterox injection consisted of, but I found a few articles explaining how the drug came to be.

The testing phase of the Veterox drug was cut drastically in comparison to the normal process a drug must undergo via the FDA. It was approved because of the emergent situation, but it was also interesting to note that they cited several animal studies on nonhuman primates conducted in the weeks prior to Veterox's release and proclaimed with a high degree of confidence that Veterox was a safe and effective drug against Z3C7. So with haste, the first human trials began on December 24. The government deemed children the highest priority and thus decided on a few children's hospitals around the nation to conduct the trials.

Although I had heard about the Veterox trials during a history class in grade school, I didn't recall much about the topic. I definitely didn't know that it had been tested on children or that my mother's friend was involved in creating it.

It seemed to be a topic akin to the Holocaust. History books told the basics of this dark time in the world but seemed to gloss over the horrifying details. Only after doing my own research did I find out about Josef Mengele and his horrendous experiments on human beings in Auschwitz. I never saw any pictures in my history book depicting the deplorable conditions in Auschwitz and other concentration camps. There were no photographs showing human beings so starved for food that the only thing remaining of their bodies was literally skin sticking to bones on their skeletons. Despite the direness of the situation, those details were what resonated with me, and I ventured to guess it would have resonated with my entire history class instead of inciting yawns of boredom.

I remembered wondering, after reading some Holocaust survivor accounts, what would have been worse to endure in those camps—survival or death?

It was impossible to compare the Holocaust to a flu pandemic. One was completely preventable and at the hands of fellow human beings. The flu wasn't man-made. Well, at least I didn't think it was man-made. I really hoped not. Anyway, if there was one similarity, it was that both times people likely questioned if it was better to live or to die.

I had often pondered what it would be like to go through a pandemic. What kind of decisions would I make? How would I react? Actually, I had run the scenario through my head often. I was a daydreamer. That type of subject was not uncommon for me. Whenever I sat in waiting rooms, stood in line, rode in the car, practically anytime that I was alone, I'd plot out my path through various destructive events.

Maybe the scenario was an armed gunman coming to take the grocery store hostage or surviving a plane crash. I had a plan for each specific scenario. Whenever I traveled by air, I made sure to sit in the back of the plane, browse through the safety pamphlet to know the features of the specific aircraft, and always counted the number of rows to the nearest exit. In the event of a crash, I knew to brace. Most plane crashes weren't survivable, but in the few that were, bracing had been shown to play a significant role in one's chance of living.

That was just how my brain worked. I had a feeling most people contemplated things like I did, although maybe not as intensely. In most of my concocted scenarios, I was the heroine type—the one that bravely saved multiple people and still managed to escape safely. It pretty much summed up my personality; I was pulled to help others while still attaining self-preservation. Though, in the back of my mind, I knew that I would most likely die trying to help other people rather than escape to safety. I couldn't imagine just running past an injured person and not feeling compelled to do something.

Would I have survived the pandemic? It was doubtful. I was neither the most cunning nor the most ruthless, two traits that seemed to correlate with survival. To me, these were the most interesting parts of a survivalist mentality. I'd seen television shows about those very passionate people who had huge stockpiles of food and a secret bunker to ride out an apocalypse not blinking an eye about killing another person. What would the world look like with a population made up of the most selfish people in the world?

My mind slipped from the topic onto a similar tangent. I was curious. Were there any survivor accounts of the plague?

I came across an article called, "A Mother's Horror: Diary of a Pandemic Victim." I couldn't stop myself from reading it.

At the beginning of the article, there was an introduction explaining that the diary had been found after the pandemic, in a house owned by a family with the last name of Acrio. It appeared that both the parents and their four children had been found dead inside the house. The article provided excerpts from the diary:

December 3

It's been four weeks since the pandemic began. I don't know why I'm writing about it. A part of me wants there to be a record, but I also just need the outlet. I'm not sure how to start. My husband, Juan, and I have four children. Adonia is four. Atlas and Aida are almost three. Pilar is eight months.

For the first few weeks, we didn't know if we would have food and water. The supplies started to arrive, and we all became more hopeful. We were given bleach and trash bags, food and water. The soldiers told us how to sanitize water. The trash bags were for collecting poop, since we have no running water and nowhere to dispose of it. I have been using T-shirts and safety pins as diapers for Pilar.

We live in a poor neighborhood. Juan works as a car mechanic, and I stay home with the kids. Most weeks we struggle to buy groceries. Without food stamps, we wouldn't be able to. Beyond a few weeks' worth of bottled water that I had stored in case of an emergency, we had no supplies to begin with. Today we were informed by the soldiers that they are pulling out of the area. They've run out of water, and no food supplies have arrived. I fed the kids a can of peaches and one of green beans for dinner. Juan and I didn't eat.

December 4

A soldier stopped by our house today and gave us several cans of mixed vegetables, some beef jerky, and several cans of pears.

He said he was sorry and that he wished there was more he could provide for us. We were the only ones in the neighborhood to get food.

December 5

The soldiers are gone, and it's gotten worse. I've heard several gunshots today. Many men are roaming the streets outside, trying to scavenge food. Juan had to fire the gun several times to scare people away from our house. We only have ten bullets. I try to keep the kids away from the windows, and we sing and play to try to drown out the noise outside.

December 6

Juan left the house today to go find more food. He didn't have a choice—only two cans are left from the soldier. I was terrified when he left and corralled the kids in the bathroom. Juan showed me how to use the gun in case I need to. He came back an hour later with nothing. The houses he searched had been ransacked already.

December 7

Juan has started to show symptoms of the virus. He's running a fever. I'm not feeling well. I don't know what to do. We can't expose the kids. I don't know what to do with the kids. We are leaving the house to try and find someone who will take them in.

The next entry appeared to be made later the same day:

Nobody will take the kids. They saw we were sick, coughing and sweating. Several people yelled at us to go home. One said he would shoot us if we walked past his block. Juan can barely breathe.

His lips are turning blue. He said I needed to get the gun out. I've been crying for the past several hours. I don't know what to do!

December 8

Juan is very close to passing. He's struggling for every breath. I watch his chest rise and fall, waiting for the moment to arrive. I'm having a hard time breathing. Adonia and Atlas are sick. I'm crawling on the floor to them, trying to provide comfort. I don't know. I don't understand. What am I supposed to do? I know I'm going to die. I know Juan is going to die. NOBODY WILL HELP US! Nobody!

In a picture of the original diary, I could see the ink smears, the tear stains, around the words "Nobody." The entry continued:

Juan just died. I think I have to do the unthinkable. Once I die, the kids will be suffering alone. If they do survive, they will die of starvation. What will they do when they find out that their parents are dead and nobody is around to care for them? What if my three-year-old and the baby survive? I imagine them running around, looking for someone to feed them. Little Pilar would be stuck in a dirty diaper for days and days, dying in distress. They can't watch me die. They can't watch each other die. I'm throwing up from the thought of what I am about to do. I want them to be at rest. I want them to die peacefully. I only have five bullets.

I couldn't finish the last paragraph. My own tears started falling from my eyes. I couldn't remove the image from my mind. I felt the desperation. I felt the sadness. It was wrenching my heart.

{6}

Six

My alarm clock went off, and I awoke at six in the morning. It was Monday, and school would start in an hour and a half. I hadn't slept very well, waking up frequently throughout the night, but I forced my mind to put it all behind me for the day. I wandered into the bathroom to take a hot shower and get ready for school. As I dried my hair, my thoughts slipped back to my mom. Did she know about the Veterox trials? What happened to the kids who received it? I was sure that my dad had the answers, and I knew that I couldn't stop myself from asking the questions.

I headed to my closet and picked out a pale-blue strapless dress, a white cardigan, and black ballet flats. Quickly, I walked over to the mirror and applied my makeup, just eyeliner and mascara. I grabbed my bag and headed downstairs.

I heard Rosa's voice. "Evangeline, it's seven forty-five, we need to leave soon. What do you want for breakfast?"

"I'll just have a peanut-butter granola bar. I'll eat on the way," I answered back.

"Okay," she replied.

When I finally reached the kitchen, Isaac and Rosa were standing by the door. Rosa threw me the granola bar, and we headed out the front door.

My dad insisted that Rosa or Isaac walk me to school every day. Being that I was twenty years old, it seemed kind of obnoxious, but I didn't really mind the company.

Red, white, and yellow tulips lined the sidewalk, and bright-green maple leaves spanned the previously unshaded ground. The blue sky made the lush green grass somehow even greener. As May crept by in Nebraska, the earth started to breathe again. The world, after months of dreary, cold, and cloudy days filled with the brown-and-white colors of winter, came back to life. Springtime in Nebraska was my favorite.

Rosa was wearing her normal pencil-skirt-and-blouse combination. Isaac was dressed in a dark gray suit, a white button-down shirt, and a navy tie. He caught my eye as I glanced over at him. We both quickly turned our attention back to the sidewalk.

"What do you think school was like right after the plague?" I asked.

"Much different. The entire school system changed," Isaac said.

Rosa jumped in. "Prior to the plague, kids were only required to go to school until they were about eighteen. Once school started up again, there were a lot of kids who needed to be educated fast to help increase and strengthen the work force. The requirement changed, and students were required to attend until a career was established. For some, that meant eighteen or nineteen, if they chose technical specialties, but for most education continued until at least twenty. College courses were integrated into high-school studies, making it faster to pursue whichever career you chose."

Rosa continued, "Doctors, teachers, plumbers, engineers, and janitors...they were all heavily needed. Prior to Z3C7, it took eight-plus years of education after high school just to become a medical doctor and then four or more years of residency after that."

It didn't surprise me that Rosa was familiar with the old educational requirements for doctors. She, herself, was one year shy of becoming a psychiatrist.

"As you know, the entire process is started much earlier, and now by twenty-six, you can be a specialist in the medical field," she said. "It was actually one of the best things to come about after the pandemic. It also took away the financial burden that the previous system enacted. It was impossible to charge anyone for school at that point. Nobody had anything left."

I knew that Rosa would be a wonderful psychiatrist. She seemed particularly attuned to other people, and she enjoyed listening to and analyzing other people. I don't think anybody in my family was surprised to find out she would be going down that route. Psychiatry was a perfect fit.

Isaac, on the other hand...well, I hadn't expected his career choice quite as much. In only a few short months, he would become a homicide detective.

Between the two of them, the discussions in our house were interesting, to say the least. I'd heard countless details about murders, suicides, and the truly mentally ill. I could confidently say neither of those two fields suited me. The near constant sadness and anger would have quickly overwhelmed me. It was hard enough to hear the stories secondhand. I couldn't imagine actually having to witness them in person.

My thoughts came to a halt as we arrived at the school. I said good-bye to Rosa and Isaac. They both turned and hurried away. As I walked toward the front doors of the school, I glanced over my shoulder, looking back toward Isaac. I was surprised to meet his eyes gazing back at me. A smile crossed his face. He turned back and continued speaking with Rosa.

I was baffled by this sudden attention from him. My mind could not decipher the meaning. It felt like a switch had been flipped—and not just in him. I was excited and equally nervous, like the sixteen-year-old version of me had been when a boy first showed interest.

I remembered the time well. Even as far back as elementary, when my friends held mock weddings at recess and I was always the bridesmaid, I'd never felt terribly attractive. In junior high, I watched as all of my classmates went through boyfriend after boyfriend. At that point not even one boy had ever asked me to dance, let alone go out.

It wasn't until just after my sixteenth birthday that a boy, Lucian, out of the blue started to pursue me. Every day at lunch he would watch me, making sure that I noticed his gaze. It made me so nervous that I didn't eat lunch for two weeks. That should have been the first red flag. Finally, one day he asked me out. At the time I didn't entirely understand the attraction, as I was still a nerdy teenage girl. I assumed that he was probably attracted to my rapidly increasing breast size, which was confirmed on our first date when he tried to feel me up.

He was sorely disappointed. Literally. When his hand started to move toward my chest, my immediate reaction was to pull his hand away, but I "accidently," grabbed one of his fingers and yanked it back pretty hard. The next day at school, mysteriously, two of his fingers were taped together. It was pretty satisfying.

I finished walking the rest of the way to the front of the school and took my place in line. I had arrived a bit later than I normally did, and the line to check in was long. School security was a pain. Luckily, it didn't take terribly long to reach the checkpoint. I placed my fingers under the hand-sanitizer machine and rubbed them together until they felt dry. I swiped my finger across the white touch pad and sang "my" song in my head. The security system was very unique.

The week before we started school every year, all students were scheduled for an appointment with school security. During the appointment, a security member scanned your fingerprint and compared it with the years prior to ensure accuracy. Then they would record baseline isometric data. During that process, you had to choose a song. It could be any song in the world. Nobody knew what song you had picked, nor did anyone have access to that information. It was completely between you and the computer or whatever it was—I wasn't good with techy stuff. My song was always the same, "These Boots Are Made for Walkin'."

A fingerprint could be copied, but a song was completely unique to each individual, making it nearly impossible to trick the system. Nobody sang a song in the exact same way. Even if you could've figured out what tune it was, the odds of being able to replicate it identically were almost zero. I wasn't entirely sure how the whole system worked, but I did know it also had the capability to monitor your vitals, like pulse, temperature, and blood pressure. If you happened to be running a fever, it would automatically notify the nurse, who would then escort you to her office to evaluate the situation. Supposedly it helped to combat contagions and, therefore, reduce the amount of sick people.

My schedule this year was challenging. I was considered an advanced medical-specialty student. I had chosen my specialty early on. I wanted to be a physician for the elderly, a gerontologist. Many of my classmates took longer to decide, but it was mandatory to declare a major by the age of seventeen.

All curriculum after that decision was tailored to your career, mixed with some basic humanities classes. Volunteer work or shadowing in your career interest was involuntary. After a few years of gaining experience in your field, you could then pursue and earn a degree. In a few years, I would be a medical doctor and by twenty-six, a specialist.

My thoughts were interrupted suddenly by a female voice.

"Hey, Evangeline!"

I smiled, knowing immediately who it was.

"Hi, Charlotte!" I replied.

"What did you eat for breakfast?" she asked.

I rolled my eyes in response. I wasn't surprised by the question, as she seemed to be eternally curious about food. Surely she could predict my answer by now; I'd had the same peanut-butter granola bar that I had eaten every day for the past month. She thought it was odd that I didn't mix things up more often. I had explained to her that I never had the time to eat a proper breakfast. I was always too busy putting on my makeup or doing my hair.

"Well maybe you shouldn't worry so much about those things. I've seen you without makeup, and you look really pretty. Why do you even put on makeup? You know you would probably be smarter if you ate a good breakfast once in a while," she'd replied, without missing a beat.

That was typical Charlotte, masking any sort of criticism in a glowing compliment. Charlotte was my best friend. She was very kind and maybe a bit of a social outlier, not unlike myself.

The day we met was one of my favorite memories. One afternoon when I was in sixth grade, I was walking down the hallway toward my next class. I saw a group of girls talking to Charlotte. One in particular, Sophia, was saying cruel things to Charlotte while

Charlotte grabbed her tablet out of a locker.

"Shouldn't you be in a home for mentally retarded kids or something? It's not like you're even going to become anything of worth anyway. You'll just be one of those annoying people who clear the tables and clean the restrooms at a restaurant. Maybe they will let you take orders when it's not too busy, when people won't be annoyed that they have to repeat their order five times for you to get it. I don't understand why anyone would want to pay for you to sit through classes that you're clearly too stupid to even understand," Sophia had said.

Sophia then turned back to her friends and said, "Look at her face. God, she's so ghastly looking."

I'd been standing a few feet away, completely horrified at the awful things she'd just spoken to this poor girl. I'd learned firsthand how mean middle-school girls could be. I mostly tried to steer clear of them.

Charlotte had stood for a second, gazing at the girl with her big brown eyes. If she was furious or even upset, her face showed none of this.

"Sophia, I really like the color of your eyes! You're so beautiful!" Charlotte had replied. There had been no sarcasm in her voice; it was said with utter sincerity. Sophia looked confused.

I was angry, and I couldn't resist commenting. I looked Sophia in the eyes. "Hopefully someday your fucking brain catches up with your stunning good looks."

Fuck, I thought. Did I just say fucking?

Sophia glared in my direction, and the gaggle of girls walked away. Charlotte and I were left standing there.

"Thank you for standing up to her, but I didn't need you to," Charlotte said.

"What was I supposed to do? She deserved that comment. What kind of person says those types of things?" I said.

"You might be surprised. Anyway, all you've done is given her justification for being mean. There's no point in being mean to a mean person. It only makes them meaner. Sometimes when you say something kind, it makes more of an impact. Imagine what a miserable time it would be in her brain. I think she could use a compliment more than I could," she said.

Clearly, I had not been expecting her response.

"Well, yeah, that's true," I stammered.

Charlotte continued, "I know there is something wrong with me. I know that. I'm not that smart, and maybe I will spend my life cleaning up after people. I'm just hoping it's not in a restaurant. I can't say that I should be here," she said.

"What you've just said in the past five minutes is one of the most valuable pieces of wisdom that I've ever heard. If you shouldn't be here, then ninety percent of the kids at this school shouldn't be here, including me," I replied. We were friends from that day on.

Since I was a bit late to school this morning, there wasn't much time to talk with Charlotte, like usual. We had very different class schedules, so I didn't see her most of the day. In the afternoon, we both volunteered at a care facility for special needs and the elderly nearby.

"Hope you have a good day!" Charlotte said as she walked away.

"You too! See you later!" I replied.

{7}

Seven

I was taking American History 1945–Present. The eight weeks of my history class were almost over, and I was thankful. I felt like the oldest student in the class, and I didn't really care for the subject. It wasn't that I didn't like history, but American history was a bit boring. World history was so much more interesting to me. I'd deliberately put off taking the course for the last few years. My counselor had finally told me that I couldn't wait any longer and that it was mandatory.

Luckily, general-education classes only lasted eight weeks, and I only had one to go. This was the class I had to write the plague paper for. It was the only redeeming aspect of the course.

Mr. Stalnik interrupted my thoughts. "Evangeline, how's your paper coming along?"

Everyone turned to look at me. My face started to burn, and I was sure that it had turned a lovely shade of red. I hated being singled out.

"Um, it's going well," I muttered.

"That's good. Would you care to let us in on what you've spent the last forty minutes daydreaming about?" he asked.

Well, he had a point. I hadn't been on task all day. My thoughts kept running over the Veterox vaccine trials. Something seemed off. What was the Veterox vaccine, and why did it seem like the topic was intentionally avoided? I knew Mr. Stalnik would have a viewpoint on this.

With some hesitation, I told him, "I've been wondering about the Veterox vaccine."

I watched to see if there was any change on his face. For a small moment, it looked like his body tensed up, but as I continued on with the question, he seemed completely calm and at ease, so I continued. "What happened with the Veterox vaccine? Why isn't there any information about it?"

Without any hesitation, Mr. Stalnik responded. "That's a really good question. I, too, used to be very curious about the Veterox vaccine. The truth is there isn't much to say on the topic. During the time of the plague, Veterox was a very minuscule part of the events, so I think the attitude in speaking and writing about the plague is to include what's important. It's important to know how the plague came to be and how it was eventually eradicated. It's also very necessary to tell the human side of the story, as gruesome and sad as it may be, because that's how we connect and understand the event—especially for students like yourselves, never having experienced what life was like during that time.

"That's what I'm trying to convey in this project. The Veterox vaccine trials consisted of a very, very, small trial that, in the end, was a failure. People died, but, honestly, quite a lot of people were dying during that time. If you want to focus on the scientific aspect, look to Dr. Leonis Bouclet, the man behind the vaccine that actually worked. However, the real point of the story, in my opinion, is the human one. After all, the vaccine for Z3C7 was available far too late, long after the plague peaked. Science failed, but humans didn't. In my opinion, that's the story. Anything else that I can answer for you?" he asked.

"No, I think that's all," I responded.

Just then, the loudspeaker beeped to inform us that it was time for lunch. I gathered up my pen and notebook. As always, I was the last one left in the classroom. My mind was buzzing. I thought Stalnik might be lying. In my experience, whenever someone used the words, "the truth is," or "honestly," usually they meant the exact opposite. He had done a good job of avoiding the question and diverting the attention surrounding Veterox. He never mentioned that the trials were conducted on children.

Maybe I was overthinking the situation. After all, it was more a crime of omission than outright lies. He had good points. The Veterox vaccine had amounted to a millisecond of time in the 8,765 hours of that year. I walked out of the classroom and down the winding hallways toward the cafeteria.

I grabbed a tray from the nice cafeteria ladies and sat down at a table nearby. A kiwi, a ham-and-cheese sandwich, a carton of milk, and a salad sat on the gray tray. I was hungry, so despite my disdain for the food, I ate it all. Today my normal group of friends were gone on a biology field trip to a body farm, which I was actually pretty envious of, so I sat alone.

For years, I used to sit by myself at lunch. I tended to avoid socializing and had a general lack of friends because of it. There were a couple of reasons why, but one was because of my aversion to small talk and gossip. To begin with, I wasn't good at it. I came off disinterested and awkward. Not terribly surprising considering that I was, indeed, disinterested. Unless you were truly trying to analyze the psychology of a person without bias, I didn't want to hear about it.

Besides, everyone knew that trying to understand any girl under eighteen was futile. On the other hand, the motives of a teenage boy were fairly straightforward. Largely this assumption was based upon the millions of dads that seemed to take particular interest in the motives behind any boys dating their teenage daughters. It was hard to pull off lying to a liar.

The other reason sounded absurdly lame. To me, people were emotional vampires. I felt wiped out and drained around them. Having no downtime seemed to amplify the effect. The only thing that helped me cope was being alone. I would escape into books or daydream. When I wasn't daydreaming about how to heroically escape death-defying situations, I was thinking about other topics.

Most nights, I went to bed really early, around nine o'clock. It took me hours to fall asleep. My mind slipped from one tangent to another seamlessly.

A few days ago, I was watching *The Middle Ages*, an aptly titled historical film. At one point, the narrator explained the typical clothing women wore in the 1300s. A smock, hose, kirtle, gown, surcoat, girdle, cape, hood, and bonnet were the norm.

I wondered how long it took for them to get dressed and if they required assistance. What was a kirtle? This led me to wondering if anyone wore makeup, and if so, what was it made from? If not, what did they look like naturally? Wasn't it sad that I didn't know what women looked like without makeup? Movies never gave a very realistic view.

What kind of shoes did people wear back then? It looked as though hair was kept in elaborate braids, but how did they secure them? No bobby pins, no hair ties. What about teeth? Did some form of toothpaste exist? How many people had straight teeth or even all of their teeth? Without an orthodontist's assistance, my teeth would look horrendous.

Thinking about teeth led me to food. I assumed it would be bland. What did they have, salt and meat? What kind of spices were used normally?

My mind was incredibly hard to turn off. My curiosity always led me on a search for answers to the most mundane questions. It turned out people in medieval times did use a form of toothpaste. Swishing with wine or vinegar, chewing herbs, and disguising bad breath with mint were all popular ways to keep teeth clean.

The sheer amount of energy my mind exerted over a television program was mind-boggling. Socializing was like that for me. My mind poured over every facet of the interaction, analyzing, interpreting, and responding.

My antisocial behavior was perceived by others as pretentious and uppity—the nice way of saying they thought I was a bitch. For years, I didn't know that people felt this way about me. When I found out, it really bothered me. I considered myself a smiley and happy person, albeit quiet. To have such a negative effect on people led me to believe that I was doing something wrong. I wanted to change.

Maybe that was contrary to the opinion that, as they said, "You shouldn't judge a book by its cover." I'm not sure that advice applied very well in this situation. Whether people liked it or not, many times the cover was what drew them into a book.

I needed to appear friendlier and more open, so I did what I was great at and spent my time researching the topic. I read books and articles about socializing. I made changes. I held my shoulders back, stopped crossing my arms, and just smiled more often. It worked. People started to talk to me more often, and, oddly enough, I started to enjoy it.

As much fun as it was to have friends and the camaraderie that came along with them, I still struggled to cope. I couldn't deny that I still had internal issues to be dealt with, but I had become pretty good at creating the illusion of normalcy. Sometimes creating that illusion actually made me feel normal.

After lunch, I headed down the white hallways, meandering my way to the lobby area to wait for Charlotte so that we could walk down to our volunteer job together. I'd started working when I was sixteen. It wasn't necessarily my choice. Actually, I had no say-so in it, because my dad had made up a plan to instill work ethic in me.

The first year I had to detassel, which meant a lot of physical labor. I would wake up around five in the morning, walk to the pickup spot, and board a school bus to rural Nebraska farm country. An hour or so later, we, as in thirty or so of us teenagers, would arrive at the cornfield that we would be working that day. I would walk along and pull the tassels off of the corn, plant by plant, row by row, until it was midafternoon. Then I'd board the bus back to Lincoln and go home.

I cried almost every single day, and on the days that I wasn't crying, I was too busy being angry. Hate was too weak of a word to describe the emotion, but my dad insisted that I continue on until the end of the season. He was unrelenting. I'm not sure how he was able to endure being woken up by a raging teenager at five in the morning every single day.

In the end, I never missed a day of work. My dad said it would be one of the best accomplishments of my life. Although it was one of the biggest, it was not the best. I never wanted to detassel again, and I would forever appreciate the people who did physical labor and hoped to never be one of them. Maybe most importantly, though, it taught me what it was like to work very hard. I learned, albeit the difficult way, to work through mental obstacles. It would turn out to be tremendously helpful but only in hindsight.

The next year, my dad let me choose between two different

volunteer opportunities. The first was at Spes, a "shelter for the displaced." In other words, it was a homeless shelter. The other option was a care facility for the elderly, aptly named "Haven." I couldn't pick between the two, so I decided to interview at both to see which one I would prefer. Spes was first, only because they were able to fit me into their schedule right away.

I knew Spes wasn't for me almost immediately. The manager who interviewed me gave a few insightful pieces of advice. His speech was long but well worded.

He said, "If you're looking for a place that gives immediate gratification or, really, if you need gratification that you're doing good, then this volunteer position isn't for you. The problem with volunteering in a homeless shelter is that there is a large spectrum of people with a small spectrum of problems," he explained. "Some are going through financial difficulties, but the majority are veterans, people dealing with addiction of some kind, people who have mental issues, or all of the above. There are occasionally families who need the shelter too, as a short-term house until they are able to afford to live elsewhere, but overall what you get is a lot of people who, despite all your effort to get them to a better place, will go on living the way they do. It's hard to break those cycles, and in ninety-nine percent of cases, you can't. Some people can't handle seeing that, and that's OK."

I'd known right at that point I wasn't the type of volunteer Spes needed. Haven it was.

I sat down in one of the black chairs in the lobby. I looked up at the clock. Charlotte was late, which was uncharacteristic. She was almost obsessively punctual. While I waited, I heard a familiar voice and looked over to see Rosa standing with her back to me, talking on her phone.

"We'll talk about it later. You're making a big deal about a situation that you knew was inevitable. Trust me," she said, talking into the phone. She paused. "I think we both know what this is about...No! I'm not trying to analyze you. I'm late for an appointment—I need to go," she said, then touched her phone to hang up and shoved it in her purse.

It wasn't odd to hear her on the phone with one of her patients. She was always on duty. One of her clinical duties was to consult as a school psychologist, so seeing her here wasn't unusual.

"Rosa," I said. She turned in my direction immediately.

"Oh, Evangeline—I didn't even notice you," she said, seeming shocked to see me. "Are you headed to Haven?"

"Yes, I'm just waiting for Charlotte," I replied. Just then Charlotte walked into the lobby.

"Ah, I'm heading in to speak with Mr. Nighburn. I'll see you later," Rosa said and turned away from me.

"All right. Bye," I replied, but she was already through the doors.

Charlotte was walking toward me, beaming.

"Hey," I said.

"Hi, Evangeline. Did your day go well?" she asked.

"Yep, although the end of the day was kind of peculiar, but I'll explain later. How was yours?" I asked.

"Good. You have a really large booger hanging off your nose." she said, without skipping a beat.

If people around us hadn't heard the comment, they certainly would have noticed the look on my face.

My hand immediately went up to my nose and sure enough, a giant green blob was hanging from my right nostril.

Charlotte laughed. I could hear a few snickers coming from other kids just down the way.

"God I wonder how long that has been there? Luckily I didn't eat with anybody at lunch."

Charlotte was a true friend, the kind that had no qualms about telling you the honest truth, even if it was embarrassing.

"How is it that I always have the mortifying moments and you never do? Your embarrassing moments are like—oh you have paper stuck to your shoe. Mine are like—oh you have your underwear tucked into your dress," I said

She dissolved into a fit of laughter. The sound of her giddy laugh was infectious and so I couldn't help but join her. We laughed the entire way to Haven.

The day I arrived at Haven to start my volunteer work, the first person/patient I met was Sausagesia, pronounced literally saw-sej-seeya. She was as unique as her name conveyed, a vibrant and very funny elderly lady in her early sixties. Between her and Charlotte, I had no reason to be absent from volunteering.

As an elderly care facility, Haven catered to a wide variety of people. Many had Alzheimer's disease, but all the residents had health problems of some kind. A few were very advanced in age and needed assistance. Even after several years of working with them, the Alzheimer's residents were the hardest for me. It was such a devastating disease.

A few months ago a resident named Aidan passed away from Alzheimer's. For several months, I had helped to care for him and watched him go downhill. He came to Haven in the early stages of the disease, still able to walk and take care of himself without much help. His wife, Marianna, explained to us that she wasn't comfortable caring for him anymore, because he would frequently wander off and not remember where he was. Plus, she was seventy-three and had her own health problems, but she visited him every day. He always spoke of how much he adored her. Their kids, the two out of five that remained, visited weekly.

Every afternoon, Marianna would walk in and say, "Hey, good lookin'! How's your day going?"

Aidan's face would light up, and he'd smile. Then he would remark about how she was the good-looking one and tell her about his day.

A few months after he arrived at Haven, Marianna came in one afternoon for her daily visit. I escorted her to his room. I usually stayed for a little bit during visits with the residents who had Alzheimer's, to make sure everyone was safe. Things could change so rapidly from one day to the next.

She walked into the room and said, "Hey, good lookin'!"

Right away I could tell something was wrong with Aidan. He didn't answer her and walked over to me. "Who is that lady? I don't want her in here. I don't know who she is. I'd like to be alone. Get her out of here!" he said.

I looked over at Marianna. Her face fell; the sadness welled in her eyes. She was shocked and confused and sad. I'm sure she knew that it was a matter of time before the Alzheimer's progressed, but it was one thing to mentally prepare. To be emotionally ready for your husband to reject you after forty years of marriage was impossible. She was devastated.

After that day, Marianna still came every afternoon, but she wasn't the same. I could see the anxiety when she walked through the doors not knowing what to expect. Some days Aidan would remember her, but most he would not. When he passed away a few months ago, he was bedridden and slept most of the day.

It terrified me to think about losing control over how I felt, what I remembered, and how I was treated. It was possibly my worst fear in life. The only thing that surpassed my fear of Alzheimer's was to have a stroke and be stuck in a vegetative state, not being able to communicate but still being aware and alert inside of my head.

I once read the story of a man who was in precisely that situation. With the help of an fMRI (functional magnetic resonance imaging)—that big white tube used in hospitals to scan the brain and/or body—his doctors were able to deduce that he was, indeed, able to think and reason, although he was unable to communicate using his body.

My own body tensed up at the thought. It would be maddening. What would you do every day? How would you pass the time? It would be so lonely having just your own mind to converse with. Would you need to sleep eight hours like a normal person? What if you had an itch? On a lighter tangent, what if somebody turned on the TV in your room to a channel that you absolutely hated, and you had to sit and watch or hear it all day for years? The horror. No, seriously, the horror. I hoped that I was overthinking the situation.

Charlotte, in contrast to me, loved to work with the Alzheimer's patients. One day a few months ago, I watched as she was working with a resident with particularly advanced Alzheimer's who forgot her name every five minutes. Patiently, Charlotte answered the same questions over and over again.

"Who are you?" he would say.

"I'm Charlotte. How are you doing today?"

"Good. Why am I here? I'm ninety-five and still alive!" he replied.

Then a few minutes later, he would ask, "Who are you?"

Charlotte, unfazed by the question that she had answered twenty times previously, would reply in the same kind voice as the time before.

Later that day, I asked her why she continued to answer his question over and over again.

"They can't remember my answers. When I answer kindly, they have five minutes of feeling at ease. Imagine if you didn't know the person who was giving you a bath? Wouldn't that be scary or at least confusing? I hope that if I was that person, people would try to be nice instead of ignoring me."

The mere fact that I even had to ask the question was shameful. She was right, obviously. I always wished that I could be more like her.

Charlotte and I walked through the glass front doors of Haven and slid our electronic badges through the reader then put them back around our necks. Usually, we walked down to the changing room and put on our turquoise scrubs. It was never a good idea to wear normal clothes. One bodily fluid or another always ended up spattered on my shirt by the end of the shift.

I looked at the computer screen in the nurse's station to see who I was assigned to for the day. "Sausagesia Lake," I read. She was my favorite. I walked toward her room at the end of the bright-green hallway.

"Hi, Sia! How are you doing?" I asked.

She was wearing a pair of navy-colored pants and a lavender blouse. Her frail body looked a bit thinner than it did a week or so ago, but her cheerful attitude seemed unchanged. She always wore dark-purple eye shadow that made her light-green eyes stand out. Since I'd met her, I had never seen her go without makeup. Her shiny black hair was always curled. The lady was unrelenting.

"I'm doin' well! It looks like a wonderful day outside," she replied in her slightly southern accent.

"It is a gorgeous spring day. Have you not been outside today?" I asked.

"Not yet, dear, you know how it is when Malley is on duty," she replied.

Sia didn't like Malley, the head nurse who was on duty today. In all fairness, Malley was a great nurse. She just didn't seem to be able to prioritize or delegate responsibilities very well, so we were almost always behind on the schedule. It didn't matter. I never tried to change Sia's opinion, because it was futile.

"Well, shall we venture outside then? I'll grab you a blanket and your wheelchair, and we will go on a little walk," I said.

"That would be wonderful!" Sia replied.

Once she was settled comfortably in her wheelchair, we strolled out the back door of Haven. A cement path led to a small green garden. The flowers were blooming, and the trees were bright green.

"How is school goin'? Anything or anyone new and interesting?" she said with a laugh.

My lack of a love life was a frequent topic of our discussions. I'm not sure who wanted me to have a new boyfriend more, her or me.

"Nothing new in the romance department. Actually, I'm working on a rather lengthy paper about the plague," I said.

"Oh? Well you know I did survive the plague, right?" she replied.

"Gosh, no, I didn't, but I suppose I should have known that. You would have been thirty-five or so during it, right?" I asked.

"I was. Actually I had just turned thirty-five a few days before Z3C7 hit the United States. It was quite an ordeal. Would you like me to tell you about it?" she asked.

"Yes, I would! Please do," I replied.

"Goodness, it's been a long time since I've thought about it. It was a difficult time. It wasn't fun. Well, no, it was a bit more fun toward the end," she said.

"Fun? Ha, what exactly would make a plague a bit more fun toward the end?" I asked.

"Sex, of course. This is the side of the story you won't read in any historical account," she said.

I laughed. "I won't lie; I'm intrigued," I said, smiling.

Nodding at me, she began her story:

"When the first wave went through the United States, people were scared, petrified. Many of my family members died. A lot of my friends died. As you might imagine, nobody wanted to bring a baby into the world at that time. Birth control wasn't necessarily a priority medication. Actually, it wasn't available at all. In November, when it started, everyone mainly focused on surviving. I don't even remember most of those first thirty days; they flew by so fast.

Needless to say, sex wasn't on our minds. I don't think anyone was willing to risk getting pregnant in such a tumultuous time. It was almost a guaranteed death sentence. However, after a few months, there was a noticeable change in society. When President Monahan died, I think it shocked us into realizing that this virus could kill pretty much anyone. Goodness, if the president of the United States of America died of Z3C7, we were all screwed—please forgive my language. Influenza was the great equalizer.

At that point, most of the remaining survivors developed a completely different mentality. We all felt that, frankly, if we were still alive, well, we must be invincible and if not, then who cared? The fear was gone, replaced by some odd sense of confidence. If we were going to die anyway, why not enjoy the time we had left?

In our neighborhood, people started socializing. My husband and I started having sex again. We conceived our set of twins in that later part of the second wave. Thankfully, a bit more normalcy returned before I delivered Adalia and Adolphus."

I could see the joy in her eyes as she spoke of her children.

"Once the plague ended, I think we all had a sense of purpose," she said. "We were responsible for putting society back together. I felt like I was a needed and integral part of the community. I miss that. I think a lot of people who lived through it do. Once society was back up and running, it was like coming down off of an adrenaline high. We had become used to being busy every day, and then it abruptly dropped off.

"For me, the downtime was a real enemy, because it was when I started to think and feel overwhelmed with sadness. I started missing the people who didn't survive. I'm betting if you go and look it up, if such statistics even exist, there was an increased suicide rate during that time. Living through the plague was difficult, but surviving it was, at times, much more precarious," she said.

I was enthralled by her story. I'd never thought about the smaller details during that time. The shift in thinking over the course of the plague made perfect sense to me. Fear, in a time where you would think it reigned supreme, stepped out of the equation and was replaced by fearlessness. It was so distinctly human to waver from one emotion to the complete opposite.

"Out of curiosity, what was the best and worst thing you saw during that time?" I asked.

Sia paused, her eyes gazing up and to the right. I remembered reading somewhere that when recalling a memory, a person looks up and to the right, but when telling a lie, the eyes go up and to the left.

"The worst? Well, of course it was not having Coca-Cola." She smiled. "No, the most difficult day for me was when our neighbors, Alaina and Liam, lost all four of their children within twenty-four hours. Two days later, both Alaina and Liam killed themselves.

"The best? I suppose it was the notion that humans can still be kind and selfless even in dire circumstances. I doubt that we would have survived without the help of our neighbors and probably vice versa," she said.

One question still lingered in my mind. "Do you remember the Veterox vaccine?" I asked.

"Yes, but I don't really know much about it. When it hit the news that a cure was imminent, everyone was ecstatic. Everyone agreed with the plan the government had devised to test the vaccination. The first round was to be started at a children's hospital/camp...actually I'm not even sure where. I think it was something like four hundred doses for the kids and another six hundred doses to be distributed among the parents. There wasn't enough to cover every parent, so a lottery system was used to be fair.

"It didn't matter, because the test trials proved the Veterox vaccine wasn't safe. Apparently all of those poor children and parents died from taking it. It was upsetting, but to be honest, something like sixty percent of those people would have died regardless. I didn't know anyone directly involved with the ordeal, and I don't remember it being widely publicized. It's not like we could dwell on it," she explained.

Obviously I'd been overthinking the situation with Mr. Stalnik. In hearing Sia's account of the plague, I realized that my perspective may have been skewed. I couldn't wrap my mind around the fact that the Veterox vaccine had gone unnoticed. It seemed impossible. That was the thing though, Veterox vaccine was given during a time of chaos, in the midst of rampant death and disease—something that I couldn't entirely fathom.

I walked Sausagesia back into Haven and to her room.

"Why did your parents name you Sausagesia?" I asked.

"Well, that's not actually the way you pronounce it. My parents intended it to be 'Sawsa-Jesia.' It sounds oddly pretty, doesn't it? That's why I never changed it. For some reason though, nobody could pronounce it that way, and I finally just gave up constantly correcting them," she said.

"What! Sausagesia gave up on something? I never thought I would see the day!" I replied, smiling.

She laughed. "I don't waste my time on unimportant battles anymore."

I could tell she was tired, so I tucked her into bed and turned the lights off.

"Hope you sleep well! I'll see you on Friday," I said. My birthday was tomorrow, so I would have the next few days off.

"All right, Miss Evangeline. Can't wait to see you then! Have a safe trip home, and happy early birthday!" she replied.

"Will do! Thank you!" I said.

What time was it? I checked the clock on the wall of the hallway. 4:07 p.m. I was supposed to end my shift at four. Charlotte would still be waiting for me in the break room. She usually went home without me if I was more than fifteen minutes late. I walked through the doors to the break room, and as predicted, she was sitting down in a chair, watching TV.

"Can I borrow a dress of yours for tomorrow night?" she asked.

Every year my dad, Rosa, Isaac, Charlotte, and I went out together for my birthday dinner. This year I chose an Indian restaurant that had opened up a few months ago. I loved Indian food.

"Sure, which dress did you want?" I replied.

"I don't know, whatever you think would look good on me," she said.

"I have an emerald-green wrap dress that would look great on you. Green always looks good on brunettes," I told her.

"Thanks for letting me borrow it! What time tomorrow night?" Charlotte said.

"I think around five. Since it'll be Tuesday night, I don't think we will have to wait very long," I replied.

We walked out the front doors of Haven and continued down the street. Charlotte's house was about a block and a half away.

The air seemed heavy with humidity. It reminded me of the days when Charlotte and I wanted to be tornado chasers. One spring weekend in junior high, we had watched a movie about a team of meteorologists in Kansas who spent their time driving into storms, trying to predict tornados. We were thirteen and had passionately decided that it was our fate to be storm chasers together. I think we even tried to make up business cards.

Charlotte must have been thinking the same thing. "It feels like a good night for tornados," she said, smiling.

"I think we'd be dead by now if we had gone down that route," I replied.

"Yes, probably, but it would have been a fun way to die," she said.

"Only if it were an EF-5 or something crazy. It would be disappointing to die in an EF-1, and that would have been our luck," I said.

We arrived at Charlotte's front door.

"Tell Autry and your mom hi for me. I'll have the dress ready for you when you come by tomorrow afternoon," I said.

Autry was Charlotte's younger brother. He suffered from a severe form of autism and required a lot of care. Her dad divorced her mom several years ago and then ran out on them. Financially, they weren't doing very well. Hence she borrowed my clothes often.

"OK, see you then!" Charlotte replied.

{8}

Eight

The clouds were rumbling through the sky during my walk home. Thankfully, my house was a short walk from Charlotte's, only six and a half blocks. My dad was home, and it looked like Rosa and Isaac were too. That was odd, I thought. They were rarely home this early. Surprise birthday party?

I wouldn't put it past them. They were always up to crazy antics around my birthday. A few years ago, they surprised me with a trip to Canada. We all boarded the plane and took off for Vancouver. I only figured out that we were actually headed to Egypt midway through the eight-hour flight, when we hadn't landed. They'd successfully persuaded the gate agents and flight attendants to play along with the ploy. In hindsight, I *had* thought that it was weird that we somehow had priority boarding and were the first ones on the plane.

When I reached the front door, I could hear people talking inside.

"She's here," Rosa said.

Everyone quieted down immediately. It has to be a surprise party, I thought. I trudged through the door, fully expecting there to be a room full of people exclaiming, "Happy Birthday!"

I walked through the living room. Nobody popped out. The air seemed tense. My stomach started to churn, and suddenly I felt really nervous. I stepped into the kitchen. My dad was sitting at the table, with Rosa standing next to him, and Isaac stood across the room with his arms crossed.

"What's going on?" I asked. "Were you arguing? I thought when Rosa said, 'She's here,' it was maybe a surprise party for my birthday, but obviously that's not the case."

"Well it will be a surprise—that's for certain—just not of the birthday variety," Isaac said.

Rosa glared at him.

"I'm really confused. Would someone please let me in on this conversation that seems to be going on between you all?" I asked.

The roomed seemed heavy with emotion.

Rosa spoke, "I suppose I can start us off. I know you've been wondering a lot about some details of the Veterox vaccine. We mostly agree"—she stared back at Isaac—"that there are items we need to discuss in terms of that. Information that may answer some of your questions—"

Isaac cut her off. "I really want to emphasize that I don't think this is a good decision. I'm going along with it, but this is not how I would choose to play out the situation. It's a huge safety risk for Evangeline," he said.

That last sentence didn't make me feel better. This can't be good, I thought.

"I know you have concerns. I don't discount them, but I do trust Rosa. You know she has a unique insight into these things," my dad replied to Isaac.

Isaac shook his head. "And that's the only reason that I'm even going along with this right now. I think we should hold off a bit longer, but clearly I am missing something."

"Jesus, can we just get on with this? I feel like I'm going to throw up, because I'm so nervous at this point," I said.

My dad spoke:

"Yesterday when I was talking with you about Z3C7, we didn't quite get to the Veterox vaccine trials. I did that purposely, because I didn't know what I was going to say.

Okay, let's start back where we left off yesterday. Two months after the first wave started, Dr. Ethan Crailene got in touch with your mom. He said he had successfully created a vaccine for Z3C7 and that the initial tests in mammals had gone very, very well. Your mother and Ethan talked for quite a while, going through the basics—what the vaccine was, how many trials had been undertaken, what the government was going to do.

It turned out that Ethan had called her because he wanted Camp Espoir to be the first test site for the trials. The children in our camp would be the first recipients of the Veterox vaccine. He explained that government approval was imminent and that the first fifteen hundred doses would be ready in the next seven days. Violet told him that she would call him back with a decision. Ethan told her that he needed an answer within the hour. She called me into the room after she hung up with Ethan and asked me for my opinion.

We discussed it for a while, weighing the pros and cons. I told her, "I don't know, Violet. I think we have to go for it. Do you think that the government has vetted the vaccine enough?"

She replied, "Yes, I feel like they know it's safe, but there aren't any long-term studies to draw from, so I can't be certain. There's no question the testing phase of the drug is highly inadequate. It would never have passed the FDA under normal circumstances. However, these aren't normal circumstances. I think we have enough evidence that the drug hasn't caused any adverse side effects to feel good about moving forward with it."

I agreed with her. In retrospect, I'm not sure we were capable of turning the vaccine away. It was hope. If we hadn't tried, how many kids would have died? Of course, it was the more risky route. We could have waited for the trials to conclude and Veterox to be available to the entire population. Though that brought up other issues. How long would that be? What if the government ran out? The natural reaction for Violet and me was to want to move forward immediately. I'm not sure ethically if it was the right or wrong decision. Unfortunately, it wouldn't be the only ethical question we would have to answer."

I interrupted him. "What was Veterox?"

"Do you mean what was the Veterox vaccine made of?" he asked.

"Yes, what was in it? I've tried to find out from other people, but nobody seems to know any information about the trials, let alone the drug's components," I said.

"That's for a very good reason. I couldn't tell you what was in it, because I never knew. The government didn't allow for me to know those details. Actually, only a select few knew the formula: your mother, Ethan, and maybe his wife. Probably a few government people but that's it. I say that pretty confidently, because if there were more than a dozen people who knew the formula, you would have been able to find out what it was last night, at the click of a button. Believe me; somebody would have spoken up about it."

Last night? I never mentioned that I had done any research last night. Was he now monitoring my computer?

He continued on:

"So after Violet decided to participate in the trials, the ball started rolling really fast. Within twenty-four hours, Camp Espoir went on lockdown. Actually that's a little dramatic, because nobody was begging to get into a hospital/camp full of severely sick people anyway, but soldiers did arrive to enforce the lockdown. Ethan and his wife, Vivienne, and several doctors from the government arrived on the scene to help with the intake of extra patients. We were still admitting people during those first forty-eight hours, to fill the six hundred slots, but that was halted when it went public that Camp Espoir had been chosen to conduct the initial trial. After that, nobody was accepted, for obvious reasons. That didn't stop people from coming and begging to get in. We sent them on to the nearest hospital, because that's all we could do. It was an awful feeling, turning all of those people away.

A few days before the vaccine was to arrive, we held a meeting with all of the parents at the school gym inside of the camp. We explained the rules. Every child would get a shot of the Veterox vaccine. One parent of every child would get a shot of the Veterox vaccine. The remaining doses would be doled out by a lottery system to any remaining family. The lottery winners would be injected in a separate room from the original participants.

Security tightened to insane levels. Your mother and I had bodyguards at all times. We couldn't go to the bathroom without an escort. They actually went into the stall with us. No joke.

Early in the morning on December twenty-fourth, the vaccines were flown in from an undisclosed location. The plane landed at Chicago O'Hare International Airport, and the cargo was then loaded into armored cars. Shortly thereafter, the entire convoy drove along the route to Camp Espoir. A lot of the kids were so sick that they couldn't be transported anywhere, so it wasn't a viable option to move the operation to a more secure area. The convoy arrived, and the vaccine was moved to a room where guards stood watch.

There were about twenty nurses on staff, and I think maybe ten of them were helping us do the injections, while the rest were assigned to the normal patient-care duties. Ethan and Vivienne took the first two doses, along with all the doctors and nurses. Your mother and I decided to decline our two doses so that two more parents could receive them.

Altogether, the vaccinations took around six hours to complete. Ethan and Vivienne left soon after they were finished to rendezvous with government officials.

During the first few hours, patients were monitored continuously. Nobody had shown any adverse reactions, and remarkably, a few of the children started to get better. Three hours later, the number of those who were recovering increased. Four hours later, everyone was showing signs of improvement. We were ecstatic.

The security teams remained in place as a precaution, and it was decided that no outside visitors would be allowed in for twenty-four hours, though some family members had decided to stay in the waiting area. A few of the staff had gathered together in the gym, celebrating the news.

Around six in the evening, a nurse came over the loudspeaker, calling, "Dr. Rolieux to room 121. Code blue."

Immediately we started running down the hall toward room 121. A young girl, Layna, was sitting in her bed. She didn't appear to be in distress.

"Why did you call a code? Is this the right room?" Violet asked the nurse.

"Yes, it's the right room," the nurse replied. "Layna, honey, can you show Dr. Violet what you showed me?"

The girl nodded her head, put out her arm, and waved her fingers in a circular motion. A green marker on the dry-erase board near the door lifted and began to float in the air. It crossed the room and landed softly in Layna's lap.

"I'm not sure what to say. She is telekinetic? This just started happening?" Violet stammered. Her cell phone interrupted her. It was Ethan. She answered it immediately. His voice boomed through the speaker on the phone.

"Violet. I'm calling to tell you that government personnel are on their way to quarantine the entire camp. Vivienne and I are experiencing some, err, side effects," Ethan said, sounding worried.

"Let me give a guess; you are telekinetic," Violet replied.

"So you're starting to see the side effects there as well? No, we're not telekinetic, but we have similar issues. I'm not allowed to say what they are right at this moment, but I'll fill you in later when we know more. Make the necessary preparations for evacuations. People will be there very shortly, I imagine.

"It's an emergency situation. Please make sure nobody else is allowed into the building. Any visitors need to be taken out immediately. Everyone who has had the vaccine needs to remain inside. You and Xander will probably be flown to a separate location to be briefed. I'm sorry, Violet. Things are about to go crazy. I'll talk to you soon."

He hung up.

"Did you hear all of that?" Violet asked me.

I told her that I did and that we needed to focus on getting everyone ready. I went through the patient roster to see if there was anyone left on supportive measures, since they would need extra care during transportation. I told Violet I would call down to security and make sure everyone in the waiting area was evacuated. I asked if he had given a time frame.

"No, just that it would happen soon," she replied.

I called down to security, and they were overwhelmed, so I decided to go down to help them while your mom readied the patients.

I started running down the hall. "I'll meet up with you in a bit," I yelled back to her.

Less than thirty minutes after Ethan called, a brigade of government officials arrived. They weren't the kind of mean government people you think of from the movies. Everyone was kind and methodical about transporting the children and their parents. All fifteen hundred Veterox recipients were accounted for and transported to the airfield close by. All of the remaining families were contacted to let them know there was a situation and were told they would be contacted again later that evening with information. Officially they were told that "because of precautionary reasons," they were being evacuated and sent to a receiving hospital for quarantine and observation. They were informed that the new location had more resources and medical equipment to deal with potential adverse side effects. When all the patients and parents had been transported to the airport, it was our turn.

A shiny black BMW pulled up to the camp's front door. A woman stepped out of the passenger side and introduced herself.

"'I'm Aviana Mal. I'm an agent with the CIA, and I'll be taking you to a secure location to be debriefed," she said, smiling.

"Can you tell us where?" I asked.

"Yes, I can. Let's continue this conversation in the car, where we have a bit more privacy," she said.

Your mom and I got into the car. I remember the seats in that car were so comfortable. It was frigid outside, and the seats were heated. It had been some time since I'd last sat in such luxury.

"We will be driving to the airport and flying to Hawaii," she told us. "Hawaii, as you may or may not know, is now the government headquarters. It was relatively unaffected by the pandemic, because it was quarantined so fast. The location made it easy to secure. Most of the remaining US government has relocated there."

"Where is everyone else going?" your mom asked.

"To a medical compound in Oregon. I'm sure you're worried about how they are doing and what the conditions will be like for them. You'll be able to speak to officials when you arrive in Hawaii. Once everything has settled down, I'm sure you will be permitted to fly in and see the compound. I assure you nobody will be mistreated. It's a very nice facility on the coastline of Oregon. Do you know the movie *The Goonies*?"

We both nodded our heads.

"Remember the big rock in the ocean at the end? I think it's called Haystack Rock, but it's near Cannon Beach, Oregon. Anyway, that's where the facility is located," she said.

"Please don't be offended by this, but I'm a bit concerned by your openness," I said. "I guess it just doesn't feel right that you are answering our questions so...thoroughly."

"I think that's a common misconception. The movies really do us no justice in that department. I've been instructed to answer your questions as honestly as possible. There's no point in keeping you two in the dark. Besides, consider me the newest member of your family. I'm now assigned to your wife for the entire duration of her life," she told us.

I suppose I can skip forward a little bit in the story, for the sake of time. Nothing of interest happened until we arrived in Hawaii. Neither your mom nor I interacted very much beyond what was necessary. Everything had happened so fast...we were just in a state of shock.

Once we arrived in Honolulu, we were immediately escorted to a hotel…I remember how gorgeous it was. It must have been a Four Seasons or Ritz Carlton prior to the plague. It was unnecessarily lavish, especially considering the conditions most of the United States and the entire world were living in at the time. We couldn't really enjoy being in such a nice place, because we felt so guilty.

We didn't even have time to enjoy it anyway. An hour after we arrived at the hotel, we were taken to a secure military location to be debriefed. After being escorted to a facility a few miles away from the hotel, we were led into an elevator and then into a very large conference room. The room was white and windowless, very minimalistic. A long glass table sat in the middle of the room, with fifteen or so chairs pushed in around it.

Aviana introduced us to the handful of people congregated at the end of the large conference table. "This is Adrian Tallis, the acting director of the Central Intelligence Agency. Adrian, this is Dr. Violet Rolieux and her husband, Xander Rolieux."

Adrian was wearing jeans and a green T-shirt, not what you would expect from the director of the CIA. He smiled and reached out to shake our hands as he said, "Thank you, Aviana. It's wonderful to finally meet the world-famous Rolieux. I'm absolutely astounded at the amount of work and care you two put into Camp Espoir. On behalf of my wife and I, thank you for the care our daughter received at your camp. She was one of the very, very, few that did pull through, and we are doubtless about where our gratitude should lie."

"Well you're welcome. We had no idea your daughter was among our patients. What is her name?" Violet asked.

"She went by Ilena, but that's precisely the point. You both provided such a high caliber of care to every single patient it didn't matter their background. Believe me, there were plenty of patients in your care that were sons and daughters of high-level government, and even a few world, officials. We all knew Camp Espoir was the best place in the United States for children."

Aviana interrupted our conversation and led us toward the only other woman standing in the room. The woman had bright blond hair pulled back into a twist. Black glasses framed her blue-green eyes. She was wearing a fitted navy-blue dress that fell just below her knees, and at the very top, placed near her heart, was a pin depicting the flag of the United States of America.

"Xander, Violet," Aviana said, "this is the President of the United States of America, Odelia Lincoln."

I was immediately taken aback by her youth. She couldn't have been more than thirty-five years old.

"Jesus, how many people died in order for you to become president?" I blurted out. I froze immediately, realizing what I had just said. "I'm so sorry...err, I didn't mean to say that. At least not in that way. I mean, you are really young, and I'm genuinely curious, but I didn't mean it as an insult," I explained.

The president's eyes softened, and a huge smile flowed over her face. "Finally, somebody that's brutally honest," she said. "I was the secretary of the interior before this entire...ordeal with Z3C7. The president, the vice-president, the speaker of the house, the president pro tempore of the senate, the secretary of state, the secretary of the treasury, the secretary of defense, and the attorney general all got sick, so I guess the answer to your question is eight. A few are in comas, but the majority passed away."

Silence filled the room as the shock of her words reverberated through the air.

"I'm so sorry to hear that," your mom replied.

"Well, unfortunately this country has seen its share of travesty in the past months, and losing a large part of the government, I would wager to say, is a small matter in comparison. When Z3C7 hit, besides the upper, essential government officials, everyone went on leave for obvious reasons. We had no children, so my husband and I decided to volunteer with the military. We were placed on the front lines of the food-and-shelter operation. Leni and I rode together on the supply trucks going out to give people basic necessities, like food and water. It's needless to say, but I know firsthand the conditions this country is facing, and they are horrifying. My husband did end up dying from Z3C7 just over a week ago, and then, in a twist of fate, I became the president of the United States of America."

The conversation was abruptly halted by a voice over the speaker. A projector screen slid down from the ceiling, and the video feed became visible. Four people appeared on the screen.

"If you will all be seated please," said a male voice.

Your mother and I grabbed seats close to the end of the table. The president, the CIA director, and two other men sat down across the table.

The man's voice continued, "This is General Leighton Ortega of the special-command operations center. This meeting is taking place at 1100 hours on the twenty-fifth of December. The attendees in Hawaii include President Lincoln, CIA Director Adrian Tallis, General Mitchell Laderis, CDC Director David Galento, Agent Aviana Mal, and Dr. Violet Rolieux, who oversaw Veterox trials in Camp Espoir, accompanied by her husband, Xander Rolieux. Attendees on site in Oregon are Doctors Ethan and Vivienne Crailene, as well as two medical directors here, Dr. Rose Dee and Dr. Collin Eswa. We are here to discuss a resolution to the Veterox trials."

President Lincoln spoke first. "I've been informed that there are quite a number of unique side effects from Veterox being reported, some a bit unbelievable. Can you elaborate on that for us please?"

Ethan responded, "No doubt you've been informed of the telekinesis. It hasn't been limited to just one or two of the subjects. All fifteen hundred people who have received Veterox are showing signs of...I suppose an elevated intelligence level, brain activity, and peculiar talents. I don't know that we want to go into depth on our findings yet. President Lincoln, perhaps in a secondary, more confidential meeting we can discuss the details. In short, these test subjects are completely clear of the Z3C7 virus but are exhibiting signs of pretty significant intellectual changes."

The room went quiet for a moment.

President Lincoln spoke again. "So if I am understanding you correctly, Veterox did work. It did stop the virus, but it did so with particularly odd side effects. Has anybody died?" she asked.

Dr. Eswa spoke, "Yes, three children have died. We saw a large brain-activity spike before each of the children developed massive brain hemorrhages, which could not be reversed. To answer your first question, yes, Veterox did work. There are no signs of Z3C7 in any of the test subjects," he said.

The voice of General Ortega once again resonated through the air. "Our concerns at this point are the side effects of Veterox and how we proceed on. It is the opinion of Dr. Crailene and myself that the trials should be immediately halted and all of the remaining Veterox vaccine should be destroyed, along with any other relevant information."

Your mom interrupted. "Why? I'm confused as to why we would halt a vaccine that clearly works, that will save millions of lives, all because of a few side effects?"

Ethan replied, "Because these aren't just side effects. Telekinesis and telepathy are two good examples. It doesn't matter what kind of miracle drug Veterox is or was. Ethically, we cannot give people a vaccine that we know will give them, for lack of a better word, powers. Nobody can say that this drug does no harm. We have no idea.

"Maybe even more importantly, we cannot know what possible security risks it would pose for the entire world. Surely you have all seen what damage people have done to one another during the last few months. What happens when somebody truly evil gets ahold of this drug or pays somebody with these so-called intellectual powers to work for them? I'm not sure whether it's worse to die from a nuclear bomb, a biological weapon, or influenza, but at least in the latter case, we would have good people still standing. It only takes one terrorist to take this drug and use it as a weapon. There is no scenario in which Veterox should be continued."

I looked over at the president. A tear was rolling down her face, followed by another one and another one. She just as quickly wiped them away.

"Are you crying, Odelia? For crying out loud, you are really fucking crying?" the CDC director said in a mocking voice.

Your mother was livid. There were not many things in this world that bothered her, but when she felt somebody was being needlessly cruel, she would not let it go.

Violet shot back, "Are you actually making fun of someone for crying? Are you a fucking sociopath? Do you feel no emotion about the fact that we are making the decision to kill millions of people, when we have the power to keep them alive? Do you not have any feelings of sadness about playing a hand in the death of even one person? Apparently you're the type of person who feels emotion is a weakness. Quite frankly, it's very obvious that you haven't done any work on the front lines or lost anyone close to you, because if you had, you wouldn't have just made that comment."

President Lincoln glanced over in our direction and smiled. She looked back into the projector and spoke. "Ethan, I do agree with you. I am upset. I won't lie. As obvious as the right decision may be to some of you, to me both sides are equally troubling."

The president turned to your mother. "Violet, what is your opinion?"

To my utter astonishment, your mom replied, "My decision would be to destroy the vaccine and focus on dealing with the fourteen hundred and ninety-seven people who are dealing with these so-called side effects. I don't think we will ever feel guilt-free in making this decision, and we shouldn't expect to. The loss of life that will continue on after this should always resonate with us. I'm going to be honest, Odelia. I think that Xander and I should be excluded from further meetings. We need to be able to have some deniability that is plausible. Neither of us should know the full extent of the side effects or what is happening with those fourteen hundred and ninety-seven people.

"As long as you can guarantee and provide some proof that these victims and their families are being well cared for—and I mean the absolute best care—I'll take the fall for the vaccinations. We will tell the public whatever story you decide is best. I will say I think the most appropriate course of action is to tell the public that all fifteen hundred recipients died as a result of the vaccine. Fight death with death. Nobody wants to pursue a drug that causes death a hundred percent of the time, but if there is any glimmer of hope that it might have worked, any survivors, people will hold on to it."

Adrian, the CIA director, said angrily, "How? How do we go about the whole process? Forgive me, but I don't see a scenario in which we can keep fourteen hundred and ninety-seven civilians at a military compound forever without their consent—"

"Well I think we have to make it appealing," Ethan interrupted. "Obviously we can't come right out and say that they can't leave. It has to be a multifaceted approach."

Ethan's wife, Vivienne, agreed. "I'll come right out and say it; I think we will have to lie a great deal. While we'll need to emphasize the great aspects of being a vaccine recipient and the value they have to the country and world with their newfound "talents," we also need to make up a dire reason why they can't be around anyone in normal society. We could tell them that everyone who has come into contact with the participants has died.

"It might not be as hard of a con as it sounds. I'm sure the shock of suddenly acquiring 'powers' has put them at odds with what they know about the capacity of their brains. It defies logic that they would suddenly gain all of this power with a simple injection—could it be too good to be true? Surely there has to be a downside, right? We can play on that doubt."

Your mom replied, "And I don't think it will be that difficult of a cover-up to pull off with the general public. There aren't enough people around to investigate. I think once the story goes out that Veterox was a failure with a one hundred percent mortality rate, it will likely fade away."

President Lincoln stood up and walked toward your mother and me. She said, "Thank you both! I very much appreciate your advice. I think that it's probably time for you to leave, if you don't wish to know anything further. I'll be in contact with you through Aviana when we decide what we would like you two to tell the public. I imagine by late this evening we will have that decision made, so you can expect to hear from me at that time."

Your mom and I stood up. I shook President Lincoln's hand. Odelia gave your mom a hug and whispered something in her ear. We walked to the door and were escorted back to our room by the secret service and Aviana.

Once your mother and I were alone in our room, I asked her, "What's going on, Violet?"

"Xander, I don't know if I made the right decision to take us out of that meeting. I'm trying to think of our future, and if we had stayed, there was no going back. We would be permanently involved in a very sensitive matter. I think they are moving forward with the right decision, but if we know the details, we will be inextricably involved. We are going to have to be the face of this incident, regardless of the outcome, because the public will have questions, and we are the only people still standing that can answer. I want to lie as little as possible. It's going to be hard enough to do so with the current information we have. Imagine if we knew everything."

I told her that I understood, and I did, at least in part. I knew that she'd made the right decision in an ethically very gray area. We might get the chance to have a life because of it."

My dad paused. I thought he was finished with the story, so I spoke. "I'm a little in shock. So, the entire ordeal must have gone successfully, because I have yet to find any information about Veterox via books, the Internet, or teachers. Why did you conceal this from me for so long? I don't really understand."

"To answer your first question, yes, it did go well. Your mom and I made a public statement about Veterox later that evening. We informed the media that it had failed, that all fifteen hundred people had passed away, that the government was dealing with the fatalities, and that the government was in the beginning stages of conducting an investigation into what went wrong. All of our records were destroyed, and no names of the trial participants were ever officially announced. Families did come forward to announce that their children were among the dead, and don't get me wrong—people were upset. However, there were just too many other terrible things happening."

I could tell he was trying to find the words to explain the situation better.

"Understand that the circumstances were much different than they are now," he finally said. "I know that it sounds farfetched, at the least, to think that the government was able to stage such a massive cover-up. It would be impossible to accomplish today. However, back then, there wasn't much of a media presence left. People were getting news from one station, which itself was a pooled-together group of journalists from various other news organizations. Things were disorganized at best.

"In some ways, the colossal failure of the initial cover-up was part of our great success. People didn't trust in the government. Therefore, when the news came out that Veterox had killed all of its participants, it seemed like par for the course. As sad as I am to admit it, fear worked to our advantage."

"It just doesn't seem that plausible. Does it?" I said, turning toward Rosa and Isaac. "I assume that you all know about this Veterox vaccine ordeal already, correct? Do you really believe that people didn't figure out something was a little bit off about the circumstances? Wouldn't it be easier for the government to just kill everyone in the study and leave it at that?

"How do you know that wasn't the case—what if they killed everyone and covered it up? I mean, that seems like the most logical path. Too risky to keep a large group of people hidden. Besides, isn't it likely that we would have heard something from a Veterox by now? It's been twenty-five years," I said.

A smirk appeared on Isaac's face and then quickly vanished. Neither Isaac nor Rosa answered my question.

86

"Yes, that's logical. I can see how you might think that. I can't be absolutely certain that the majority of the Veterox, as you call them, weren't killed, but I can say with absolute certainty that some are still alive," my dad said.

How would he know that? What did that mean? My brain was running faster than my mouth could keep up with.

"What?" I finally managed to say.

"Let's back up again," he said. "After the Veterox ordeal was over, at least publicly, your mom and I went back to work at Camp Espoir. About seven months after the plague began, things started to calm down a bit. The majority of people who died did so in those first seven months. So in the natural ebb and flow of life, things started to return to normal. Then early in the morning on June sixteenth, we received a call from Ethan Crailene."

My dad paused again.

"He asked us if we would be willing to take in a pair of Veterox twins that had been born a few hours ago. He explained that the parents had both died and that he wanted the babies placed outside of the Veterox compound. He said that he couldn't go into detail about the situation and that he needed an answer within the next ten minutes. We said yes."

My mind was spiraling. Isaac and Rosa's birthday was June fifteenth. I felt nauseated. My ears were ringing. I was going to throw up.

"She's going to be sick. Get a bowl!" Rosa yelled at Isaac or my dad; I wasn't sure which one.

Isaac grabbed a glass bowl from one of the cupboards and quickly handed it to me.

"Couldn't you have picked a less transparent bowl?" Rosa said, laughing.

I couldn't hold it down anymore. I was just thankful I wasn't throwing up on the floor.

Isaac glanced over at me and smiled. He began to laugh, which annoyed me.

"I told you this was not a good idea. She's throwing up over finding out we're Veterox. Imagine what she's going to do when she finds out the rest," he said.

"The rest? What is that supposed to mean?" my voice croaked.

Rosa grabbed the bowl from my hands and took it over to the sink. Isaac handed me a paper towel.

My dad cut in. "I told you earlier about the special abilities the Veterox exhibited after the vaccine trials, the ones we didn't want to know about...Rosa and Isaac have them. Obviously you've put together that Isaac and Rosa were the twin babies we adopted. They started to exhibit unique talents around age two. Well, that's when we started to notice them at least. In part, that's why we waited so long to have you. It took us a while to get a handle on the situation," he said.

"What kind of unique talents?" I asked.

My dad looked over at Isaac. "Isaac, well, I guess I'll turn this one over to you," he said.

Isaac looked cautiously at me. What emotion was that on his face? Anxiety?

"I think I can convey it best by showing you, okay? Don't get sick," he said, his arrogance returning.

All of a sudden, he started running, almost sprinting, across the kitchen. He was fast, but if that was his talent, then he oversold himself. But he wasn't slowing down, and the wall was less than two feet away. And then, just as I was sure he was going to hit the yellow plaster, he disappeared. Within a few seconds, he reappeared, standing right next to me. My eyes widened. "Invisibility powers?" I said, stammering.

"In short, yes. It's more than that, but for simplicity's sake, yes, I have—what did you call it?—'invisibility powers,'" he replied.

"Yes, that makes it so much simpler," I said, sarcastically.

"Let's not use the word 'powers.' It makes it sound like I'm a superhero or comic-book character. I'm much more of a James Bond," he said, grinning.

"Ha, I sincerely doubt that. I haven't seen any of your lady friends around here. Are they invisible too?" I replied, laughing.

"Maybe that's just how I prefer to sneak them in."

My teeth dug into the bottom of my lip. Isaac's eyes flashed with delight.

"Well, I suppose it's my turn," Rosa interrupted us. "I'm telepathic, meaning that I can read minds. I can't read the past, but if you are recalling a memory in the present, I'm able to hear that. I can feel emotions as you experience them. Would you like me to show you an example?" she said.

"Uh, well, I suppose. I don't know. Am I the test subject?" I asked.

"Don't worry; it's nothing you will notice. I mean, I've been doing it for the last twenty-some years," she replied.

"Oh, well that makes me feel a lot better. Just get on with the test. I already believe you anyway. Isaac just ran through a wall, so mind reading seems relatively normal in comparison. I suppose that's why you knew I was going to throw up?" I said. I was slightly annoyed.

"Yep, but you were also just really pale, and anyone who saw the blood drain out of your face could probably wager a good guess that you were going to get sick," she said.

"Great, thanks. Let's just get on with this. What color, number, and name am I thinking of?" I replied.

"Thirty-seven, yellow, Marilyn," she answered correctly, without missing a beat. "But more importantly, why are you so angry? You're so upset." She looked concerned.

"You're the mind reader; shouldn't you know that?" I replied caustically. Adrenaline surged through my body, and my hands started shaking.

I exploded, "Why am I upset? I thought this was a surprise party for me! Surprise! Rosa has been able to read your mind for the past twenty years and, therefore, knows extremely personal details about you. Sur-fucking-prise! Isaac has probably, you know with his power of invisibility, snuck into my room to read my diary!"

Isaac laughed. "First off, I really don't think *you* are our main target. Your life is not that interesting, and I would be horribly bored watching you twenty-four hours a day. Secondly, I have read your diary. It was a few years ago. Once I came upon the details of your attraction to a certain person, I stopped."

My heart had to have skipped a beat, but you wouldn't have known it from the amount of blood rushing to my face. I was mortified. This was insane. Was this really happening?

Isaac realized right away that he had gone too far. His eyes burned back into mine, and I could tell he was upset. The sparkle in his eyes from a few minutes ago had been replaced by something, but I couldn't place it. Vulnerability? Sympathy or maybe empathy? It didn't matter. I was too angry to care. A tear rolled down my cheek. Many more followed in quick succession.

"I don't even know why I am fucking crying! I'm so angry at you all! You lied to me for the past twenty years. I'm not exactly sure which is the most horrifying—that I was so oblivious the last twenty years not to notice that you have superpowers or that you all know very, very embarrassing and personal thoughts of mine. This is like the worstest nightmare ever!" I said.

"And now I just said 'worstest!'" I tried to stifle my laughter, because that was the last thing I wanted to show, but I couldn't. For a brief moment, humor had been restored to the situation.

I paused to corral my emotions. "Why would you not tell me? I don't understand why I got left in the dark?" I asked.

"If you had known, would it have made a difference?" my dad asked.

"That is an absurd question. Of course it would have made a difference. I could have protected myself. I could have asked Rosa to tell me all of the answers to my tests!" I said, knowing Rosa would take offense to that last part.

Rosa scoffed, "It doesn't work that way, and obviously, even if it did, you know I wouldn't give you them."

"Well maybe not twenty-five-year-old Rosa but fifteen-year-old Rosa might have—"

"Precisely, Evangeline!" my dad interrupted. "There are many reasons why we chose not to tell you. First, there are inherent risks for our whole family's security. Do you think it would have been a good idea to tell you at five years old that Isaac could walk through walls and that your sister could read minds? Would you have taken that risk? I don't think it would be fair to expect a five-year-old or even a ten-, fifteen-, or eighteen-year-old to keep that secret. Secondly, and equally important, knowing all of these things would have been largely to your detriment. Let's say we did tell you about Isaac and Rosa being Veterox when you were younger. Your entire development as a normal person would have taken a wild detour. I certainly couldn't have told you in good conscience that Isaac would never spy on you or that Rosa would never listen to your thoughts. I couldn't control how Rosa used her powers. As you might imagine, she wasn't all that willing of a participant. Once Isaac moved back here a few years ago, we did discuss telling you, but nobody thought it was the best choice at that time."

I rolled my eyes.

"How would you have coped with the idea that nothing that you thought or felt was private? It would have been a horrible existence. Even now, as a mature twenty-year-old, you're going to struggle with these issues to some extent. However, Rosa and I...well even Isaac, we all think you can handle it. I know you're mad. It's justified. I also hope you can understand my reasoning. I'd like to say that I was just protecting you, but when somebody says that, it always comes out sounding like a bad excuse to justify questionable behavior. The decision was right. I don't have any regrets. Look at you; look at all of us right now. It could have been a lot different. I was truly trying to protect all of you," he said.

I wanted to argue with him, because I was angry, but he had made very logical points, and I couldn't help but think that he had made the best decision, given the circumstances. I knew that my anger and frustration were mostly due to the fact that I hated not knowing things. I was a curious person. I wanted to know everything.

I sighed. "OK. Fine. I agree with you. You're right, but I'm still angry. Is this why Mom was killed?" I asked.

"I don't know. Yes...probably. We can't say definitively, but it seems as if the banquet bombing was planned by someone who knew about the vaccine. It's possible your mom wasn't the main target. I think it's likely that there were several people of interest attending that banquet, and she was just the unlucky one to be killed.

"To clarify, we didn't have contact with the Veterox until several years after Isaac and Rosa were adopted. The gala was the first time everyone had united since the trials. As you know, Isaac left shortly after your mom died. He went to live in the Veterox headquarters.

Isaac can probably answer your questions concerning them much better than I can," he said.

I gazed over at Isaac, but I could tell he was purposely avoiding eye contact.

"Why are you allowed outside the Veterox headquarters?" I asked.

"Rules have changed a bit in the last fifteen years. I have clearance," Isaac said.

It was a vague answer but I could tell he wasn't going to be any more forthcoming, so I changed the subject.

"I assume Charlotte needs to stay in the dark about all of this?" I asked.

"Well, I don't think Charlotte would handle it very well," Rosa answered. "I think for the time being we need to keep her out of the situation. It's safer for her. God forbid, if our security was compromised and she knew everything, she might become a target," Rosa said.

"Okay. So, what's next?" I asked.

"Well actually, I think Isaac and I would like to talk to you in private, individually. Would that be all right with you?" Rosa asked.

"Sure...err, I suppose that would be fine," I stammered.

My dad looked a bit relieved. "I'm going to head to bed I think, as long as you don't have any further questions for me tonight. We can talk more tomorrow night after dinner, if you'd like," he said.

"I'm sure I'll be able to come up with a few questions," I replied back, smiling. "Good night, Dad," I said.

"Good night, my almost twenty-one-year-old," he replied. He walked up toward his room.

Rosa wanted to go first and asked to speak to me in my room. We walked up the stairs, silently. The windows in my room were open, and crisp spring air flowed through, rustling my curtains. The sun had gone down, and the streetlights were illuminating the roads and sidewalks. I could see the lights of the old capitol building on the horizon.

We both sat down in the aqua-blue chairs, which were adjacent to the windows. So many times before we had sat in this exact spot, reminiscing about boys or debating about whether parallel universes exist or just watching the snow falling down onto the trees.

Rosa's voice startled me. "Parallel universes don't exist." A smile crept across her face.

I scowled.

"I just wanted to talk to you because I know that tonight must be really confusing and shocking," she said.

"Are you trying to act as my therapist now? Gee, I suppose that was an ironically perfect field for you to go into," I snapped.

"Actually, being a psychiatrist is really frustrating. You'd think everything would go a lot easier, knowing the things that I do, but it doesn't. I went into the field thinking I'd be well suited to it, but it's very challenging. Most things are easy for me to pick up on, like schizophrenia and bipolar disorder. The therapeutic aspect is a bit more difficult. The people who don't require medication but need so-called 'talk therapy' can be frustrating. You can't just tell them what's wrong and expect them to change. They have to realize the behavior themselves and want to change. That's the hard part. And…it's hard to be constantly surrounded by troubled minds. Some days, it's difficult to be a happy person," she said.

"Can't you control who you hear and whatnot?" I asked.

Her eyes brightened up a bit. "Yes, to an extent. I'm still learning to block. There's maybe a forty-foot radius to my powers. Well, I can go beyond forty feet, but it's pretty hard to tune in individual voices at that point. Unfortunately, I'm not able to block the voices completely.

That's why my bedroom is on the ground floor, and if you think about it, it's on the opposite side of the bedrooms on the second and third floor. It's pretty much the only place that I can go and be alone in my own head," she said.

Well that sounded awful. If I had to be around people, or, maybe worse, their thoughts, fourteen hours a day, I would turn into a loon. I have a hard enough time socializing with anyone besides my family or Charlotte or maybe Sausagesia for more than an hour.

"It's not that bad," she said, responding to my thought.

"What do minds sound like? I mean, does my mind sound just like my voice?"

I could tell she was more than happy to answer. Her eyes sparkled.

"Interesting question. No, not initially at least. I can't tell the gender of a mind right away. It's not a male voice or a female voice. I guess that's the closest way I can describe it, a non-gendered voice. However, it becomes fairly easy to discern a female mind from a male one after you hear the cadence and the general topic of the thoughts. Women talk a bit faster and are much more descriptive...there's more feeling to what they say. It's a little less hectic to read a male mind. It's kind of like going from color to black and white. I guess, think about how Isaac talks and then how Charlotte talks. You can kind of imagine that if you switched their voices, you'd still be able to tell the male versus the female one just by what they are saying and how they are emphasizing certain words.

"Anyway, with people that I know, like you and Isaac, your minds sound like your normal voices. Again, imagine Charlotte saying, 'Hey, how are you?' Do you hear it in a monotone voice, or do you hear it in her own voice? I think it's just natural to pick that up," she said.

Fascinating, I thought.

"It is, isn't it!" she said, responding to my thought again.

I wondered if I would ever get used to that.

"Probably. So let's talk about the elephant in the room, whether I'm always listening to your mind. I don't think the answer is going to provide you much comfort, but anytime that you're in the requisite forty feet of me, yes, I am. I try to ignore it as much as I can. I've found ways to distract myself, which does help. That's why I cook a lot. That's also why I'm usually in my room after eight every night. Do I know all of your secrets? Yes, I think I do," she said.

I was mortified. My rosy cheeks were probably giving away how I felt. Ha, I thought, catching myself. I doubted it was my red cheeks giving it away.

"Here's the thing, Evangeline. There's nothing for you to be embarrassed about. Trust me. Having a crush on Isaac is not that dark of a secret, and being that it's your darkest one, you have nothing to worry about. Really, your mind is joyful and interesting and one of the kindest that I've ever had the pleasure of listening to. The amount of information you think about is literally astonishing. Sometimes when I come up here to talk to you and we just sit in these chairs, looking out the window, I'm listening in. I've learned loads and loads of random and interesting information from you," she said.

This was the most peculiar conversation. Was this really happening? In some strange way, I really hoped so.

Rosa interrupted my thoughts. "I think Isaac is on his way up here. We've covered most of what I wanted to talk to you about, but we'll have the next forty years to go over any questions you have," she said, smiling. "Just to warn you, Isaac seems a bit…anxious," she added.

My stomach suddenly clenched up.

Rosa's laughter roared through the room. "Oh goodness, you two. I feel like I'm going to throw up just from being in the same vicinity as you both! It's going to be OK. I promise. You know I can read minds," she said, giving me a wink.

I heard a knock at the door.

"She's in here. Come in. I'm just leaving," Rosa said. "I'll see you tomorrow morning."

She glanced at me then stood up and walked toward the door. Isaac and Rosa exchanged glances and then walked in opposite directions. Rosa closed the door, and Isaac sat down in the chair. I shifted in my chair uneasily.

"So I can walk through walls," he said, flashing a smile.

"Yeah, I was a little bit surprised that you actually used the door to come in here," I replied, trying unsuccessfully to remain cool. I started twirling my hair. It was a nervous habit of mine.

I continued on. "How exactly does it work? Can you walk through anything? Do you leave footprints on the ground when you are invisible and walk through the snow, like in the movies?" I asked.

He laughed. "No to the footprints question, but, yes, I can walk through anything. At least, I've never encountered something that I couldn't pass through. Weight becomes nonexistent once I go, as you say, invisible. It's a bit of a strange feeling during the transition. I suppose the closest human thing to it would be a tingly goose-bump sensation," he said.

Suddenly it dawned on me why Rosa had always harped on him for leaving without telling her. I knew he did have a habit of disappearing in the early morning hours. Occasionally, on sleepless nights, I would hear Isaac and Rosa arguing over his constant need to wander off.

"Is that why you always go out at night?" I asked.

"Yes," he replied. "As a Veterox, I only need about two to three hours of sleep a night."

"What do you do all night?" I asked.

"I travel," he replied.

"Are you going to tell me more than that?"

"Not tonight." He paused.

"Remember when I told you that sometimes you cannot forget the things you find out?" he asked. "I was saying that from experience. I've had this so-called power for the last twenty-six years. I've seen a lot of things. I've traveled to a lot of places. In many ways, I've become desensitized to the world around me."

"What's the worst thing you've ever seen?"

"Are you sure that's something you really want to know?" he responded.

I nodded confidently.

"A few years ago, when I was in the Middle East, I saw a public beheading of five children and two adults, using knives," he said.

Jesus. I felt like I was going to cry again. I tried to think of a cowboy hat, of an ice cube, anything to distract myself. He would never tell me anything else if I cried in front of him over this. A tear defied my willpower and slid down my cheek.

Isaac noticed immediately. "I'm sorry, Evie. I shouldn't have...told you that," he said. He reached over and placed his hand on mine, then suddenly pulled it back.

"It's okay. I just wasn't expecting it to be that dark. When did you go to the Middle East? What's the best thing you've ever seen?" I asked, trying to lighten the mood.

His eyes burned into mine

"I've been to the Middle East several times. The best thing I've ever seen? Well, that's actually a good story. Several years ago, I was walking down Capitol Parkway around the 32nd Street area. It's kind of a blind intersection. A car pulled out in front of oncoming traffic, which was going about forty-five miles per hour, and it ended up causing a major wreck. Seven cars were involved; three of them were just absolutely crushed. I didn't think anyone out of those three cars would survive. It was just a mangled mess.

By the time I got to the cars, four or five people were already there, helping the victims to safety. Someone had called the police, and you could hear the sirens in the distance. One of the cars had slammed into a light pole, and the two teenage victims weren't able to get out. Nobody wanted to move the young girl and boy, in case of spinal injuries and such.

Then something horrific happened. The front of the car burst into flames. Immediately a man and his wife ran over to the car and started frantically trying to get the car doors open. They called for someone to help, but everyone was sort of frozen in fear. I ran over, and together, the husband and I knocked out the passenger-side window, so we could enter the car. His wife was a petite lady, and she told her husband that she thought she could get inside the car and cut the seat belts off. I ran to ask if anybody had a knife. A lady gave me a tiny pair of scissors that she had in her purse.

By the time I got back, the wife had already jumped into the burning car; her husband was holding on to her legs so he could pull her out if need be. I remember her telling him that she loved him "just in case something happens," and he told her that he loved her too. I handed the wife the tiny scissors, and she actually managed to cut the belts of both teenagers.

A few other bystanders finally decided to run over and help us. We pulled both the boy and girl to safety. The wife did sustain some pretty bad burns on her arms and torso. Actually, some of her hair was singed off. I think it was that couple's act of selflessness that left me questioning my negative view of people. I was astonished that they sacrificed themselves so freely for two complete strangers. I knew it wasn't a logical decision, because there was a high probability that one of them would not make it out alive. Yet they still made the decision to try. I don't know…up until that point I seriously questioned living in this world."

Goose bumps rolled down my arm. I remembered that accident from several years ago. It wasn't that far away from where we lived, maybe half of a mile.

"So I suppose we should discuss my choice to read your diary a few years ago. I'm sorry. It's something I very much regret," he explained.

"Well, you were wrong about my attraction to you. Far overblown," I lied.

"Really? I don't think that's a true statement, and if I am being honest, I hope it's not," he said.

My eyes met his. My ears started buzzing. Was he joking? I couldn't tell.

"There's a reason why I went to the effort of reading your diary, Evangeline. Part of me wondered…" he admitted.

My stomach was once again in knots, but this time the anxiety was mixed with a pleasant feeling.

I started in. "What does that mean? I'm sorry; time is moving cruelly fast tonight. I'm trying to process all of this, and I feel like my brain keeps being pounded the moment I feel even a tiny bit saner. You were right. I was lying about my…err, affinity for you. Forgive me for just asking such a novice question, but are you really attracted to me?"

"Without question."

His bright-green eyes sparkled brightly.

"What does that mean? Could you please elaborate?" I asked.

"No. Not tonight," he replied. He stood up and walked toward the door and then abruptly disappeared.

Is he still here? I wondered. Suddenly, I heard Rosa's voice.

"Isaac, can I talk with you?" she said.

"Yes, let's go out for a walk," he said, answering back.

She must have been listening into the entire conversation. I heard the door close and could see them out the window, walking down the sidewalk together.

"Close," I whispered, and the curtains glided shut.

I thought about how absurd the whole situation was. The universe was trying to make a very poignant statement, but I wasn't sure what it was yet. I walked to my closet and grabbed my pajamas. I didn't think my mind could take much more. I needed the alone time to process the barrage of information that I had just received this evening, but I didn't want to think anymore. Maybe when I woke up everything would be clearer. I climbed into bed and whispered, "Lights off."

{9}

Nine

I woke up tired from a long but unsatisfying night of sleep. I didn't remember any dreams, but that wasn't uncommon for me. I hadn't had dreams for a few years, or at least I'd stopped being able to remember them. I wasn't convinced that I was even capable of having them anymore.

It was light outside, and the sun seemed to be much higher in the sky than normal. I glanced over at the clock. It was 11:07 a.m. Birthdays had their perks, one of which was no school or work. My dad once told me that before Z3C7, neither kids nor adults automatically got birthdays off. I had no idea why it would be changed post-plague. Maybe they valued the day of birth a bit more after seeing half the world die.

I noticed a white piece of paper on the floor in front of my door. I walked over and picked it up. The neat, perfectly spaced handwriting was easy to recognize:

E,

I didn't want to wake you to say good-bye this morning. It sounded like you were having good dreams (smiley face)! I will meet you at The Oven this evening around five. Happy Birthday!

Love, R.

Upon second thought, I decided to go back to bed. Charlotte would be here at three to get ready for dinner. I set my alarm clock for two.

"And don't forget to wind the clock," my alarm clock blared into my ears a few hours later.

I crawled out of bed and walked into the bathroom to turn on the shower. I grabbed a towel and stepped into the water. The water flowed down my head and dripped onto the tiled floor. I closed my eyes and focused on breathing. I thought it was supposed to be a relaxation technique, but it had no effect. I turned off the shower and stepped out, grabbing a towel to dry off.

I stood in front of the mirror naked and brushed my long brown hair. Once it was tangle-free, I grabbed my red lip liner and carefully drew a line around the outside of my lips and then filled them in. I opened up the tube of red lipstick that I normally wore and smoothed it over the lip liner. I loved the way it contrasted with the blue in my eyes.

Classic vintage looks had always appealed to me. I tended toward a 1950–1960-type style. I liked wiggle dresses, hair rollers, and red lipstick. I could run in heels, though I normally just removed them and ran barefoot when need-be.

That probably gave away my utter lack of athletic ability. I wasn't necessarily a clumsy oaf. I ran cross-country one year. Well, I ran one race. My pace was so incredibly slow that I fell back to last place just a mere mile in. In a moment of pure, adolescent embarrassment, I faked a hurt leg so that I could ride back in the medical truck trailing behind me. It was much easier to play the injury card than to feel the scrutiny that I was sure awaited me at the finish line.

I thought about what dress I was going to wear, but I couldn't decide on one definitively. My nerves were on edge. I pinned my hair up and finished my makeup while pondering my dress of choice. I fully realized the absurdity of the moment, worrying so much about the dress I was going to wear when I should have been processing everything else. It was a trivial detail, but one that successfully distracted my attention away from the chaos in my mind.

The Veterox part wasn't even that upsetting. I had always secretly thought that people could have powers. I knew that it sounded idiotic, but many fields of science and medicine defied logic. Things that seemed like fiction often turned into nonfiction. Unless I knew that something had been proven not to exist, I didn't assume anything. So it wasn't the powers that I was surprised about; it was the fact that Rosa and Isaac were the recipients of those aforementioned powers.

I glanced at the clock. It was ten minutes to three. Charlotte was going to be here any minute. Two black garment bags at the end of my closet caught my eye. I unzipped the first bag. It was a navy-blue shift dress with an asymmetrical neckline. Although it was a gorgeous dress, it wasn't right for tonight. I unzipped the other bag. The dress was perfect. I remembered buying it a few years ago with some of my leftover detasseling money. I was pretty sure that I'd never worn it. The dress was a bright, vibrant orange color, with lace detail at the neckline and hand-sewn glass beads spattered throughout but particularly at the waist.

The shoes were the easy part. I grabbed my favorite pair of nude, shiny leather peep-toe heels.

Three o'clock rolled around, and I knew Charlotte's arrival was imminent. She was always on time. Of course, she wouldn't be coming empty-handed. I could almost certainly count on her lugging a huge box of perfume over to the house.

I'm not sure when it started, probably well before I knew her, but her main hobby in life was collecting vintage perfume. She had amassed quite a number of bottles. It was actually sort of fascinating.

After Z3C7 killed half of the population, you could imagine how much "stuff" was left over. A very popular government incentive allowed for anyone to lay claim to items in an abandoned house, provided that they would oversee the cleanup of the property. One couldn't just go steal items from a house, a permit from the government was required, but basically if you wanted to own any items in the property, you would be legally responsible for the cleanup as well. The majority of clothes were actually reused and fairly valuable after the plague, because factories hadn't been functioning for months. Wooden antiques were also a popular item. Even in thrift stores today, you could still find quite a lot of pieces from the plague days.

One item in particular seemed to pop up more often at thrift stores than others—perfume. After the plague, perfume seemed to be thrown away en masse. Used perfume bottles were worth practically nothing. Nobody wanted it, except Charlotte and me, apparently. I had to admit, it was kind of a fun treasure hunt.

The door buzzer rang, interrupting my thoughts. I grabbed my phone to verify that it was Charlotte and pressed the screen to unlock the front door. She knew the drill, and a few minutes later, I heard the knock at my door.

"Come in," I said.

I grabbed the green wrap dress and walked out of my closet.

I heard Charlotte's voice. "Um, could you open the door for me?"

I opened the door, and there she stood, as predicted, with the green chest of perfume sitting precariously in her hands. She actually did have some valuable bottles, like two bottles of Chanel No. 5. Chanel was a wildly popular and expensive brand that went under during the plague, and so it was still somewhat sought after, even twenty-plus years later. But Chanel No. 5 wasn't a favorite of Charlotte's or mine. It was too strong and, well, old lady-ish.

"This is for you. Happy birthday, Evangeline," she said, handing me a small box-shaped gift, wrapped in white paper.

As I unwrapped it, I already knew that it was perfume, as per our tradition of gift giving, but I wondered what she'd picked this year. I took the glass bottle out of the box. White flowers adorned the cap.

"I'll spray it on, and you try to guess the different scents," Charlotte said.

Thanks to her, I had become awfully good at picking out the different notes of a perfume. It'd evolved into a game between us. She lifted the perfume up and sprayed it on my wrists.

"Violets, something fruity, a tiny bit of vanilla, and cedarwood?" I asked.

"Close. Strawberry, violet, jasmine, musk, and vanilla. It's called Daisy. I thought of you when I came across it last month at Aardvark Thrift," Charlotte said, smiling.

"Thank you so much! I do love the retro feeling. *Jeg elske dig*," I replied.

"*Jeg elsker ogsaa dig*," she answered back.

Jeg elske dig meant "I love you" in Danish. What could I say? We were odd ducks. Several years ago Charlotte and I decided that it would be fun to pretend like we were foreigners. We walked to our local mall, and although we had no idea how to speak a different language, we proceeded to speak to each other in a pretend one. We just made it up as we went, thinking we looked like infinitely cool foreigners.

I didn't realize just how absurd we probably looked until one night, several years ago, when I saw an episode of a reality cop show in which a similar situation occurred. A police officer had received a report of a stolen tire. He located a man who seemed to be speaking in a different language to his friend. The man looked Hispanic. The officer walked over to the man and asked if he knew anything about the tire and if he could ask his friend about it. The Spanish-speaking man turned to his friend and asked, "Where-o you put-o the tire-o?"

The officer responded, "I don't speak Spanish, but I'm pretty confident that's not Spanish."

We were that man. In any case, we had managed to learn two Danish phrases as a result of the mall incident. Even though we did love each other, we mostly just tried to tack it on to every conversation because it was obnoxious. The habit hadn't completely faded away.

I placed the bottle of perfume on my vanity and turned back to Charlotte. "Okay, I pulled the green dress from my closet for you. Do you want to go try it on in the bathroom?"

"Yeah, I'll be right back," she said.

I handed her the dress, and she walked toward the bathroom. Our body types were wildly different, yet we were somehow both able to fit into a size zero. Charlotte was a few inches taller than my tiny five-foot-four-inch frame. We were both very slim. Her skin was a beautiful brown color, many shades darker than my ghastly pale tone, and she had bright brown-colored eyes. She was much more boyish in body type, and I was very curvy. Nevertheless, we could wear the same size clothing, but it was amazing how different the same dress looked on each one of us.

The door to the bathroom opened, and Charlotte emerged in the green dress. She looked stunning.

"Are you trying to impress somebody at the Indian restaurant tonight?" I asked, smiling.

She looked shocked. "How did you know?"

I laughed. "Well you don't necessarily wear a dress all that often!" I replied. "What's his name?"

"Patak. He clears tables at The Oven, and he's studying to be a special-education teacher. We just met a few days ago, in the office at school. He doesn't know I'm coming there tonight. I'm so nervous," she said. She smiled sheepishly.

"Oh you'll be fine! You look beautiful. That's so exciting—are you going to ask him out?"

"If I have the courage."

"I'll ask him for you before we leave, if you want."

"I'd like to do it myself, but don't be surprised if I take you up on that offer," she said, smiling.

"Well, we should probably get going. We're meeting everyone at the restaurant. Who knows what traffic will be like?" I said.

I grabbed my car keys on the way out and locked the front door. My preference was always to walk rather than drive, but The Oven was downtown and too far to venture via my feet.

It was a beautiful spring night. The air was heavy with moisture, typical of the stormy spring nights that brought massive thunderstorms rolling through the prairie. I could see huge thunderheads, big, billowing, bright white clouds that reached high in the sky.

I hated backing out of the driveway. My tiny green car, the kind that was fuel efficient and barely went above fifty-five miles an hour, always sat to the side of our driveway, since it was so uncommonly used. That meant I had to back out of the driveway on a sort of curve, and I wasn't good at it. So when nobody else was around, I just swung the car around onto the lawn and drove forward down the driveway. My dad hated it when I drove on the grass. I pulled onto the street, and we were off to The Oven.

"Geez, you drive so slowly!" Charlotte said, interrupting my thoughts.

"No, I drive defensively. I don't want to get into an accident," I said.

"Well you'll have no problems accomplishing that," she replied.

It was just a short, few-minute drive downtown. I parked the car outside of the restaurant, and Charlotte and I walked in.

{10}

Ten

As I walked through the doors, my heartbeat sped up and my stomach ached from anxiety. I saw Isaac. He was dressed in a dark gray suit, with a white shirt and orange tie. A silver clip with his initials engraved in it held the tie back. Rosa and Dad were sitting across the table from him.

Isaac looked up. He smiled at me, and I felt the warmth of blood as it rushed to my face. I smiled back, embarrassed.

I knew that I was acting like that annoying type of girl who fawned over boys. I had always made fun of that type of girl in my mind, so this was a baffling and somewhat mortifying situation. Worse yet, I actually felt giddy inside. I was thinking shamefully immature thoughts and conjuring up various romantic situations. It was cringe worthy.

I noticed Rosa staring at me. A smile appeared on her face, and I realized she had just heard everything I'd thought. I shook my head.

I sat down at the table between Rosa and my dad. Charlotte sat directly across from me, with Isaac to her right.

The restaurant's walls were painted a shade of deep crimson. The dark, glossy tables were adorned with candles. Ornately woven carpets covered the floor in a sort of staggered, nonsymmetrical pattern. Indian music played in the background. I recognized the distinctive sound of the sitar intertwined among the other instruments. The smell of cardamom and spices filled the air.

"How has your day been? Did you sleep in?" my dad asked.

"It's been good," I replied. "Well, I haven't been up for most of it, but it's getting a lot better now! Charlotte gave me a really neat bottle of perfume."

"I have your present at home," Rosa said. "What do you normally order here? It's one of the rare times I don't know. I like chicken and maybe a tomato-ish sauce? What's that soup that comes before the meal?" she asked.

"It's mulligatawny. I would suggest chicken tikka makhani or chicken tikka korma. Order a side of buttered naan," I replied.

I answered a few more Indian-food-related questions, and then the waiter came to take our order.

"Chicken tikka korma, a buttered naan on the side, please, and I'll just have water to drink," I told the waiter.

Charlotte always came here with me, so she knew what to order. I glanced at her and then at the boy cleaning tables and then back to her. She nodded, smiling.

I saw a smile cross Rosa's face as well. It was going to take me a while to get comfortable with her mind-reading powers. No private conversation would ever be private. Rosa glared at me. I shrugged.

I needed to go to the bathroom and it was a good excuse to escape the situation.

"Hey, I'm going to go to the restroom. I'll be right back," I said.

"Me too," Isaac said.

He followed close behind me. Once we were out of earshot, he said, "That dress looks very nice on you. Happy birthday." His eyes were bright with excitement.

"Thank you. You look quite alluring…err…attractive in that suit. We match a little bit, with that orange tie of yours," I replied, stumbling over my words.

"I have your present back at the house as well. I was hoping to have a little alone time with you later this evening, if that's okay?" he asked.

I regained my composure. "Yes, I'll make sure we do. I'm going to go into the bathroom now. I know you're tempted to, but don't follow me in," I said, grinning.

He looked at me with a sly smile on his face and continued on to the male side of the restrooms. As I reemerged from the bathroom, Isaac was standing next to the wall, waiting. I moved closer to him so that we could walk back to the table together. It was a peculiar feeling, being so close to him. There was palpable tension between us.

Suddenly, I could hear a low, rumbling noise. It sounded like a freight train barreling down the tracks. Then a piercing voice reverberated through the air.

"ISAAC, GET EVIE OUT NOW!" screamed Rosa.

It was the kind of shrieking sound that is so chilling it jolts through your body. The hairs on my neck stood up. Before I could even interpret everything she had said, Isaac grabbed my hand and pulled me forward. He was running in a full-on sprint, and I couldn't keep up. I felt a tingly sensation run through my body, and then everything went black. When my eyes opened again, we were somehow back at our house, in the middle of the kitchen.

"What happened, Isaac!?" I shrieked.

"I don't know, Evangeline," he said. He rarely used my full name.

"I'm not entirely sure. I've never transported before. I didn't even know that I could. I need to return to the restaurant to see what's going on and help out if I can. Lock the doors, and stay here. I'll let you know when I find out anything. Please, just stay calm," he said. He disappeared again.

I immediately ran over to the television and flipped it on. I was sure the news would be breaking by now. There was nothing on channel ten, so I flipped to eight. The familiar sound of trumpets interrupted the current show, and a news lady appeared on the screen. Her name, "Belle Rinkasely," flashed on the bottom of the picture.

Her voice sounded very serious. It was the kind of tone that journalists took on when something bad had happened. I could always feel the intensity of the situation through their voices.

"We're sorry to interrupt your programming, but we have some breaking news to share with you. We are getting reports that a tornado has hit in the downtown area of Lincoln. People on scene are reporting multiple casualties and a wide path of destruction near 8th and R Street. Our reporters are trying to gain access the scene but have been unable to get past 16th Street.

"Again, a tornado seems to have hit downtown Lincoln, with multiple casualties being reported from first responders. Our police contacts are saying that if you are in the area of downtown Lincoln, they would like your assistance in helping victims. Please do not try to enter downtown Lincoln if you are not in the direct vicinity of the Haymarket, as this will cause traffic delays that could hold up first responders transporting victims to nearby hospitals. We will update you as we get information. For now let's push it over to Huckleby, our head meteorologist, for more information about the storm. Huckleby?"

A tall man, I'd guess in his upper fifties, appeared on screen. He started to speak. His voice sounded upset.

"I'm Meteorologist Huckleby Jones live in the storm-prediction center. Doppler radar indicates that a very strong tornado touched down around L and 6th Street at 5:42 p.m. The tornado continued to gain intensity and started to track in a north and easterly direction into the Haymarket area of Lincoln. We have reports that no sirens were sounding in that area, although they were going off in the rest of Lincoln.

"Our radar is predicting an EF-4 to EF-5 strength of tornado. Remember an EF-1 is the weakest type, with winds around 65 mph while an EF-5 can pack winds in excess of 200 mph. In my opinion, the hook echo on the radar, which many times gives us a good idea the strength, is appearing very large, which is indicative of an EF-4 to EF-5 tornado." He pointed towards an areas on the radar that was lit up with green, blue, and red blobs. "If this proves to be true, most buildings in this storm's path will have been leveled. Not just homes but actual concrete buildings, like hospitals and structures engineered to withstand very strong winds. I'm concerned about the older buildings down there—"

Belle Rinkasely interrupted, "Huckleby, we have to cut away. We have some live shots coming in via helicopter. Let's listen in."

The high-pitched humming noise of the helicopter suddenly echoed out of the television.

"Yeah, we are right over the scene of destruction," a male voice said. "Sadly not much remains of the Haymarket area. As you can see"—the camera closed in on an area close to the Indian restaurant we had just been in, where nothing was left standing—"most of the buildings down here are gone. There looks to be debris everywhere. First responders are slowly trickling in..." he said, his voice fading away.

My ears started to ring. Shock poured over me in a wave of

electricity that cascaded down my arms. There was no warning. Not a single person had time to hide somewhere safe. In an EF-2-strength tornado that might be okay. In an EF-5, nobody survived that wasn't underground.

Come on, Isaac, I thought. I wished he'd at least call me with some news. The realization of what this meant finally hit me. If Isaac wasn't going to tell me over the phone, it was bad news. If Dad, Charlotte, and Rosa were being transported to a hospital, he would have let me know immediately.

I ran to the door and grabbed Rosa's keys. Her white Saab was the only one left in the driveway. I didn't care that Isaac had told me to stay. I had to get down there. I bolted out of the front door and onto the lawn.

Isaac appeared in front of me.

"Isaac," I said.

"What are you doing?!" he asked frantically. His face was pale.

"I was going—" I said, but he interrupted me before I could explain.

"Evangeline, go and pack a bag. Get clothes and toiletries, and grab food. I need to get a few things for myself. Meet me at the front door in ten minutes," he said in a frantic voice.

I wanted to ask why. I wanted to ask what happened, but I could tell by the urgency in his voice that he wasn't joking around. Besides, I knew the truth of the situation. They'd all died.

"Okay." I replied.

We both hurried through the front door. I sprinted up the three flights of stairs and barged into my room. Isaac ran in the opposite direction. Once I reached my room, I grabbed a suitcase from the closet and stuffed it with a few outfits. I didn't know what to pack, so I just grabbed whatever was readily available. I pulled a bag of toiletries out of the bathroom and threw it on top of the clothes. I needed to leave room for food, so I zipped up the bag and began to roll it out. I saw the bottle of perfume Charlotte had given me earlier and quickly took it off the buffet and shoved it into the front pocket of the bag. I hurried out the door.

My suitcase loudly plopped down the stairs behind me, but I managed to make it down to the first floor in mere seconds. I hurried into the kitchen and unzipped my suitcase. I went through a checklist in my mind: bottles of water, energy drinks, granola bars, fruit, peanut butter, bread. That was all I could manage to fit inside my bag. Isaac wasn't waiting at the door yet, so I grabbed a reusable bag from a drawer in the kitchen and crammed more snacks and water into it. I could hear Isaac's footsteps getting closer, so I dragged everything to the front door.

"We're going to take Rosa's car," he said.

I'd assumed as much. We grabbed our suitcases and headed to the car. Isaac loaded them into the trunk, and I sat down anxiously in the passenger's seat. He got in, started the car, and backed smoothly out of the lane. I wondered where we were going.

We had only made it down the street a few blocks when the car slowed down and turned into the driveway of another house. The garage door opened, and Isaac pulled next to a glossy black car.

"We're going to switch cars. I'll grab your suitcase. You just get into the passenger's side," he said. I was confused but did as he asked. I opened the door and walked over to the other car. I slid into the black leather seats and waited for Isaac. He loaded the suitcases into the trunk of the black car and then grabbed some items from Rosa's car and opened the rear door to place the items in the back pocket of the passenger's seat.

"If you could, please reach into the glove box and pull out the envelope for me," he said as he got into the driver's seat.

I opened the glove box and located a white envelope. A pink registration slip was underneath the envelope, and I noticed that the name on it said, "Ezra Crailene." I'd never heard of the first name, but, of course, the last name I recognized immediately. I wondered how he was connected to Ethan. I handed Isaac the envelope, and he placed it in the seat pocket behind him.

He placed his thumb on the ignition, and the engine started. The garage door closed as we backed out of the driveway and onto the street once again. This time we didn't stop, and soon we were merging onto the interstate, heading west.

{11}

Eleven

Several minutes passed by in silence before Isaac spoke. "I have a lot to tell you, and it's going to be confusing. There's a reason for what we're doing, and you'll see why, but I can't give you every answer now. Do you understand what I'm saying?" he asked, looking over at me.

"What happened at the restaurant, Isaac? I need to know," I said, ignoring his question.

He paused.

"Charlotte and your dad are no longer alive. I don't know where Rosa is. She wasn't at the restaurant when I returned," he said.

My mouth dropped open. "What do you mean she wasn't there? Are you sure about my dad and Charlotte?" I asked.

"Yes, I'm sure. When I found them, it was clear that Xander and Charlotte had tried to escape the building. They were several feet away from our table. It looked like your dad was trying to protect Charlotte by shielding her with his body, because he was on top of her when I found them. One of the side walls fell down on top of them."

The buzzing returned to my ears. I felt like I had been punched in the stomach. I gulped, trying to hold back tears, but I couldn't stop them, and I knew that I shouldn't. One giant tear fell down my cheek, the precursor to a waterfall that swiftly enveloped my face. Isaac glanced over at me, and his face fell. He pulled over to the side of the road. My hands were shaking.

He turned his head toward mine and looked into my eyes. "I'm so sorry, Evie. I wanted you to know the truth, and I apologize if I went too far. Their last seconds were spent together, and maybe they weren't ideal, but they didn't die alone. Your dad adored Charlotte, and I'm sure he did everything possible to protect her. I've seen a lot of death and a lot of awful things in my life. Life doesn't deal fairly. In fact, far more often than not, it's unfair. I'm truly sorry, Evie."

I could tell his words were sincere, and I knew that he was sorry for me, but he didn't seem that broken up.

"Why aren't you upset?" I asked, trying to keep my voice from cracking.

"I'm used to death." He paused. "Maybe I'm also better at hiding my emotions."

His eyes stared back at me, glistening a bit more than normal. He quickly looked back at the road and pulled onto the interstate.

"Is it my fault? Did finding out about you and Rosa last night cause this? Is that even possible?" I asked him.

"No, of course you're not responsible for the situation. However, I'm certain that it was not a coincidence. It's called weather modification. Rosa's talent makes her a very valuable target. It's possible they were after you too, which is why we had to leave so abruptly," he said.

I wondered what they would want with me. My mind was a chaotic mess. I couldn't think in any linear way.

"What is weather modification?"

"I can't fully answer that question for you yet, but simply put, it is done by Veterox who can control the weather," he replied.

I wasn't satisfied with the answer, but my brain swiftly changed tangents.

"What will they do with Charlotte and Dad's bodies?" I said. My voice cracked again.

"It's OK," he said. "They'll be taken care of. Charlotte's will be released to her mom, and Xander's will be taken to a crematorium, as per his wishes. It's all being arranged. You and I will be considered missing and presumed dead. It won't be all that hard to pull off, because in a tornado that strong, sometimes human remains can be difficult to find. It will give us a few days," he said.

A few days? I wondered.

"How long will it take to get wherever we are going? Where are we going?" I asked.

"Probably around twenty-four hours. I'll drive straight through the night, because we cannot risk being seen at a hotel. Once we arrive in Oregon, we'll stay the night at a safe house. Our rendezvous will take place the next morning."

"How do you know what to do, where to go?" I asked.

"There's always an emergency plan of action. I know it very well, because I'm the one that came up with it. There are several redundancies built in. Right now, my job is to ensure your safety. This is the way I feel we are most secure. It's a complicated system. I'll explain more tomorrow night."

"No, explain it now. Please."

"I've already been in contact with others, and we're working in tandem. It's not just me. It involves the upper echelon of the intelligence community, and truly, I cannot tell you more than that right at this moment," he said.

I didn't want to engage in an argument. I had no energy left. He didn't either, and so we just sat there as time swiftly sped by.

It wasn't that I didn't have a million questions running through my head, but they seemed to be suppressed, pushed back by shock. I felt numb and, at the same time, overly sensitive. The last few moments before the tornado hit ran in a cycle through my mind, like a movie. Isaac's description of the scene provided the imagery for Charlotte and my dad's last moments.

I didn't want to think about it anymore, so I decided to focus on my surroundings. I watched out the windows as we passed town after town—you could see the grain elevators from the interstate. A brown cow was grazing in a bright green pasture nearby. I could see a huge balloon-shaped water tower jutting up from the ground, just off the side of the road.

Before I knew it, darkness had slipped over the landscape. I wasn't sure how much time had passed. The clock read 11:31 p.m., so it must have been a few hours.

I wrestled around in the seat for a while, trying to find a comfortable position so that I could go to sleep. Finally, after thirty minutes of adjusting the seat, I realized that I would never find a comfortable position. It wasn't a physical problem. My mind was restless. It was something that I could never seem to control, even on my best days, let alone tonight.

"Is there something wrong?" Isaac asked, breaking the silence.

"I just can't get comfortable, and I can't turn my mind off, and I want to get out of the car and run until I collapse onto the side of the road and fall asleep."

"Well, that might be a *bit* dramatic and probably not a very good idea. Take a deep breath," he said.

I did as he said, but it didn't really help.

"Reach into the seat pocket behind you."

I twisted my arm around the seat and stuck it into the deep pocket like he had asked.

"Do you feel the little envelope? Pull it out, please. I grabbed a few of your sleeping pills. You're going to need to get some rest. A lot of things are going to happen in the next few days," he said.

I glanced at the clock. It was almost midnight. The bottle was a few years old. I had been prescribed the pills for insomnia problems, but I'd never taken one. I wasn't very comfortable with the idea of taking pills to fall asleep. I knew the root of my sleep problem was my inability to turn off my mind, which wasn't a good excuse to take a pill, but on this night, I was willing to make an exception. I just wanted the day to be over. I didn't want to be awake anymore. I grabbed a pill and drank it down with a sip of water.

I didn't immediately fall asleep. For a while, I watched out the window as cars glided by. If I looked closely, I could see the lights of the tiny villages nearby.

Ten minutes went by pretty quickly. I looked over at the dashboard of the car, and it appeared to be moving, like waves. I looked over at Isaac and noticed that if I stared at him long enough, his body seemed wavy too. Was this what it felt like to trip out on acid? I felt so happy and carefree. I must have looked a bit off.

"Are you all right?" Isaac asked. He was staring at me oddly.

"I am. I really am," I said merrily. The three hundred pounds of extra weight I had been carrying on my shoulders had disappeared. Nothing bothered me.

"Are you sure? You look a bit peculiar...grinning like a sort-of Cheshire cat," he said, trying to hold back a smile.

"Do you have a big penis?" I blurted out. It didn't seem like a weird question to me…at the time.

Isaac started laughing. I joined in, because it sounded fun.

"Well, hmm, I'm not exactly sure how to answer that. I bet that pill is starting to work now; maybe if you close your eyes, you'll drift off to sleep," he said, still smirking.

"Okay. Yeah, I think that might be nice. Good night, Isaac," I replied.

"Good night, Evangeline."

{12}

Twelve

I woke up and glanced at the clock on the rosewood dashboard. It was almost eight in the morning. I looked out the window for a road sign to tell me where we were.

"Ogden, Utah," Isaac said, interrupting my thoughts. "We're about twelve hours from where we are going. How did you sleep?" he asked.

That sleeping pill had worked pretty well. I didn't recall waking even once. The last thing I remembered…oh. Fuck.

Isaac's laughter rang through the car.

"Your face is turning such a lovely shade of crimson. I assume that you remember?" Isaac looked at me, his eyes bright with mischief.

"Yes, mortifyingly, I do remember, and if I recall correctly, you maneuvered around that question quite deftly. Did you want to answer that question now?" I grinned back at him.

He smiled. "I think I will pass on that one, for now at least. But I would like to point out that I kindly lulled you into sleeping instead of taking advantage of your very honest state of mind. Who would have thought a sleeping pill would turn out to be a truth serum with you?"

he said.

We laughed for a few minutes, which provided a much-needed release from the very stressful topics of the last forty-eight hours.

"Would you mind if we kept talking about these light subjects for a while? The distraction is nice." I said.

"Sure," Isaac replied. "What's your favorite color?"

"Cherry red, you know, the color my room is painted," I said, "and yours?"

"Orange like the fruit," he replied. "Since you seem to be fond of asking these two questions, I'm going to turn the tables. What's the best thing that's ever happened to you and the worst?"

"The worst...well"

"I'm sorry. Absurd question to ask you right now. Replace that...what's your most embarrassing moment?"

"Hmm...I suppose the best thing would be when you all surprised me with the trip to Egypt for my birthday. It was pretty amazing to see the Great Pyramids at Giza and the Sphinx. You know me and my obsession with history."

I paused.

"The most embarrassing...well, I have had few that could qualify for that award. One in particular does come to mind though. One morning, I was late getting off to school. I'd thrown on a lavender dress and was hurrying to meet you and Rosa downstairs. We all started walking down to the school and I realized about halfway there that I had forgotten to put on underwear. My dress was long enough, falling at my knees so I didn't think it would be a huge problem and it wasn't, until Charlotte and I were walking over to Haven. You know those grates that are sometimes placed on the sidewalk—a sort of vent type thing?"

"Yes, I think I can see where this is going," he said, smiling.

"Well, yes. Before that day, it had never expelled air. Suffice it to say I wasn't expecting the sudden rush of wind that sent my dress fluttering up, ensuring anyone within a quarter mile of me got quite the show. Charlotte laughed so much. She giggled on and off the rest of that afternoon."

"I'd like to get that thought out of mind. Next question—name your favorite movie."

I thought about it for a minute or two.

"*Elf.* I used to watch it with dad every year around Christmas. I still get excited when it comes on. What about you?" I asked.

"I would have to go with *Band of Brothers* which is actually a miniseries but it's still on top of my list."

"Oh I completely forgot about that one—it was really good. Which character would you be if you could play any of them?"

"Without a doubt, I would be Richard Winters," he said, smiling.

I rolled my eyes. Richard Winters was the heroic general.

"Of course you would think that highly of yourself. I won't lie; the actor who plays him, Damian Lewis, is quite attractive...and he's British, which is always a plus..." I replied.

"Oh really?" he said. He sounded jealous. I smiled.

"Enjoying this, are you?" he asked, smiling back.

"I am. You're usually so indifferent and unmoving. I'm not used to seeing emotion on your face," I replied.

"I've never had a lack of emotion regarding you. I was just better at keeping it under control," he said.

"Why now?"

He didn't answer. Instead he changed the subject.

"What is your favorite book?"

"You first," I said.

"*Children of Men* or *1984*. Ironically, I very much enjoy the dystopian type of novel," he said. "Yours?"

"*The Giver*, but I also love *Children of Men*. That might have been my second pick."

I paused for a moment then asked the question that was nagging at me. "What's going on between you and me?"

The atmosphere in the car changed from lively to uneasy.

"Evie, I'm not sure. Yesterday I knew the direction we might be heading. There's no question that I'm absurdly attracted to you. I can feel the electricity between you and I, and it's incredibly hard for me to push it away. However, right now I can't pursue that aspect as I'd hoped. Emotion is rarely logic based, and at this moment I can't take the chance it will distract me from what I need to do.

My job is to get you to the Veterox rendezvous in Oregon. Once you are safely in the VHQ, I need to focus my energy on finding Rosa. You know that if the situation was reversed, nothing would stop her from finding me. She'd pull every resource she could, and that's my intention as well. Once I can ensure you are both safe…" He paused and turned to look at me. "I'm not interested in anybody else."

I was silent for a moment then said, "I know I should be able to separate out logic from this situation, but it's difficult." Tears flowed down my cheeks once again. "I don't want to be alone. The only positive thing that my mind can manage to process right now is that you're alive and here with me. How do you know that where I am going is safe?"

"I wouldn't take you there if it wasn't safe. Trust me. It's the most secure place you could be on the planet." He sighed. "I don't want you to be alone either. I have two options, and I'm not picking the choice I most want."

That last sentence resonated with me. Continuing to be upset would make him feel worse, and that was not the option I wanted to pursue. There would be plenty of time to be sad later on. I understood.

"Isaac, it's fine. I'm not mad at you. I'm hurt, but I know that's not your intention. Rosa's life is at stake here. I would be an extremely crass person to put my hurt feelings ahead of someone's life, especially Rosa's," I said.

I watched out the window as the bright-green landscape of Idaho disappeared. My thoughts wandered over the past three days. I hoped Sausagesia was doing all right. I'm sure the nurses had told her that Charlotte and I weren't returning. I wondered how Charlotte's mom was doing. Not good, I imagined. I couldn't stand to think about my dad, but I'd taken a small amount of comfort in knowing that he was with my mom.

Isaac's voice interrupted my thoughts. "I have to pull over to get some fuel. We're not too far away from the safe house. Could you reach into the back pocket of my seat and pull out that white envelope?" he asked.

I reached back and felt around. My fingers came across the envelope, and I pulled it out.

"Open it, and grab me sixty dollars, please," he said.

I ripped the envelope open and saw a sizeable amount of cash. I pulled out a few bills. They were all one-hundred-dollar bills.

"Geez, how much cash do you have in here?" I asked, handing him one of the bills.

"A lot. We can't use credit or debit cards right now for tracking purposes," he said.

He pulled off the interstate into a little gas station on the right side of the road.

"Can I get out and stretch my legs?" I asked.

"Of course," he replied.

The orange dress that I so deftly picked out yesterday afternoon was starting to wrinkle. I had taken my high heels off, but the other shoes I'd brought were in my suitcase, which was in the trunk, so I placed the heels back on my feet and slid out of the car. Isaac's eyes met mine as I stood up. He looked down at my dress and then turned away quickly.

"Are you trying not to look at me?" I teased.

He glanced back with a smirk on his face. "Yes," he replied.

We got back into the car and headed down the interstate once again.

"Have you been to wherever I am going?" I asked.

"Yes, it's home for me. I lived there for over ten years. I don't think I can describe the VHQ. It's a beautiful place. Some things will be similar to what you're seeing now, like the vibrant green colors and the trees, but it's also going to be jarringly different," he said.

"Why can't we go there right now? Why do we have to wait until tomorrow morning at the rendezvous point?" I asked.

"Well it's a bit more complicated than just arriving at the Veterox headquarters," he explained. "Certain security precautions have to be taken. You will have an escort into the VHQ. I won't be with you when you depart. Technically, the entire city is not visible to anyone outside of the VHQ."

"It's an invisible city?" I asked.

"Yes, well, you can think of it that way. I couldn't tell you the exact science behind it, but it was designed to be undetectable by anyone who doesn't know it's there," he replied. "It's only accessible once a day. Tomorrow's time is in the morning. As a security precaution, the schedule is changed daily."

How does he know all of this, I thought.

"How were you able to set up the meeting?" I asked.

"Well, I'm able to communicate with the VHQ through a chip

implanted in my body," he explained. "I don't use it often, because of security reasons, but in a situation like this one, it enables me to contact Ethan directly when I'm outside the VHQ. He's been keeping me up to date with the latest information on Rosa and setting up the rendezvous. You're the first human in many years to be allowed inside the VHQ, and because of that, it required presidential authorization," he said.

Presidential authorization?

"Why am I allowed in? If so few people are allowed inside the VHQ, why am I getting special treatment?" I asked.

He sighed. "This is one topic I can't discuss with you, at least not at this moment. You're going to learn all about this tomorrow. I'm sorry. It's for your own safety. You'll understand why soon enough," he said.

The whole conversation irritated me. I wanted more information than "it's for your own safety" provided. I was tired of being in the dark.

"You're very controlling," I said, slightly annoyed.

"Yes, I am," he replied.

He didn't speak for a moment. I could hear the sound of Elvis's voice on the radio in the background.

"It's my job to be steely, Evie. I need to have control of this situation so that I can think clearly and develop a plan of action. I'm not intending to make you angry—"

"Well you are," I said, interrupting him.

"I don't know what to say. You are sorely mistaken if you think I derive pleasure in keeping secrets!" he said, his tone upset.

"I'm not sure what you derive pleasure from, honestly," I said.

His expression shifted. He laughed.

"Watching you blush. Wondering what it will be like to touch you," he said.

He'd successfully changed the mood.

"'Will be like'? So you are assuming that you're going to get to touch me?" I replied.

"I am. I know that you feel it just as much as I do. It's futile to resist. I'm just delaying it. Believe me; I've tried, in vain, the past two years. It's like being a south-pole magnet trying to escape a north-pole one," he said.

I smiled, knowing exactly what he meant.

I saw the sign for Portland, indicating we were only a few miles away. Soon, we passed over a bridge on the Willamette River. As I looked down at the water, I could see several ornate bridges in the distance. The greenery, the water, and Mount Hood on the horizon made for a spectacular, scenic view. We continued driving as the sun went down, and I wondered how close we were to the safe house.

As the city lights faded away in the rearview mirror, we exited the interstate. The car drove slowly up a winding road. I assumed we were going up a mountain and I wondered what kind of a place we were going to. When I thought of the word "safe house," I imagined an outdated, old cabin in the middle of nowhere.

Suddenly we came upon a gate. As we pulled up behind it, Isaac rolled down the window and said, "VHQ code red." A pole rose up from the ground and opened to reveal a scanner. Isaac turned to face the pole, and a light beam appeared to scan his face. The gates opened, and we drove in.

The lane curved to the left and to the right, and I caught a glimpse of the house ahead. It certainly wasn't an old cabin. The lights in the house and garage turned on automatically as we drove closer. The house towered three stories high; each level had a glass wraparound deck. The siding of the house was some sort of dark gray stone, accented by huge glass windows that pointed in every direction. You could see the dark wood floors gleaming as the lights inside brightened up the house.

"I was expecting it to be a little more...rustic," I said to Isaac.

"Just wait until you see the VHQ tomorrow," he replied. "I'll grab our bags out of the trunk. Go ahead and take a look inside. When you get to the door, you'll need to look into the scanner, so it can identify you. It should open automatically, but I'll be right up if you have any problems."

I put my heels back on and got out of the car. The crisp, cool air rushed past my head, and a shiver ran down my spine. I ran up the stairs to the front door.

{ 13 }

Thirteen

It was like a mystery mansion. I located the scanner, which was to the right of the door. It must have been motion activated, because it turned on just as I looked into it. The blue light moved across my face twice, and then it turned off and the front doors opened.

I was enthralled. What could I say? It was like fulfilling a science-fiction fantasy. For someone who frequently read science magazines, this was like crack, and after the last two days, I'd take any thrill I could get.

I heard Isaac coming up the stairs. He pulled the bags through the door, and it closed behind him.

"This is magnificent! I've never seen a house like this," I said.

He seemed unimpressed. "Shall we go find the bedrooms? I think they're on the third floor."

The bottom floor looked to contain the living room, a bathroom, and one bedroom. At the end of the hallway, to the left, was an elevator. This place kept getting better.

Isaac waved his hand across the motion pad, and the elevator doors opened. We entered, and Isaac touched the third-floor button.

The elevator opened up again a few seconds later, and we walked onto light gray stone floors. On each side of the hallway, there were two large black doors. I picked the one on the right side, which opened up into a very large bedroom full of glass. The bed was facing the windows, and the view was breathtaking. Looking out of the pristine glass, I could see the city lights of Portland in the distance. I sat down on the bed.

"I take it you've claimed this room," he said, laughing.

"Maybe, let's go see what the other room looks like."

We walked across the hall and opened the door to the adjacent room. It was the exact same layout but faced the opposite way. It was equally as beautiful, but I preferred the other room.

"I'll go with my original pick. Is that all right with you?" I said, smiling.

"Sure, whatever makes you happy. It's nice to see that smile back on your face," he said. "I'm going to go shower, and I'm sure you'd like to as well. I'll meet you downstairs in the kitchen when you're finished. It's on the second floor. Then I'll start cooking dinner," he said.

I smiled and walked back to "my" room. The bathroom was just as grand as the rest of the house. I had the choice between a bath and a shower, but I picked the latter.

I got undressed and opened the shower door. The water instantly started falling from the ceiling, like raindrops, big, warm raindrops. The view was stunning. Normally one might not want a huge glass window facing the outside in a shower, but this shower was so big that you could scoot all the way to the other end, where it was doubtful that anyone could see you. I didn't want to do that. I sat down on the ledge and gazed out upon the dark, mountainous landscape.

Once I finished showering and drying my hair, I walked over to my suitcase to grab some pajamas. I didn't remember what I had packed. I kind of just threw a mixture of everything in during the chaotic exit. I rifled through the clothes. Inside was a navy-blue dress, tights, and a pair of flats—which I would wear tomorrow—a black bra, a nude bra, and several pairs of panties. I picked out the nude bra. The only thing resembling pajamas I could find was a sort-of chemise. It wasn't the most modest of attire, but I didn't really have a choice. I slipped the white cotton nightgown over my head. It flowed down to my knees, and it was fairly opaque, so it seemed fine to me. It was a little bit lower cut on top than I would've liked, but it was far from obscene.

I grabbed my flats and slipped them on. I didn't like being barefoot. The feeling of cold tile on my feet grossed me out a little bit. I wandered out the door and down to the elevator. I waited for the door to open and pressed the number two. Within a few seconds, the elevator opened again.

The smell of garlic filled the air, and steam rose from the stove. The kitchen was situated at an angle from the elevator, and I could see Isaac working hastily between the stove and the counter. He was wearing an orange T-shirt and dark gray pajama bottoms.

I peered out the large glass windows, which were lining the back half of the second floor. They weren't normal windows, appearing more like glass walls. The room stuck out a little bit, giving the illusion that it was floating out in space. I walked over to the table to get a better look at the scenery outside.

Isaac's voice suddenly pierced the silence. "Evangeline, are you trying to torture me? Do you not have normal pajamas?"

A small smile appeared on his face, but I could tell he was trying very hard to hold it back.

I blushed. "No, unfortunately, I do not. It seems I did a poor job of packing," I said, "but I'll admit it's a little bit satisfying to see you squirm."

"Are you cold?" Isaac asked.

"No, it's not too bad down here. Why?" I said.

"Well, it looks as if you might be a bit chilly," he said, flashing a smile.

I looked down. I'd forgotten to put on my bra, and it was quite apparent. Isaac started laughing.

"Well, just for the record, this was not my intended look." I replied. "I'll be back in just a minute."

"I'm making lemon-butter chicken and pasta; is that all right with you?" he called after me.

"Yep, that sounds good," I replied back.

I finished putting on my bra and grabbed a blue cardigan out of the suitcase for good measure. I took the elevator back downstairs and walked to the dining-room table. Isaac had already placed my plate on the end of the table, and he was grabbing his own as I sat down.

"Would you like a glass of wine?" he asked me, glancing at my new outfit as he spoke.

"Sure. What kind is it? It's a little peculiar that this house in the middle of nowhere is stocked so well, isn't it?" I asked.

"I picked out a pinot grigio from the wine cellar. I'll have to take you down there later. I assume VHQ had the house stocked because we were arriving today. Wouldn't it be nice to live up here?" he asked.

"It really would," I agreed. "Do you think it's odd that I haven't felt very sad today about Charlotte, Dad, and Rosa? Is there something wrong with me?" I asked, abruptly changing the subject. The truth was that I felt guilty about feeling happy.

"I think with grief, at least from what I have seen, experiencing it is very different from person to person. The only wrong way is letting it slow you down so much that you can't move forward. You'll feel it eventually. Right now, you're pushing it away, trying not to think about it. Maybe you haven't even had the time to. Regardless, you shouldn't feel guilty about being happy. Life isn't that black and white. Happiness and sadness can, and often do, exist at the same time," he said.

"I know," I said, but I didn't really.

Isaac placed his hand on my arm. "Evie, what do you think Charlotte, your dad, and Rosa would want for you? I don't think they would want you to be devastated. I'd wager to say they would give anything to see you happy instead of sad right now. Don't spend too much time worrying. You're going to feel the emotional loss at some point. Enjoy where you are right now."

My heart ached equally with the feelings of loss and joy.

As we finished cleaning up our dinner dishes, I glanced at the clock. Eleven thirty. It felt later, but then I realized we were in Pacific Time, two hours earlier than Central. We both walked to the elevator and rode it up to the third floor.

"Did you go out on the balcony yet?" Isaac asked.

"No, I didn't even notice," I said.

"I'll show you. It's a little chilly outside, so you might want to grab a blanket."

We walked into my room, and I grabbed one of the fuzzy blankets off of the bed. He walked to the glass windows, and I saw the door he was talking about. It opened automatically. Two chairs sat on the metal floor of the balcony. I sat down in one, and Isaac sat down in the other.

"Can you imagine what it looks like in the daylight?" I said.

We both sat in silence for a while, enjoying the happiness of the moment. I tried not to think about the events of the last few days, but sadness started to creep in.

"Isaac, will you sleep with me tonight?" I asked pensively.

"Why?" he said.

"I don't want to be alone," I said.

"I'm not sure if that's a great idea," he replied, "Lying right next to you might be torturous."

"I promise I won't try to seduce you," I said, smiling.

"Evangeline, you don't even have to try. That's the problem. It's hard enough not to touch you when we're in the same room. In the same bed...I don't know that I could resist."

His words hung in the air for a second as I grasped what he was saying. I imagined us lying together on the bed, being in close proximity. My body tingled from the thought. I knew the truth—that it wasn't just my loneliness that wanted him in the bed with me. I wanted him to touch me. I knew I had to walk away. Passion was a strong emotion, one especially illogical. He didn't want that yet.

I stood up and walked over to him. I touched his hand for a moment. "I need to go get a drink. I've got to cool down," I told him, and I quickly walked through the door.

I went down to the kitchen and grabbed a glass of water. I heard footsteps behind me, and I turned around, knowing it was Isaac.

"I'll lie with you until you fall asleep," he said.

"Thank you," I replied.

{14}

Fourteen

I woke up to the sun streaking light in every direction. Isaac was still lying next to me, asleep. It was six, a few hours before I was leaving for the VHQ. I wandered onto the balcony to take one last look. It was more beautiful in the daylight.

I went back inside to wake Isaac. I touched his arm softly. "Isaac, it's time to get up. We have a few hours before our rendezvous."

His dark-green eyes slowly opened. "Okay," he said. "Thanks."

I grabbed my clothes from the suitcase and headed into the bathroom to change. I slid the navy-blue dress over my head and tugged it down to my knees. The sleeves hit just below my elbow, and the dress was snug but not too tight. I grabbed my tights and pulled them on.

I decided to pull my hair back into a messily styled bun. I put on some eyeliner and mascara, then dotted my lips with a bit of red lipstick. Once I was finished, I gathered my clothing and toiletries to pack back inside my suitcase and returned to the bedroom. Isaac was gone, probably getting dressed himself.

I opened my suitcase and stuffed everything back in. The bottle of perfume Charlotte had given me for my birthday tumbled out as I closed the zipper. I sprayed a bit of the perfume on my neck and wrists then placed it back in the bag. She would have been happy to know that I was using it.

I heard a knock at the door. "Come in," I said.

Isaac was dressed in a pair of dark jeans and an orange sweater, with a white collared shirt underneath. He had something in his hands, a wrapped gift. He handed it to me, and I sat down on the bed to unwrap it.

"This is your birthday gift. I grabbed it from the house before we left," he said.

Inside of the box was a small, razor-thin electronic tablet. A pair of bright-red headphones were connected to it. Obviously he'd already known my favorite color well before yesterday's conversation.

"Tap it to turn it on," he said.

I placed my finger on the screen and tapped gently. The screen lit up with letters. "Evie," it said, in large font. The letters soon disappeared, and another screen opened up. A list of books popped up under the heading "My Audio Books." I saw the title *The Learning Series: Quantum Physics, Astrophysics, Ancient World History, Linguistics, and Human Behavior.*

"I know that you love to read, and I had initially thought that you might like to listen to these courses on your walk from school or from the nursing home or when you go running. Now, maybe you can listen to them before you go to sleep or to distract you from all of the changes," he said.

It was the perfect gift.

"A few months ago I was just telling Rosa about wanting to take a course in quantum physics because it had always interested me," I said.

"I know; she told me. That's when I decided to get you this," he replied. "You can also listen to music on it and check your e-mail. I don't think it will be a problem to get into the VHQ. Speaking of which, I'm confiscating that nightgown of yours. I'm going to have enough competition as it is." He smiled, but his eyes betrayed him.

"Fine," I said. I pulled the cotton chemise out of my suitcase and handed it to him. "But don't lose it. I want it back when you return."

The clock read 8:30.

"Do you have everything packed up?" he asked.

"Yes, I think so," I replied.

"OK, I'll meet you at the front door in ten minutes."

"All right," I replied.

He left, and I checked the bathroom again for any remaining toiletries. I felt nervous. Soon I'd be on my own. I wheeled the suitcase down the hall to the elevator. I entered and pressed the button for floor two. I needed to grab some water. The doors opened, and I walked into the kitchen one last time. I grabbed a bottle of water from the refrigerator and drank it down quickly.

Then I saw the set of knives sitting in the block on the counter. I grabbed the smallest one, a paring knife. What if I needed to protect myself? What if something went wrong? I didn't want to be defenseless. Fear started to take over. I lifted up my dress and shoved the tiny knife into the waistband of my tights. I checked to make sure you couldn't see the shape of it through my dress. Then I walked over to the elevator and waited for the doors to open.

When the elevator touched down on the ground level, Isaac was waiting for me by the door.

"We are actually heading to the garage. Follow me," he said.

I walked nervously behind him. As we entered the garage, he hit a small white button.

"Step over here," he said, as he guided me to the correct spot. The ground below us started to move, and we descended.

"Once we get to the bottom, you'll see where to go. I can't follow you from the elevator. The meeting point is just a few steps away. In exactly five minutes, you will be met by the Veterox. They look just like I do, like normal human beings. I'm not sure who is meeting you beyond that point. I'll get updates from Ethan to ensure you are safely inside," he said. "It's going to be okay, Evangeline."

He grabbed my arm and pulled me into him, wrapping his arms around my body in a tight embrace and breaking my fearless façade. Tears fell from my eyes and dripped down my face. Isaac wiped them away.

The elevator stopped as we reached the bottom.

He pushed the hair back from my ear and whispered, "You're safe. I'll be back," he said.

I hoped that he was right, but everything up to this point had gone awry. We parted, and I stepped off the elevator with my suitcase. The elevator started to rise again, and I didn't look back. I walked forward toward a small concrete bench.

{15}

Fifteen

It has to be 8:47 by now, I thought. I wondered if I was in the right spot. I decided to walk a bit further down the long cement tunnel in front of me. I started dragging my suitcase on the concrete floor. Suddenly, a bright light filled the tunnel, and I heard the sound of footsteps coming down the corridor. The light blinded me. I stopped walking and let go of the suitcase for a moment. I raised my hand up to shield my eyes so that I could try to see who was coming.

My hand didn't get much further than chest level. Suddenly, I heard a popping sound, and I felt searing pain in my lower abdomen. I grabbed my stomach and fell to the ground. I'm sure it appeared fairly dramatic. I heard voices running toward me. My hands felt wet. Was that blood? It had to be blood.

"What in the fuck happened, Finn?" an angry male voice asked.

"My initial body scan showed she has a knife, and she was raising her arm in the air. Her body language was threatening. I didn't know if she had another weapon or was going to pull the knife," the guy named Finn said.

"Where did you shoot her?" the first male voice asked.

"In her lower abdomen. I don't think I hit any major organs. I wasn't shooting to kill," Finn said.

"Thanks for not killing me," I said to the two men sarcastically. "I do have a knife." I paused to catch my breath. "But I wasn't trying to hurt anyone. I just brought it for protection," I tried to explain.

The first man looked me in the eyes and spoke calmly, "My name is Ezra Crailene. I'm Ethan's son, and I'm a doctor. I need to pull your dress up to see where all of the blood is coming from," he said.

"It's probably coming from the bullet wound, because Finn shot me!" I replied.

Ezra laughed. "Yes, I'd imagine so," he said, smiling.

I started to feel faint.

"Evangeline, I'm going to pull your dress up now; is that okay?" Ezra asked again.

"Yes, I think so. Just don't look at any other body parts besides the bullet wound," I replied.

He laughed again. "I promise to use the utmost discretion," he said.

He pushed the dress up to my mid-thigh and then asked Finn for a knife.

Jesus, not my dress, I thought. In this moment, my brain failed to realize that it was covered in blood and that I might not even be alive to wear the dress later anyway. He cut a small hole and ripped it all the way up to the top.

"That is not what I would call discretion," I said.

He smiled. I could feel his hands touching my stomach. An odd feeling of electricity filled my body, followed by intense pain when he pressed on the wound. I winced. He pulled his hands away quickly and looked confused.

"Tell me where it hurts the most," he said. He pushed on the area surrounding the wound again.

"Right there," I said.

Ezra's face started to go blurry.

"Your face is really blurry. Are you melting?" I asked. I don't know why I thought he was melting.

"She's losing consciousness, Finn. She's bleeding out. We need to get her to Violet Hope right now. Contact Ethan, and let them know we will need an air evacuation once we pass into the VHC. Page Dori. I think the bullet probably went through her intestines, but I fear that it might have ripped through the superior mesenteric artery as well because of the amount of blood. The knife is also protruding from the side of her body. She must have fallen on it. We need an open operating room as soon as we arrive. She needs to go straight into surgery."

He turned back to be me. "Evangeline, I need you to stay awake as long as you possibly can. You've lost a lot of blood and are going to feel quite light-headed. We need to transport you across the VHQ threshold, and then, as you may have overheard, you will need to have surgery. Hang in here with me," he said in a calm voice. I passed out shortly thereafter.

I remember waking up in the helicopter for a few minutes. Ezra's voice rang through the air. He was communicating with the hospital via some sort of phone, though I couldn't see it. I could hear his conversation.

"Dad, she's with me. We're about two minutes out. Did you get in touch with Isaac? Then we are waiting until she is conscious to ask her? OK, yes, I understand. Do we have an operating room ready, and does the anesthesiologist know about her being only half Veterox? I think it'll be Dr. Slobode. Yes. Thanks," he said.

Maybe that last sentence didn't occur. Again, I passed out. We must have landed safely, because when I regained consciousness, I was in a hospital room with people running around. I didn't see Ezra.

A nurse noticed that I was awake. "Honey, you're at Violet Hope Hospital. We are getting ready to wheel you into surgery in a few moments. You're going to feel very sleepy," she said in a calm voice.

She plunged a vial of cloudy white liquid into my IV line. My eyes closed, and I fell asleep.

{16}

Sixteen

I woke up groggy. I gazed around the room. It looked more like a hotel room than a hospital room. Ezra was sitting on a couch, typing on a tablet. He was way more handsome than I remembered.

"You're really handsome," I blurted out.

He looked over at me. "Well you have quite a lot of morphexine in your system, so we'll see how you feel about me in a few days," he said, smiling. "Between one and ten, how is your pain level right now?" he asked.

"A three," I replied back.

"That's excellent. If it gets any higher, please let me know right away," he said.

I nodded.

"You were really very close to dying on the way here. There were a few moments in the helo that I didn't think you would make it into surgery because of the blood loss. Once you were in the operating room, I repaired a hole in one of your major arteries. We did need to give you a blood transfusion, but everything went very well. You had

149

a small tear in your intestinal wall, which was also repaired. The knife you were carrying sliced into your side, but it was purely a superficial wound, with no damage done to any organs. It's been sutured, and it will be fine," he said.

That knife was the worst idea ever, I thought. It had gotten me shot and then stabbed me. Isaac was going to kill me when he found out.

Ezra continued, "You won't have much scarring. I was able to go in and repair everything through the tiny bullet wound. It will probably heal into about a half-inch scar on your right side. The knife wound only required a few stitches. You're incredibly lucky it was only a paring knife," he said, smiling. "Is there anyone you would like me to contact?"

"My dad…wait, is he still dead?" I asked.

Everything started to come back into focus, and I realized the answer to my own question.

Ezra nodded.

"What do you want to do about Isaac?" he asked.

I paused to think. "Is he still in the middle of the rescue operation for Rosa?"

"Yes, he is," Ezra replied.

"Then, no, not right now," I said.

Isaac didn't need the extra stress. I was alive and out of danger. It would be selfish to let him know now. I knew that he would probably be angry at me for keeping it secret, but it wasn't worth risking Rosa's life, or his own for that matter.

"I had a feeling you would want to hold off. He does know that you arrived at the VHQ safely, although 'safely' might not be the best word to describe how you arrived." He laughed. "Let me know if you change your mind."

I felt a sharp twinge in my lower abdomen.

"Are you having more pain?" Ezra asked.

I must have winced.

"Yes, a little," I replied.

"I'm going to go grab some morphexine. I'll be right back. In the meantime, you've got a front-row seat to a beautiful sunset," he said.

He stood up and walked on the beautiful, dark wood floors over to the hospital-room door. He said, "Open curtains." The cheery yellow curtains that hung against the entire back wall of the room started to move apart. He walked out of the room to grab the medication. As the curtains silently opened, the sun came streaming through the windows. Then I noticed bright-blue water and a beach. Was that the ocean?

I looked around the rest of the room, which was no less lavishly decorated than the house Isaac and I had stayed at the night before. A large gray velour couch, the one that Ezra was sitting on just a moment ago, was placed adjacent to the hospital bed, on top of a citrusy-yellow rug. The walls were painted a sandy-beige color. Behind the couch, hanging on the wall, was a huge gilded mirror. To the right of the couch was a door; I assumed it led to the bathroom. I heard a knock, and Ezra walked in.

Ezra was tall, maybe a little over six feet, and his hair was dark brown. The white coat he wore had been emblazoned with red embroidery that said, "Dr. Ezra Crailene, MD, PHD, Chief of Surgery, Violet Hope Hospital." Behind his black-rimmed glasses, I recognized the bright sapphire-blue eyes that I'd seen earlier in the morning. They looked a lot like the color of my eyes.

"I've got the morphexine. It should take effect immediately," he explained.

He took the syringe full of clear liquid and injected into my IV. It felt like a trickle moving up my arm and then through my neck and continuing down my spine. The pain was gone, but I felt odd. A little bit giddy maybe. Euphoric?

"Feeling better?" Ezra asked.

"Yes, much. Thank you," I replied. "How do I work this bed? Is there a button to press so that I can sit up?" I said.

"Just say 'up' if you want to sit up and 'down' if you would like to lay back down. Everything here is voice activated and will respond to most voice commands. There's a television in the ceiling that will descend if you'd like to watch something," Ezra explained.

"Ocean," he said.

Suddenly I could hear the waves crashing outside of the windows.

"This is ridiculous. Why does a hospital need all of these amenities?" I asked.

"Well, although it may seem like a lot, it's actually quite normal here. Every house here has this technology and much, much more. You're used to the world outside of the VHQ, and it's very different. However, you're in one of the most advanced hospitals in the world. I'm sure you've heard the name by now. Violet Hope Hospital was named after your mother. In many ways, it was inspired by her. The walls, the decorations, and the ocean are all an homage to her work at Camp Espoir."

I wanted to know more, but I was so sleepy.

"Are you staying with me all night?" I asked.

"Yes, I need to keep a close eye on you during the next twenty-four hours, so I'll be in here with you. I may be out of the room to grab some food for an hour, but I'll wait until you fall asleep. If you wake during that time and need me, just say 'Dr. Ezra Crailene,' and you'll be automatically connected to me," he said.

"Do you know how long I'll have to be in here?" I asked.

"If all is well, I'll be discharging you tomorrow evening. You'll be transferred over to our house until you are assigned a residence of your own," he said.

What had he meant by "our house", I wondered. A residence of my own? That was an odd thing to think about.

"Do you have any updates on Isaac or Rosa?" I asked.

He sat down on the couch again. "Isaac has a good lead. They are working on getting her back. I wish I could tell you more, but we're in a public hospital, and this is a very sensitive matter. Right now, we don't know if anyone from the VHQ is involved in the incident. Once we move you tomorrow night, I'll explain more," he said.

"Isaac is doing okay then?" I asked.

"Believe me, Evangeline; you don't need to worry about him too terribly much. He possess a particular skill set that's hard to beat," he said, smiling.

I wondered how well he knew Isaac, but I was too tired to start that conversation.

"I'm feeling sleepy, so I think I'm going to close my eyes. Is that okay?" I asked Ezra.

"Of course. I'll be over here, doing some patient charts," he said.

My thoughts wandered back to Isaac. I wished he was lying next to me. I drifted off to sleep.

I awoke in the morning feeling much better. Ezra was still sitting on the couch, typing on the tablet.

"How are you feeling this morning? Are you hungry?" he asked.

I didn't realize he had noticed I was awake. I wondered what his Veterox powers were. I was hungry. My last meal was with Isaac.

"I'm feeling pretty good for taking a bullet and a knife to the abdomen, but I am hungry. What can I have to eat?" I asked.

"Pretty much anything that you want. All your labs look great, and I didn't notice any problems through the night. The cafeteria can make whatever you desire," he said.

"What about a Thai red chicken curry with rice?" I asked.

"I'll let the nurse know, and she'll get it ordered for you. It will be up within a half hour. I'm going to have my colleague come in to care for you for the rest of the day. I'll be back this afternoon to discharge you. I just need to go and finish some preparations for your transfer. Her name is Dr. Isadora Crailene. She's not as good of a surgeon as me, but she won't kill you," he said. A smile appeared on his face and he started laughing.

A woman entered the room. She was wearing a navy pencil skirt and a tight pink blouse, with her white physician's coat over the top. Her hair was pulled back into a ponytail. Her dark brown eyes gazed brightly at Ezra.

"Don't listen to this fool. He's just a bit jealous that I beat him in the 'Outstanding Physician' contest this year," she teased.

She turned to me. "Hi, Evangeline, I'm Isadora. I'm Ezra's older sister. Well, as you might be able to tell from my name, I'm the adopted sister and the best looking of the bunch." She laughed.

Ezra scoffed. "Evangeline, I'll see you a little bit later," he said. He turned toward Isadora. "Dori, are you going to be home tonight? I need to know how many people to tell Mom for dinner."

"Yes, probably, pending any serious emergencies. I'm on call," she replied. He walked out the door.

"Goodness, well what a way to arrive at the VHQ! Ezra was really worried about you yesterday. He's a topnotch doctor, and when he gets worried, I know it's pretty bad. When the Com went off and I heard the code air evacuation go out from Ezra, I rushed to the hospital. I assisted in your surgery yesterday morning. We were both relived once the arterial hole was closed up and you stabilized. I'm glad Isaac wasn't around. He would have been furious, knowing that you were shot by a Veterox. Actually I'm going to stay away from him when he gets here. He's going to be really angry that we didn't tell him about it," she said.

"Do you all know Isaac pretty well then?" I asked.

"Oh, you don't know? Well, I guess I'm not sure if I should be the one telling you. I'm kind of surprised Isaac didn't. Ezra, Isaac, and Rosa are triplets," she said.

I think my jaw visibly dropped open.

"Our parents are Ethan and Vivienne Crailene. Your mom and dad took in Rosa and Isaac when they were born. It's a long story," she said.

Everything started to make much more sense. Isaac knew I'd be safe here with his family; that's why he was so adamant that I come to the VHQ.

"So how are you older than Isaac, Ezra, and Rosa if they were born during the plague? Were you born before the plague?" I asked.

"Well that's another interesting story and one that you might be especially interested in," she said. "I was born during the early, early stages of the plague. My mom was a little over thirty weeks' pregnant with me when she started showing symptoms of the flu. I don't think she was terribly concerned right away. Nobody was at that time. By the time she arrived in the emergency room, it was too late. Not much could be done to save her. A doctor by the name of Violet Rolieux took charge of her case," she said.

"My mom?" I said. Then it hit me. "You're the baby from the NICU. Her first, well, second patient with Z3C7," I said.

"Yes, I am. Your mom named me Isadora. She was assigned to Camp Espoir almost immediately after my birth. I was in the NICU for the first weeks of my life, but she called the hospital nearly every day to check on me. When the Veterox vaccine came along, it was your mom who got me moved over to Camp Espoir to be vaccinated. After the trials went awry and we were moved over here to the VHQ, she arranged for the Crailenes to take me in. She was an amazing lady, by all accounts. Your dad was amazing too. I was sorry to hear about his passing," she said.

"Thank you," I replied. The conversation paused for a moment. I thought about my dad and how much I missed him.

Isadora's voice interrupted. "Not to change the subject but I need to complete your discharge physical, and I have to remove your catheter. I'm sure you want to get up and walk around. Your IV will stay in place until Ezra comes in to officially discharge you. Actually, he might leave it in for the next few days to control your pain level."

"Sure, just let me know what you need me to do," I replied.

"Curtains," she said. The bright sunlight was replaced by the artificial light of the room.

"The catheter removal will be a little painful. I'm going to lift up your gown. By the way, aren't these the most awesome hospital gowns? I picked them out," she said.

I hadn't really noticed what I was wearing, but I looked down, and she was right. It didn't feel scratchy. It was made of a soft knit fabric and had buttons going down the front. It wasn't necessarily the most attractive piece of clothing, but it wasn't hideous either.

I loved her cheery attitude. Her smile was radiant. She was just one of those people that exuded happiness.

She pulled a pair of blue gloves out of the box on the wall and placed them on her hands. "Okay, now just relax your legs. Take a deep breath, and blow it out," she said.

I didn't really feel anything, thanks to the morphexine, but I was definitely glad Isadora was removing the catheter and not Ezra.

"That's it. All right, you can go ahead and stand up," she said. She threw everything away in a small bin nearby and then walked over to the sink to wash her hands.

I placed my legs over the side of the bed and stood up. I felt a bit wobbly at first, but it subsided within a few seconds.

"How is your pain?" Isadora asked.

"It's not bad. It throbs, but it's tolerable," I replied.

"I'm going to go ahead and give you a low dose of morphexine. We like to see little to no pain, because it tends to build if you don't stay on top of it. Do you want to take a shower? I can move your IV into the bathroom," she said.

"Yes, that would be nice," I replied.

She went to the side of the bed and unhooked the IV bag from the machine. We walked into the bathroom, and she hung the bag on another hook in the shower.

"Okay, I'll go get the morphexine. If you need anything, just call my name. The shower will turn on automatically when you enter," she explained. She walked out and closed the door behind her.

I got undressed and stepped into the shower. The water was pleasantly warm. I looked down to inspect my injuries. A clear membrane-like bandage covered both the gunshot and knife wound. There was some purple bruising around both spots, but other than that, they weren't terribly gruesome. Nonetheless, I did feel a little queasy, so I decided to make it a quick shower. I stepped out of the glass door and grabbed a towel. I slipped on a new hospital gown and opened the door. Isadora was standing by the bed.

"I brought your suitcase in. You can change clothes whenever you want. I'll have to disconnect your IV first. I picked up a few pairs of pajamas for you on my way here. Isaac told my dad that you didn't pack any. They are in the suitcase," she said.

I laughed, remembering how he had confiscated my white ones

yesterday morning.

"Yes, thank you!" I replied.

"I brought in the morphexine, and I have your lunch. It smells really good. Let me go ahead and give you the meds first, and then you can eat. I'm going to go grab some lunch as well, if you don't mind?" she asked.

"Yep, that's fine," I replied.

She was right about the pain; it was getting worse. I sat down, and she injected the medicine. Within a few minutes, I was feeling better. She walked out of the room, and I picked up my fork to eat.

As I finished my last bite, I heard a familiar knock at the door, and Isadora entered.

"Good news, Ezra's on his way to discharge you a bit early. I need to do the physical examination, and then I thought I would unhook your IV so you can get dressed. I'll bring your suitcase closer so that you can pick out your clothes," she said.

She lifted the bag onto my bed, and I unzipped it. The only outfit I had left was a bright-red, knee-length dress and an ivory cardigan. The waist was elasticized, which was perfect for my needs, since anything too tight around my abdomen would be uncomfortable. I grabbed a pair of underwear and the only bra left, a black lacy one. I hoped the dress was opaque enough that you couldn't see through it.

"That dress is gorgeous. I saw that you were wearing one when you came in yesterday. Do you always wear dresses?" she asked.

"Normally, yes. I love dresses. They're what I'm most comfortable in," I replied.

She unhooked the IV bag for a moment and wound the remaining cord around my arm so I could change.

"I just have to say, when I saw you in the emergency room last night, I was in awe of how beautiful you looked. Even after a gunshot wound and a lot of blood loss, somehow you still looked so radiant. Isaac always said you were gorgeous. He did not exaggerate. I think it's your eyes. They're such a deep blue but yet bright and cheery. I remember your mother from when I was little, and you look quite a lot like her," she said.

"Thank you, although I sincerely doubt I was radiant," I replied.

I wondered if Isaac had ever mentioned Isadora to me. I walked into the bathroom to finish changing. I pulled my hair up into a ponytail and came back out.

"Go ahead and lie down on the bed, and I'll just take a look at your incisions," she said.

I flipped up my dress so that she could see them. She pressed on my belly in several locations.

"Any tenderness besides the area right around your incisions?" she asked.

"No," I said.

She flipped my dress back down.

"Everything looks good." She paused and grabbed her tablet and started typing.

"So did Isaac finally ask you out?" she asked. She quickly added, "You don't have to answer that. I'm just really curious. I think we're all wondering. Dad said he was acting very protective of you, and naturally, we assumed that maybe there was more to it? But you don't have to tell me," she said.

I didn't mind the question.

"Well, I think we were headed down that road just before everything happened at the restaurant. There's nothing going on between us right at this moment, but I'd be lying if I said I didn't hope for something more in the future. There's a passion between us. I've never...I don't know. It's just different," I said, blushing.

"I can confidently tell you that you are not alone in those feelings. I've known that he liked you for years. Well, a few years anyway," she said.

"How?" I asked.

"Every once in a while he would come back to the VHQ and visit for a weekend. I begged the guy to come back and stay for good. He always loved it here. I had a feeling that you were the reason holding him back, so I just asked him. I knew right away, when his eyes lit up, that I was right. When Isaac is passionate about something, you know it. He wanted you. It was just a matter of time, although I have to admit, it did take him a little longer than I thought it would," she said.

I responded, "I can understand his train of thought a little bit better now than I could a few days ago. I don't know that I would have found out about the Veterox anytime soon if he'd had his way. I think it was hard for him to manifest his feelings, because he knew that in doing so, he would have to expose me to huge safety risks. Judging by what's happened in the past few days, I don't doubt he was right."

She nodded. "That sounds like Isaac. He always chooses the protector role. I think his powers place him in a unique position to view the world. They have naturally made him very tentative about people, and thus he's very cautious. Although, you probably would have found out soon enough, with you being Violet's daughter. I'm sure that forced his hand a bit."

"What do you mean? I think everyone did a pretty good job pulling off the secret for the last twenty-one years. I doubt I would have caught on," I said.

Isadora's face suddenly became serious. "You don't know? Jesus. All right, Ezra will be here soon. I can't explain just yet, but once we get in the car, I'll show you what I'm talking about. I'll be right back. I need to go make a call," she said.

She abruptly walked out of the room. This is absurd, I thought. I wanted to get off the roller coaster. I wondered what bomb was going to be dropped on me next. A few days ago, I would have wagered a bet on the fact I knew a lot about the world. It was obvious now that I only knew less than 1 percent.

My stomach started to hurt, as it always did when I got anxious. I was more of a rip-the-bandage-off type of person. When it was slowly being peeled off, I would start to hyper-analyze the facts of the situation, and it usually ended in a conclusion that was wrong and overly dramatic.

One time, when I was fifteen, I had to go into the doctor's office to get a physical and some lab tests run to make sure I was healthy. A few days later, the office called to tell my dad that the doctor wanted to meet with me to discuss the lab results. Between the time they called and when we arrived for the appointment two hours later, I had scoured the internet, searching for things like "abnormal test results fifteen-year-old," and "doctor wants to talk with me about lab results," and "blood disorders common in a fifteen-year-old," and "what kind of disorders can fifteen-year-olds die from?"

By the time we arrived at the office, I'd convinced myself that I had leukemia and was going to die. Of course, it turned out that the doctor just wanted to ask me some questions about my diet, because my lab results had shown iron-deficient anemia, so she was trying to decide whether I needed to be on iron injections or if my diet could be modified.

My mind was my own worst enemy. I rifled through my suitcase, looking for the tiny tablet that Isaac had given me. The red headphones were easy to spot. I turned it on and placed the headphones in my ears. I scrolled through the different books, trying to decide which one to listen to. I remembered Isaac had said that I could e-mail on it. I wondered. I touched the icon with an envelope on it. An e-mail account appeared, showing one new message. It had been sent early yesterday morning. The subject line read "Evie." I clicked on it immediately.

Evie,

I assume you're safely inside the VHQ if you're reading this. Hopefully, you know why I sent you there by now. There's a lot I haven't told you, and I'm sure my family is going to explain most of it before I get back. I'm sorry I didn't get the chance to tell you everything. Once I return, I promise you can ask me any question you want. I'll even tell you if I have a big penis. Kidding. You'll have to wait on that one for a while. Are you smiling? Good. I bet you're probably blushing a little bit too.

I'll be there as soon as I can. In the meantime, my family should prove to be a pretty big distraction. Don't feel bad if Dori manages to coerce you into spilling your secrets. She's very charismatic. I'm sure you can convince her fairly easily to tell you all about me. Watch out for the dashing blue-eyed Ezra. He'll try to steal you away. Don't wear that white nightgown around him. Actually, I'm confiscating that thing before you leave. I'd better get back into the bed before you realize I'm gone. Just so you know, I was right; it's incredibly hard to sleep when you're lying next to me.

–Isaac

Thankfully, I was all alone. The many faces I made reading that letter would have surely outed me as the giddy, doe-eyed schoolgirl falling for a boy. He was kind and funny and intriguing. I wondered where he was. Hopefully, I would get some information about the rescue mission tonight.

I could hear voices outside of my room, which I immediately recognized as Ezra and Isadora.

"Lilyana is going to cover call for me tonight," Isadora said.

They both walked into the room.

"OK," Ezra said, still talking to Isadora.

Isadora walked over to my bed and unhooked the IV from the machine on the wall. The only thing remaining was a small tube that was taped down to my hand.

"We're going to leave the line in, just in case we need to give you any medication over the next few days," Ezra explained to me.

Isadora removed the tape and placed a bandage over the tip of the IV line in my arm.

"Speaking of which, how do you feel pain wise?" Ezra asked.

"I'm good for now. Are we ready to leave?" I asked.

"Yep, I'll grab the suitcase. Dori will help you to the door. We're going to wheel you out the rest of the way, so you don't have to walk," he said.

"I think I can walk. I'd rather walk," I said.

"It's fine," Dori said. "I'll walk beside her in case she needs help."

I smiled at her, thankful for the gesture. She grabbed her tablet and tucked it into the pocket of her doctor's coat. We walked out the door and into the hallway. The hospital was busy, with several doctors scurrying around. I couldn't help but wonder if they were on their best behavior because Ezra and Isadora were there.

For some reason, I garnered a lot of stares. I wasn't sure if it was because of me or my two escorts. I saw the frosted-glass elevator in the small cove just to our right.

The pain in my side radiated up my body, and I suddenly thought that maybe it wasn't such a good idea to walk out. I didn't want to stop, because everyone was staring. However, I went over the options in my head, and it seemed like a far worse idea to faint in front of everyone than to ask for a wheelchair.

"Hey, I think I might want that wheelchair," I said to whomever was listening.

Isadora walked swiftly toward the doctor's station and returned with a wheelchair. It was smaller and bit more attractive looking than the kind we had at Haven. We neared the elevator, and it opened automatically.

Ezra said, "Mezzanine," and the doors closed.

I didn't even know we had descended when the elevator doors suddenly opened up and we exited into the lobby. The word "lobby" wasn't a grand enough word to describe the entrance to the hospital. The ceiling towered above us, with sunlight filtering in through the windows perched high at the top. Water flowed over the fountain that was situated in the middle of the lobby and surrounded by chairs.

"Is Ellenora here?" Isadora asked Ezra.

"She should be pulling up any second," Ezra replied.

A black SUV came into view as it pulled under the entrance wing. I recognized the winged logo with a *B* in the center. I wondered what a Bentley SUV cost. Two hundred thousand or so?

We walked out the front doors. The weather was remarkably balmy, maybe seventy-five degrees. Ezra opened the door and helped me inside, while Isadora went around to the passenger's side and got into the backseat. Ezra walked over to the passenger's front seat and sat down.

"Ellenora, this is Evangeline," Ezra said to the female in the driver's seat.

She looked back and said, "It's very nice to finally meet you. And please, call me Nora."

"Ellenora is Isaac's associate. Well, that's her title anyway. She's also a very good friend of ours," Isadora said to me.

Nora was one of the most gorgeous women I had ever seen. Her flawless skin was dark, as dark as the sky at night, and her lips were colored in a striking shade of pink. Her hair was perfectly coiffed. Small, tight curls cascaded down to her shoulders.

I had always wanted hair like that. I'd tried once, somehow convincing my dad to let me get a perm, but it was not to be. Instead of the bouncy, shiny, and thick hair that I so coveted, mine became like a limp noodle, plastered to the side of my face. It looked more like a sad clown's hair than anything close to Nora's.

I couldn't tell how tall she was, but her legs did look long and somewhat uncomfortably scrunched into the driver's seat. If I had to guess, I'd say she was close to six foot, the taller end of the spectrum. Her demeanor was confident and yet soft. I could tell by the way her dark brown eyes crinkled up when she smiled at me that she was genuinely happy to meet me. I smiled back.

"Hi, Nora," I said. "It's nice to meet you too."

As we drove away I noticed the scenery and the buildings that made up what looked like a large, sprawling city. The tall white buildings jutted high into the sky. It seemed as if we were going uphill, but the ground leveled out as we turned onto a busy street.

There was something different about the way the light refracted off of everything. The air seemed more pristine, as if it was glimmering slightly. It seemed to sharpen the scenery, like watching television in ultrahigh definition instead of standard.

"Am I imagining that the air looks different here? I know you can't see air, but it feels like I can," I asked.

"That's actually my design," Ezra said.

Isadora rolled her eyes, "Here we go. His biggest fault is his extreme ego," she said.

Ezra ignored her comment and continued, "It's actually called the S-Sphere. It serves two purposes. Isaac may have explained to you that this city is invisible to anyone outside of it. Those tiny particles that sort of reflect off of your eyes a bit, they are an integral part of how the shield works. The other part of S-Sphere is its ability to filter out viruses and bacteria. In short, it's very hard to get sick here. Ironic, isn't it?"

"So do you ever take care of patients who have infections or, well, the flu?" I asked.

Isadora responded, "It's not infallible, and if we've learned anything in the past twenty years, it's that bacteria and viruses are able to survive no matter what. Of course, with a virus it just has to run its course, but we do have some very effective antiviral medication to combat them. However, those cases are very, very few, and usually it's not viral but instead a type of bacteria that we can't treat with antibiotics—those strains that have become antibiotic resistant. So to answer your question, yes, we do see patients that have infections, but the majority of patients we see have other problems, like strokes or certain types of cancer and traumas or injuries," she said.

I stared out the windows, taking in all of the beautiful, vivid colors. I remembered what Isadora had said in the hospital about me not knowing something.

"What's the big secret that I don't know? Can you tell me now that we're in the car?" I asked.

Ezra looked back at Isadora. "Show her," he said.

Isadora took the electronic tablet out of her coat pocket and touched the screen. She started typing. I saw my name pop up on the screen as she scrolled down to the bottom.

"Here," she said, handing me the tablet. "Look in the notes."

My height, weight, and a bunch of vitals were recorded at the top. My eyes searched for the word "notes," and I finally spotted it midway down:

NOTES: Patient is 51 percent human and 49 percent Veterox. Please use caution when prescribing medication dosages, as it may vary from the Veterox recommendations.

What did that mean? I was half Veterox? Neither of my parents were Veterox. Were my parents not really my parents? I started to get angry. The deception kept getting more elaborate. I understood why I was lied to about Rosa and Isaac; however I couldn't understand why someone would intentionally deceive me about who my parents were for twenty-one years. That was truly mean.

"So I assume you know who my real parents are then? Please, go ahead and drop another bombshell on me. Apparently, that's just how my life goes these days," I said angrily. I also sounded whiny, which I didn't like.

"Oh, no, no. I'm so sorry. That's not what it means. Xander and Violet are your parents. You misunderstood. Violet was a Veterox. That's why you're half Veterox," Isadora said.

"My mom was a Veterox? What? How? Why was she not detained here?" I asked. I was speaking rapidly now. "There's no way I'm half Veterox. I don't have any special powers. I may be a little unwary, but I'm not ignorant," I said.

"You do have powers," Ezra interrupted. "You're a receiver. It's just not as pronounced in you because you're only half Veterox," he said.

"As far as your mom, only my dad and mom knew about her being a Veterox. It's a long story. Let's just focus on you for a moment," he said.

"What is a receiver?" I asked.

"How do you feel when you're around a group of people? Do they overwhelm you much of the time?" Ezra asked.

"Yes, I get overwhelmed pretty easily. I always feel emotionally drained. I need time alone to get my energy back," I replied.

"That's because you're taking on the emotions of the people surrounding you. When somebody is angry or happy or sad, you feel it. That's why a social situation is overwhelming. You're being battered by the moods of everyone around you. I'm sure it would be much more manageable if everyone was happy all the time. Naturally, I'm sure you do gravitate toward people who are more positive. What was Charlotte like?" he asked.

That's true, I thought. She was a happy and positive person. Being around her never really bothered me like it did with others. I realized he was waiting for me to answer his question.

"She was altruistic and always kind. Her presence was light and airy," I replied.

"That's the perfect example of what receivers gravitate toward before they learn how to block. We call you a receiver, but maybe a better word would be empath. You need to learn how to understand and differentiate emotions so that you can block them from affecting you. It's a critical technique, and it will make socializing much easier for you," he said.

"How? How does blocking work?" I asked.

"There are a few techniques. We can consult with an empath advisor. If I had to guess, the best type for you would be role playing."

Isadora interrupted, "It's a wonderful talent to have. Isaac mentioned that you're going to school to be a doctor. That's pretty much the perfect field for you."

"Do you think my parents knew about me being an empath?

What's the difference between a full Veterox receiver and me?" I asked.

"To answer your first question, no. I doubt your parents knew about you being an empath, but, of course, they knew you were half Veterox. I'm sure they were looking for some type of sign that you had Veterox abilities, but it wouldn't be easy to detect in you. It's not even that easily identifiable now. Isaac probably doesn't even know," he said.

"How can you tell?" I asked.

"When we first met, after Finn shot you, I had to examine your body for injuries. Do you recall a buzz-like feeling, as if you'd been shocked, when I first touched you?" he asked.

I did remember a weird feeling. At the time my mind wasn't functioning normally, but I did remember an electricity-like wave going through my body.

"Yes, I remember an odd sensation when you pulled up my dress," I replied.

He laughed. "Make sure you don't use that exact wording when you tell Isaac," he said.

I laughed. "I'll be sure to phrase it differently."

"Anyway," he continued, "that shock helps me detect your frequency. That's the best word I can use to describe the process. Think of somebody that talks really fast and is very energetic and is always in motion. Now think of someone who exemplifies the opposite of those qualities. For example, maybe they are laissez-faire, relaxed, happy-go-lucky, and methodical.

"When you're around the first type of person, you feel differently than with the second. Everyone moves at a different frequency, but they usually stay within a predictable parameter. My Veterox abilities allow me to detect your frequency. The first type of person I described tends to be on the high end of the frequency continuum, and the second type on the lower end. It can help me assess their abilities. In your case, at first I was a little bit confused, because it kept changing. That's when I realized that you were an empath. You were taking on the emotions of Finn and I, which is why your frequency kept varying."

I understood what he meant. What a peculiar ability, I thought. The way he described it made sense, but it all just seemed so illogical and a little bit, well, stupid.

"What's the purpose of having the power to feel frequencies? I mean, it doesn't seem all that valuable. So you can tell by someone's vibration what type of person they are? I'm sure a five-minute conversation could also accomplish the same feat," I said, looking at Ezra.

A cackle of laughter erupted from Isadora. "I'm sorry," she said, still laughing, "It's just that nobody has ever made fun of him in such a blatant manner. You're so audacious. Isaac has excellent taste."

In reality, I hadn't meant it as a jest. I just kind of blurted it out without thinking. To my surprise though, Ezra had a smile on his face.

"I can't deny you have a valid point," he said. "It's difficult to explain, but if used properly, it does guide me."

"It's true," Isadora said, "but his other talent is far more interesting. Do you know what osmosis is?" she asked.

"Yes, it's a process of diffusion, like when water moves into and out of a cell," I said.

"Now think of information as the water and Ezra as the cell. That's how he learns. We call it osmotic processing," she said.

I thought I understood what she meant. Ezra could absorb information.

"How does that work exactly?" I asked. I imagined him closing his eyes dramatically as he touched a book and absorbed the information in one second. Basically, the Hollywood version.

"My hands are the mode of processing I use the most. I can touch a book and learn every bit of information from it within a half hour or so, but it also works through my eyes," he replied. "For example, I can look at a picture and commit it to memory immediately. It's a pretty handy talent to have," he said.

The car started to slow down. I looked out the window of the Bentley and saw a large gray-and-white stone wall. Above the wall, towering trees with brightly colored green leaves stood densely as far as my eyes could see. They were the type of trees you might imagine in a lush forest. The ground was covered in chartreuse grass. The green color was vivid and vibrant against the dark-blue sky.

The gray-and-white stone wall started to open. Apparently it was a gate. We drove down a long and winding paved road under the cover of the tall trees, until we came upon a split in the lane. It looked as if it were a circular driveway. As the car turned slightly to the right, the house came into view. I'm not sure "house" was the right word for it. Villa seemed like a more appropriate term.

{17}

Seventeen

A four-story villa, with at least two distinct wings, sprawled out across the green lawn. The first two levels were lined in a staggered pattern of gray and white tile. The third level stood out from the rest, with deep mahogany-colored wood cladding the side of the house. The dark-red color of the wood made the traditional Mediterranean style of the house look stunningly modern. Large black windows, some rectangular and some arched, lined all three levels. Isaac was right. The safe house we had stayed in a few nights ago was underwhelming in comparison to this.

"Are you feeling well enough to walk into the house?" Isadora asked.

"I think so. Will I be able to lie down once we get inside?" I asked.

"You'll have to go through the security protocols and be issued a COM device, but that should take only about fifteen minutes. Do you need more pain medication?" Ezra asked.

I did, but I was afraid of becoming too reliant on narcotics. Pain medication was the gateway drug to addiction. "Is there anything besides morphexine that I can take? I'd like to switch to something less addictive," I said.

"Morphexine is actually non-addictive. It has many of the same effects as morphine, which is addictive, but morphexine has been chemically altered. Not only is it designed to be nonhabit forming, it will also become ineffective once your pain is gone. It's a so-called smart drug. In other words, it won't work if you're not actually experiencing pain," Ezra said.

"Did you invent that too?" I asked, smiling sarcastically.

"No, I didn't, but Isadora did," he said.

Of course.

"I did." Isadora smiled.

"In that case, I'll take some of that morphexine. I'm not joking. I would be really appreciative of the pain relief," I said.

Ezra pulled a prefilled syringe out of his bag. By now, I recognized the clear liquid. He took an alcohol wipe and rubbed it against my IV port, where he injected the syringe. I felt the familiar surge as the medicine went into my body.

Isadora opened the door and stepped out of the SUV. She walked around to my side and helped me down onto the pavement. As we walked down the short pathway to the front doors, I felt a little dizzy, but it quickly subsided.

The massive, glossy wooden front doors suddenly opened. A woman with light-blond hair appeared. Her hair was cut into a sharp, modern bob, and she was wearing an ornately embroidered, deep-purple dress and nude high heels. As she came closer, her bright-green eyes gazed kindly at me.

It was Vivienne, Isaac's mom. The resemblance between her and Rosa was uncanny. Actually, all three of her children resembled her. Rosa inherited her pale blond hair and delicate features. Ezra was more difficult to pinpoint, but there was something similar. I just couldn't tell what it was yet.

"Welcome! It's so nice to finally meet you, Evangeline Rolieux. I've always loved your parents' last name. It has such an old-world French feel to it. I'm Vivienne Crailene, if you haven't already figured that out. My eyes probably gave me away, since they are nearly identical to Isaac's." She winked. "My husband is Ethan Crailene or Ethan, as you may prefer to call him. Let's head inside. I'm sure you need to lie down. The security procedures will be brief, and then I'll take you up to your room," she said.

"It's nice to meet you too," I replied. I probably looked like a crazy lady as I stared into her emerald eyes, but she didn't seem to notice or care; I wasn't sure which one.

She led us through the front doors and turned to the right. A dark-brown door towered in front of us. She walked up to it and knocked.

"Hi, Finn. We're here for the security protocols. She's not feeling really well, so if you could try to be brief, it would be appreciated," she said and then turned to me. "I'm sure you recall Finn, the man who shot you yesterday morning," she said, smiling. "He's the head of our security team. In all seriousness though, he's a brilliant agent. He will take you through the security procedures. We'll be waiting here once you're finished," she said.

I walked through the door, and Finn closed it behind me.

"I'm so sorry about the other day. With security operating at such a high level right now, we're especially on edge. When I saw that knife, I was instantly on guard. If I may ask, why did you hide a paring knife in your stockings?" he asked.

I thought back to my unfortunate choice in the kitchen that fateful morning. "I suppose it was fear. My mind wasn't working properly. I grabbed it on my way out of the safe house. I felt defenseless because of the last few days. I just didn't want to go down without a fight, if it came to that, and in my convoluted mind, it had come to that," I said. "I'm sorry that you had to shoot me. It was ridiculous of me to bring the knife. I'm sure if the outcome had been lethal, you would have lost your job. I'm sorry."

It was the truth. I really felt bad about putting him in the position to shoot me. I remembered a few years ago, when I'd read a book on survival. One of the examples it gave was how to react in a situation like a mall shooting. You were supposed to run away, in the opposite direction of where the shots were being fired from, find an exit, and get out of the building. It said not to hide unless you couldn't physically escape. However, once you saw any sort of uniformed police, it said you should not put your arm out or point at anything. They'd be searching for the shooter, and they might take this as a threatening action, meaning you'd likely get shot. I thought back to when my hand went up in the air, while I was trying to see through the blinding light. Finn had done exactly what he was supposed to in this situation.

"Well you did have a rather rough twenty-four hours before we met. I'm just glad you weren't beyond repair. Let's get these protocols out of the way, so you can go rest," he said.

"That would be great," I replied.

"Let me get you the COM device first. This needs to be on you at all times," he said.

"What exactly is it?" I asked.

He handed me a very thin piece of plastic, maybe five inches tall by three inches wide. "It provides us essential information and is a communication device. It's undetectable outside of the VHQ. This is just an interim device. You'll have to decide whether you would like the ISA chip implanted. The ISA will eventually take the place of your COM device. We'll discuss that in a few days, but for now, the COM will do. It's essentially another step in our security system. I'll come up later this evening or tomorrow morning and explain it to you more in depth. The key for now is to make sure it's with you wherever you go," he said.

I took the device and put it in the pocket of my red dress.

"Now I'll start the body scan. Yet another security measure. Stand right here." He pointed to a spot in the middle of the room. "I understand that the school you formerly attended had the voice-recognition system as well. Please go ahead and set up the song you wish to use," he said.

I thought for a moment. I used my typical "These Boots Are Made for Walkin'" and started singing it in my head.

Finn spoke, "The scan is complete. I'm all finished. I think Vivienne is waiting outside of the door to take you up to your apartment," he said.

"Okay, thanks," I replied. I walked toward the door.

"Do you feel well enough to take a tour of the house, or would you like me to take you to your room?" Vivienne asked when I walked out.

Isadora and Ezra were nowhere in sight. I wasn't feeling all that well.

"I think I would rather go lie down for a bit before dinner, if that's okay," I said.

"Not a problem! I understand. We'll have plenty of time for a house tour later on, when you're up to it. Follow me," she said.

The house was decorated lavishly, with antique furniture scattered about. A beautiful wood buffet sat in the entryway with blue-and-white porcelain pottery sitting on top of it. Yellow sculptures added a vibrant wash of color to the room. The design style of the whole villa seemed to be a mixture of modern and old fashioned, with a lot of color thrown in. The hallway curved to the right, and we continued walking toward the end of the hall. I noticed the elevator immediately. It was nearly identical to the one in the house Isaac and I had stayed in a few days ago.

"You'll actually be staying in Isaac's apartment until we have your permanent housing ready. There wasn't enough time to secure a place for you on such short notice, but within a few weeks, I'll have something set up," she said.

As the elevator hit the third floor, the doors opened. A large wooden door stood just a few feet away. Vivienne said, "Evangeline Rolieux, Orchid," and the door opened.

I should have expected the extravagance by now. It was astounding. The gleaming dark-brown wooden floors were contrasted by seven large black windows. Outside of the windows was a large balcony that overlooked part of the ocean, and on the far right side, you could see the mountains. An antique dining-room table sat at the edge of the room, close to the windows.

Then there was the kitchen. It had every appliance one would expect and one I didn't recognize. It looked like a microwave but larger. The silver stove and refrigerator took on a dark grayish cast, probably from the stone counter top. A white subway-tiled backsplash and dark redwood cabinets made the room feel warm. A row of vases, full of orchids, sat on top of the countertops. The walls in the room were painted a dark but bright shade of orange.

Vivienne walked over to the first window on the left side. She touched what I assumed must be the entrance to the balcony, and it opened. Like giant sliding glass doors, the windows slid back, one by one, until they vanished into the right side of the wall. We walked out onto the balcony. Two dark-gray chaises sat on the stone floor of the balcony.

"Please, sit down. I'm sure you're uncomfortable with all the walking and standing you've done since you arrived," Vivienne said.

I sat down on one of the plush velvet chaises.

"I'm not the type of person that beats around the bush. I was very sorry to hear about Charlotte and your dad. Xander was a wonderful person. He's done a lot for our family, and I'm truly sad about his passing. Isaac told us about Charlotte, and I know she was a very close friend of yours. I just wanted you to know that we have taken care of Charlotte's funeral expenses and have set her family up financially for the future. We've also donated forty thousand dollars in Charlotte's name to Haven. I wish we were able to transport you to her funeral, but for obvious reasons that isn't possible. We will get you to her grave site as soon as we can. I'm sorry that you've had such a rough couple of days," she said.

I wasn't expecting the subject to come up with Vivienne. Charlotte would have been thrilled about the donation to Haven, and knowing her family would be okay financially did put my mind at ease a little bit.

"Thank you," I replied.

"Your dad has been cremated, and his ashes are being sent here. You'll have possession of them once they arrive," she said.

I still wasn't ready to come to terms with the reality of his death. In my mind, he was still alive. The last few days hadn't felt real. It wasn't a dreamlike feeling. I knew I was awake, but I felt numb. My mind hadn't had much of a chance to process the deaths of Charlotte and my dad. Too many things had transpired in the past forty-eight hours for my brain to comprehend. I was focusing on superficial things, like the color of the kitchen I was standing in or how wonderful it was to see the deep blue ocean in the distance, right that moment. Maybe it was my mind's way of coping. I didn't know. I had never had to deal with even one trauma in my life, at least not that I remembered.

"Why am I here? Is it because of my mom and dad? Is it because I'm half Veterox? Is it because of Isaac?" I asked.

"All of the above. Actually, all three reasons are equally important. Violet and Xander were dear friends of ours. They took in our children, and we would do the same, no matter the circumstances. Isaac adores you," she said, "and I highly doubt that, even if we had wanted to, we could have talked him out of bringing you here." She paused. "Your status as half Veterox is, shall I say, extraordinary. You're the only one in the world. You represent the possibility of our two races existing together, and that does make you valuable. It also makes you a target," she said.

The only one in the world? Why would I be a target if nobody knew about me, I thought. Did that mean that people knew that I was half Veterox? I was confused.

"Nobody knows the Veterox exist, so why would anyone care or have any interest in me?" I asked.

"Because there are plans for that to change in the immediate future. Soon there will be an announcement about us. A lot of information is going to come out. This is an extensive topic that maybe we should discuss a bit later on. Isaac will be back soon, and, along with the rest of the family, we can discuss everything related to the announcement. I think Isaac would want to be here," she said.

She said Isaac would be here soon, so did something change with the Rosa situation, I wondered.

"How do you know he will be here soon? What's going on with Rosa?" I asked.

"Ethan, my husband, is actually with Isaac, and it is my

understanding that they have a very solid lead. There's a very small window in which they can get Rosa back, but they're confident they can do it. In fact, it should be happening right now. Within the next twenty-four hours, they will be here, if all goes well," she said.

I wondered how Isaac was doing and where he was. How was Rosa? Who took her? Was she in pain? Did she know about Dad and Charlotte? Questions flooded my mind.

"Do you know who took Rosa?" I asked.

"No, I don't, but Isaac and Ethan do. I'm not trying to withhold information from you or keep you out of the loop on purpose, but I can't yet divulge what's going on. To be honest, I myself know very little, and conjecture will only cause worry that may be completely unnecessary."

She looked me in the eyes. "He's going to be all right, Evangeline. Isaac is a very resourceful and intelligent person. I'm more concerned with how he will react when he finds out you've sustained injuries while under our protection," she said, laughing.

Everyone seemed to see Isaac in a different view than I'd ever had of him and his family already seemed to know how much we cared for each other.

"How long have you known about Isaac's…err, attraction to me?" I asked. I was curious. The mutuality of our attraction to each other had only come to light a mere seventy-two hours ago. Of course, I had liked him much longer than that, but I was curious about how long he had thought of me in that way.

"A couple of years, but it was a very complicated situation, as you now know. Isaac is a very cautious person. I don't think he felt it was worth the risk. He would rather sacrifice his own feelings for your safety. Frankly, I'm surprised he went ahead and told you everything, although the impending announcement that I spoke about earlier might have had something to do with it," she said.

I understood his regard for my safety, but it didn't stop me from being slightly annoyed. Why did he think it was right to make such an intimate decision for me? This announcement she spoke of…was that the only reason they told me about the Veterox, because they knew I would soon find out anyway?

I wanted to avoid showing emotion in front of Vivienne. I didn't know her well enough to confide my innermost feelings. Loneliness started to creep over me. The truth was, I didn't know anyone here. My dad was gone. Rosa was being held somewhere and, for all I knew, being tortured. Charlotte was dead. I wasn't as confident about Isaac coming back as everyone else seemed to be. In fact, if there was anything that I had actually learned or comprehended from the past few days, it was to expect everything to go awry. I changed the subject.

"What are weather modifiers? Isaac mentioned them yesterday. Who are they? What can they do?"

"As the name suggests, they are able to control the weather. Veterox weather modifiers are able to manipulate the weather in different ways. In the Midwest, where the majority of crops are grown, like corn and beans, they control the amount of rain. You'll notice there hasn't been a drought for several years. Another example that maybe you wouldn't really notice, because you're fairly young, is that the amount of severe weather has significantly decreased in the last fifteen to twenty years. Tornados and hurricanes do occur, but not at the magnitude they previously did. That's because of weather modifiers," she said.

I did actually remember reading something about the lack of severe weather in the past two decades, but it was tied to climate change and, obviously, not the Veterox.

"So were they responsible for the tornado that killed Charlotte and my dad?" I asked.

"That's actually a complicated answer, but in the simplest terms, no Veterox modifiers were responsible for the attack," she said.

I sensed there was more meaning to this conversation than I was aware of. "I'm going to guess you can't elaborate."

"No, I can't, but once Ethan and Isaac return, we'll be able to. It's another safety issue," she said.

"I'm getting a little annoyed with everyone withholding information from me. I feel like the least trustworthy person on the earth. I'm sorry. I'm not trying to be mean or take my frustrations out on you. There's a lot going on in my head. I'm not used to being so powerless and so negative," I said.

"Evangeline, you've been through multiple traumas! Of course you're frustrated, dear; that's to be expected. You haven't had the chance to be sad. You've been lied to. You've been shot. Isaac is gone, and you're stuck here, in a completely foreign world, with people you've never met. You're doing remarkably well for the situation. It's going to be a tough road ahead, and you have a lot to work through," she said.

I listened to the waves crashing onto the beach. I was trying earnestly to keep my emotions under control.

"I think that's my cue to leave you for the evening..."

"Wait," I said, interrupting her, "I mean, I have one other question."

"Yes?"

"Why did you give up Rosa and Isaac?"

She was silent for a moment and then sighed.

"I'm sorry, it's just still very hard to talk about for me. After we were taken here because of Veterox, to Oregon I mean because the structure of the VHQ wasn't yet built back then, we were held in a compound. Everyone was scared—we didn't know what the future held. I found out that I was pregnant a few weeks after we arrived. I told Ethan immediately, and I knew there was something different about the pregnancy because I was severely sick and my clothes weren't fitting correctly. Ethan took charge and since he was already in somewhat of a situation of power, he was able to convince the government doctors to allow him oversight of my pregnancy. He used a stethoscope and found three beating hearts, so he knew right away that it would be a multiple pregnancy. We never did an ultrasound because we didn't want the evidence."

"How did you keep it hidden?" I asked.

"Ethan made the decision to tell the officials that I was a few more months along than he thought which helped with the belly situation. With multiples, delivery is usually earlier than term babies, thus making the timeline viable. Pretty much from the day we found out, we knew we couldn't keep them all. We didn't trust the government. We wanted to assure that they would be somewhere safe. That's where your mother and father came in. Rosa, Isaac, and Ezra were delivered on June fifteenth. Just hours after they were born, Violet and Xander agreed to adopt Rosa and Isaac."

"Why didn't you give all three up and just say the baby died?" I asked.

"Two reasons. We knew if the other Veterox found out that the first baby born after the vaccine disaster didn't survive, it would create fear and chaos. Secondly, I wanted to keep him for my own sake."

"How did you choose between them?"

Vivienne sighed again and I could tell she was trying to hold back sadness.

"Rosa was the automatic choice, being the only girl. We flipped a coin for Isaac and Ezra. It was a very difficult day…I was depressed for a long while after we gave them up."

"Do you regret it?" I asked. The words came out of my mouth and I immediately wished I could take them back.

"Yes, very much so. Early on I took comfort in the fact that I was doing the right thing for the Rosa and Isaac. After a few years, when we knew we were safe, I went through a period of immense regret. I wanted to bring them home, but I knew it wasn't best for either of them. Your mother was wonderful about updating us as much as she could."

"So after she died, that's why Isaac came here? Why didn't Rosa?"

"Yes, Isaac came back, but Rosa didn't want to leave without you. I was happy to have him back, but I've always felt an empty spot in my heart where Rosa is supposed to be. I'm glad she has you. I wish that…"

"I'm sure she does love you."

She stood up. "My cue," she said, her tone changing to upbeat. "If you need anything, just speak my name or Ezra's or Isadora's, and we'll come, probably running," she said, laughing at the end.

"Okay, thank you."

"We will be having dinner in a few hours, downstairs in the dining room, if you feel like venturing out. If not, nobody will be offended at you for laying low tonight. Ezra and Isadora are monitoring your vitals and will be checking on you periodically," she said.

Vivienne walked over to the kitchen. "Before I leave, let me show you how the FD works, in case you need it," she said.

She walked over to the stainless-steel-box appliance that had a large door like a microwave, but the door was opaque instead of clear. She touched the front of it, and it turned on.

"Consider this a sort-of food printer. It will make anything you'd like. Just tell it what you want—anything is a possibility—and within five minutes, it will be ready. The food is gourmet. You'll be hard-pressed to find a meal that's better made from scratch. That's coming from someone who loves to cook on an actual stove," she said.

She walked toward the door. She turned to look at me. Her dark-green eyes stared into mine.

"You're going to be okay, Evangeline. We're all here for you. I can see why Isaac has such fondness for you. You seem to be a lovely person," she said, smiling. She walked out the door and left me by myself.

I was happy to be alone but equally as scared at the thought of no distractions. I walked over to a door, which I assumed might be the bedroom or maybe a bathroom. I touched the pad attached to the door, and it opened. It was the bedroom. The walls were painted a bright, cheery red. It was the same color as my room back home. I supposed I couldn't call Lincoln my home anymore.

An antique bed sat in the center of the room. The deep-red mahogany wood contrasted with the ivory-colored duvet cover and the gray sheets peeking out from under the comforter. On one side of the room, windows looked out over the ocean, identical to the view from the dining room and kitchen. On the opposite side of the room stood an ornate metal lattice. The rounded design, which I thought was called quatrefoil, scaled up the wall from the floor to the ceiling. The red paint appeared through the holes in the metal.

I walked toward one of the bedside tables. A white note sat on the table:

If you want to watch TV, just say "TV." The remote is in the space below. Everything is voice command. If you have any problems, say our names, and someone will come help you. Vivienne

I pulled the gray-and-white covers back and slipped in. I didn't feel like changing. I grabbed the remote and said, "TV." A large television came down from the ceiling. I flipped through the channels, not really paying attention to what was on. I just wanted the noise so that I didn't feel so alone. I drifted off to sleep.

{18}

Eighteen

I slept the entire night without waking. I never heard Ezra or Isadora come to check on me. I assumed they were probably monitoring me from afar. The clock on the television read eight forty-five. I fumbled out of bed and walked to the bathroom. My wounds hurt considerably less than yesterday.

I entered the bathroom, which was fashioned in the usual grandiose style of the house, with white glossy tile, stainless steel, and dark wood. A large Japanese soaking tub sat a few feet away from the glass shower. I undressed and stepped into the shower. After my shower I walked back into the bedroom to look for my suitcase.

I noticed the bed had been made and a green sheath dress was lying on top of the ivory duvet comforter. My suitcase was on the floor beside the bed. I grabbed a bra and panties out of it. Thank goodness I'd packed so many pairs of underwear. I slipped the green knit dress over my head. I grabbed my makeup bag out of the suitcase and applied some eyeliner and mascara. I dotted my lips with a bit of lip gloss. As vain as it was, just the process of getting up and around, doing normal things, made me feel happier.

I touched the pad on the window, and it once again opened. Isadora was sitting on the chaise outside. When she saw me, she waved and gestured for me to join her. I walked over to the balcony and sat down beside her on the other chaise.

"I hope you don't mind; I just love Isaac's view. I came in to check on you and heard you were in the shower, so I decided to wait out here for you," she said.

As I looked down the beach, I noticed a large rock. I had seen *The Goonies*, and I recognized Haystack Rock and immediately thought of my dad's conversation a few days ago. I pushed the thought back.

"Thanks for the dress. I was wondering if I would have to wear the red one again. I'm running short on clothes, especially after Ezra cut off the navy one," I said to her, smiling.

"Oh, I suppose I should show you the closet. We can do that a bit later. How are you feeling today? A bit better? What would you like for breakfast?" she asked.

"Much better. I imagine you're going to make me eat breakfast?" I asked.

"Yes, you've probably lost seven pounds in the last few days. You need to eat," she replied.

"A ham-and-cheese omelet sounds good and maybe a glass of orange juice," I said.

She walked over to the kitchen and turned on the FD machine. She read my order into it.

"Let me go ahead and remove your IV line while we're waiting," she said, walking over to her bag and taking out a cotton ball and a bandage. She walked over and pulled the tape off of my arm, applied pressure over the IV needle with the cotton ball, and then swiftly pulled back to remove it. She placed the bandage over the tiny hole and walked back toward the kitchen.

I didn't hear any sound coming from the FD machine, but within a few minutes, a gentle bell rang. Isadora opened the steel door, and magically, or more likely thanks to science, a plate with a yellow omelet garnished with some sort of purple flower, along with the glass of orange juice, was sitting inside. She grabbed it and brought it over to me. It looked delicious, and it was. I ate it up within a few minutes. I finished the last sip of my orange juice and set the empty glass back down on the table.

"What's the plan for today?" I asked.

"It just depends on what you feel up to. I thought I'd take you on a tour of the grounds here and maybe take a ride around the VHQ, so you can become a bit more familiar with your surroundings," she said.

"How big is this place—" I said, but suddenly a voice interrupted us.

A female voice calmly stated, "Code blue incoming to Violet Hope Hospital. Lockdown procedures are in place. Code orange."

I watched as the blood drained out of Isadora's face. She frantically got up and ran over to the bedroom. I followed quickly behind. This wasn't good news, clearly.

Isadora spoke, "Connect to Ezra."

The television spoke back, "Password."

"Orchid Cranio," she said.

Ezra suddenly appeared on the screen.

"Did you call the code? What's going on? Where are you?" she asked Ezra frantically.

"It's Isaac, Rosa, and Dad. Rosa is critical, and Isaac has been wounded. We are transporting them via med evacuation to the hospital. There's a major safety threat, and the code orange is in place. Don't leave Evangeline. I've got to go. I'm almost at the VHQ

191

entrance to meet them. Can you call Emily to confirm the helo is en route to evacuate?" Ezra asked. His voice was calm but serious.

"Yes, I will contact her immediately," she replied.

"I'll update you when we are in flight, if I can," Ezra said. The screen went black.

Isadora turned to me. "Are you okay? You're looking a little pale," she said, giving me a wary look.

I nodded. But I wasn't. I was on the verge of throwing up.

"Emily is the med-evacuation pilot," she said. Turning away from me, she spoke to the television again. "Contact Emily. Code blue."

A young woman appeared. Her long blond hair was pulled back into a ponytail, and she was wearing a dark navy uniform.

"Isadora, we are en route to the VHQ entrance. Two minutes out," Emily said.

My stomach lurched as the reality of the situation hit me. I ran to the bathroom in what likely appeared to be the most dramatic way possible. I didn't want to throw up in front of Emily or Isadora. I made it to the bathroom. I was unable to hear the rest of the conversation, but it must have ended promptly, because Isadora knocked on the door shortly thereafter.

"I'll be back out in just a minute. I'm fine," I said.

"Okay, I'm going to contact Vivienne. I'll be right out here," she replied back.

I stood up and walked over to the sink to brush my teeth. I washed my face and dried it off with a towel. I had always wondered what it would have been like to have all of your family and friends wiped out during the pandemic. What happened when you were the only survivor? Would you want to go on? Maybe more importantly, would you go on even if you didn't want to? I hoped that I wouldn't have to find out the answer to that question. I walked out of the bathroom.

"I just spoke with my mom," Isadora said. "She's talked to Ethan. He thinks Rosa has an epidural hematoma from a head injury she sustained during the operation. He said Rosa was conscious immediately after the incident but then collapsed and was unresponsive. Isaac sustained a wound to the leg. The lockdown is a precautionary measure to ensure their safety. They should have arrived in the VHQ about five minutes ago. The code orange is remaining in effect until they arrive at the hospital. We will be leaving here for Violet Hope once the lockdown is lifted, which should be in ten minutes or so," she said.

Isaac was not critical. A leg wound probably wouldn't be life threatening. Rosa, on the other hand, was probably spiraling downward. I knew that an epidural hematoma was a brain injury that usually resulted from trauma. She'd been lucid, at least for some period of time, which was critical. The prognosis was usually much better for people who were conscious immediately following a traumatic brain injury than for those who were knocked out straightaway. Time wise, if they were able to get her here promptly, within an hour or so of her original injury, that was good. Although I knew a fair amount of information about epidural hematomas in theory, the biggest part of being able to establish a prognosis was through examination and knowing the patient history, neither of which I could do.

"Once we arrive at the hospital, if Rosa needs surgery, I'll probably be assisting Ezra if we get there in time. It's possible they will have already completed the craniotomy, if they had to go that route," she said.

I just hoped I would get there in time in case things went wrong. Although my abdomen hurt, I couldn't stop pacing the expansive wooden floor of the apartment. I wouldn't have felt so powerless if I could have been there waiting for them when they arrived.

"Grab some shoes, so we're ready to go when the all clear is given," Isadora said.

I reopened my suitcase and grabbed out the pair of flats I'd worn the day before. Then I heard a weird, birdlike chirping sound.

"Stay here; someone's at the door," Isadora said.

She walked out of the bedroom, ensuring the door closed tightly behind her. I could still see and hear her through the touch pad on the door. She walked over to the front door and touched the pad, probably to see who was on the other side.

"Hello? Isaac?" she said, confused.

"Dori, let me in now!" Isaac's voice commanded.

"I need you to tell me the password so that I know it's really you," she replied.

"Orchid asilosis," Isaac said. His voice sounded upset.

Isadora promptly opened the door. "What is wrong with you? We're in lockdown! You're bleeding," she said.

He rushed past her. "Where is Evie?" he said. His voice was frantic.

She pointed to the door. Knowing it was probably safe now, I opened it.

Relief washed over his face as he walked toward me. He was wearing dark denim jeans and an ivory sweater. His bright-green eyes looked at me, gazing up and down. I realized that he was searching my body for injuries. Ezra must have told him. That was why he was so frenetic.

"Isaac, I'm okay," I said.

The concern in his eyes vanished, replaced by an equally strong emotion. The electric feeling was back. He pushed me into his room, out of sight, against the red wall of his bedroom, and he grabbed my face in his hands. His lips pushed fervently into mine, pressing me to the wall. My fingers rushed up his body toward his dark-brown hair. His hands moved from my face, down past my hips. He tugged on my dress, pulling me into him so that our bodies were touching. His arms wrapped tightly around my waist.

Suddenly, his lips parted from mine. Fiery green eyes gazed back at me. "I'm so sorry that I wasn't here yesterday, Evie. I shouldn't have left you."

"Isaac, it was my choice not to tell you. You have nothing to be sorry about," I replied.

"It shouldn't have happened. Ezra should have told me immediately," he said.

"In his defense, he didn't have much time. I am under the impression that I was bleeding pretty profusely. I think he spent the first ten minutes trying to stop it. I don't really remember much. Besides, nobody advised me to bring a knife along, which is what caused the entire ordeal," I explained.

"It's not a good excuse. Well the knife thing…" He shook his head. "Regardless, you almost died. I would have wanted to be by your side if something had happened."

It was true. I would have been angry had the situation been reversed.

"Where is the wound?" he asked.

"Add an *s* to 'wound.' Besides the gunshot, I fell on top of the knife, which then stabbed me," I told him.

His eyes widened.

"Where was the knife?" he asked.

"I hid it in the top of my tights. I can show you the wounds, but I think you might object to me lifting up my dress that high," I said. I blushed.

A smile broke through his somber demeanor. He leaned in and whispered, "I'll look forward to that a bit later."

"Hey." Isadora's voice broke through the air. "You know I can hear most of your conversation, and the things I can't hear...well, I can venture a good guess as to what you're saying and doing. I don't want to witness any other firsts between you two," she said.

Blood continued to rush into my face.

"Besides," she continued, "Isaac, you're bleeding all over the floor. I guess being love struck truly does have pain-controlling ability, because that injury is gruesome."

I looked down and saw the pool of blood accumulating on the dark wooden floors. Further up his right leg, a huge laceration was visible through the side of his dark jeans. The cut was about eight inches long and tore through the muscle down to the bone. The word "grisly" came to mind.

This kind of injury was why I knew that I could never be an emergency-room doctor. Well, no, there were many, many, reasons being an ER physician wouldn't suit me. People stuck some very odd things up their orifices. The psychiatric type of crazies abounded in the ER as well. However, even if I could manage to deal with the aforementioned problems, I couldn't deal with the grotesque injuries. Of course, gerontology wasn't lacking its own gross factor. Many body parts started to fail at eighty-plus years old. They just tended to be of a less ghastly variety, at least in my opinion.

"Can you close the wound here?" I asked Isadora.

"No, I don't have the supplies. We just need to get him to the hospital. Grab a towel from the bathroom. I'll try to get a medical override. I'm not even sure why the code orange is still in effect," she said.

I went to grab a towel while Isaac laid down on the couch in the living room.

"They should be at the hospital by now. I was in the helicopter with them. The plan was to head into surgery as soon as possible. Ezra said she was getting worse. Her GCS was at a nine," he said.

GCS was short for Glasgow Coma Scale. The scale assigned numbers to the level of verbal, motor, and eye movement a patient had after a brain injury. It was a good way to assess the level of brain damage. For example, if the patient couldn't speak at all, he or she would be marked at a one, while those who could speak but were confused might sit at a four in that category. There were three different categories and the sum of those numbers made up the score. The higher the number, the better. A three was the worst on the scale, and fifteen was the best possible score. Rosa was only one point away from being considered in the severely brain-injured category.

The few minutes that I'd had of a saccharine and gleeful mood were replaced by sadness. I took the towel I had grabbed from the bathroom and applied it to his cut, pressing firmly in an attempt to stop the bleeding.

"I'm waiting for someone to get back to me about the medical override. Right now, we have to stay put," Isadora said.

"No. Please! Let's just go. I can't sit here with Rosa being in that condition. Isaac"—I turned toward him and started sobbing—"there are very few people left in this world that I love. I have to try to be there with her if something bad happens. Can't you do something? Please."

"Dori, let's go," Isaac said. "I'll issue the override. Can you call Emily and inform her of the situation?"

"Yes," she said and walked into the bedroom to call Emily.

I could hear Dori in the other room, speaking.

"Emily," Dori said.

Emily's high-pitched voice responded immediately. "Isadora? Is there something that I can assist you with? We've just landed at Violet Hope, and the patient has been taken off the med evac—"

Isadora interrupted her, "Emily, we need you to fly here immediately. Isaac is issuing you an override authorization. He needs to be transported to the hospital, along with myself and Evangeline Rolieux," she said.

"Can I please speak to Isaac to confirm?" Emily asked. Isaac placed his hand on my shoulder and stood up. He walked into the bedroom.

"This is Isaac. I can confirm that I have issued the override. Password is viola," he said.

"We will be there in a few minutes. Orchid out," Emily said, and the room went silent. Both Isadora and Isaac walked back into the living area

"Well, let's get up to the helipad. Do you need help, Isaac?" Isadora asked.

"Nope, I'm fine. Let's just get up to the roof," he said, limping. We walked out of the front door of the apartment and got into the elevator.

"Roof," Isaac said.

I didn't feel like making small talk, and neither did anyone else. Once we arrived on the roof, the elevator doors opened, and we walked out onto a giant helipad. As we waited for the helicopter's arrival, I couldn't help but think about the absurdity of the situation. I was standing on top of a billionaire's house, in an invisible city, waiting for a helicopter to take me to a hospital named after my mother, so I could see my sister, who could read minds. In fact, everyone who stood here with me had special powers. It seemed like a science-fiction novel. Who knew, maybe I had died and this was my own unique version of an afterlife. I seriously considered it a viable option. It would have made the most sense.

I heard a humming sound, and I looked around to see what direction it was coming from. The helicopter came into view as it was landing. Actually "helicopter" wasn't a good word for the type of aircraft landing before my eyes. It lacked propellers, which were perhaps the defining characteristic of a helicopter. The sleek white aircraft hovered over us while it proceeded to descend down toward the helipad. The words "Violet Hope Medical Evacuation Aircraft" were sprawled on the side.

Once it landed, Isadora led us to a door in the back of the aircraft. Inside, it was surprisingly minimalistic. There were two transport beds sitting in the middle and normal-looking passenger seats on each side. I counted ten of them in all. Medical equipment sat toward the front of the plane, and several white drawers stood on both sides of the cockpit door.

"Isaac sit here," Dori said. "Evangeline, go ahead and take the seat beside him," she told me.

We both sat down and buckled our seat belts. Isadora walked up to the cockpit door, and it opened.

"We're ready for departure, Emily," she said and walked back out.

She opened one of the white cabinet doors and grabbed a few large gauze pads. She walked over to Isaac's seat and pressed a button on the side. It reclined back and elevated his legs. Isadora placed the gauze over his laceration. As she did, the aircraft started to move up. It was a little louder than I expected, but much quieter than any aircraft I'd been on.

Isaac said something to Isadora, and she pressed a button. The white panels on the side of the cabin slid up to reveal one large window on each side of the plane. The sparkle of the dark-blue ocean caught my eye. The plane took a right turn, and I got my first glimpse of the city. I felt Isaac's hand touch mine on the armrest. The city was full of towering glass buildings and vast stone structures. A monorail track wound in and out of the VHQ. We started to descend, and I could see Violet Hope Hospital, a huge complex, below us.

Once we landed, the rear door opened, and two or three medical personnel boarded the plane. Isadora directed them to Isaac and showed them his leg.

"Evangeline, are you going with us to the emergency room, or do you want to wait for Rosa in her room? I've just been informed that she's in surgery right now. You can visit her in the ICU once Ezra feels she's stabilized, but that will be in an hour or so," Isadora said.

I wavered in my decision. "I'll go with Isaac until she's stable," I said.

She nodded and wheeled Isaac out of the plane. We walked down the corridors of the hospital, and soon we arrived in the emergency department. Isadora walked ahead and led us into a room. It looked to be a surgical suite. Isaac got out of the wheelchair and onto the bed. A pretty young woman, probably in her early twenties, entered the room in scrubs.

"My name is Anastasia. I'm going to be your nurse," she said, looking at Isaac and smiling.

Anastasia was attractive, really attractive—the type of girl that looked flawless without makeup. She had a sparkle in her eyes when she looked over at Isaac, and that annoyed me. I couldn't really blame her, but it didn't make me feel any better. Isaac must have noticed my disdain. He looked over at me and rolled his eyes, laughing.

Isadora interrupted, "I'm going to give you some morphexine and a topical anesthetic to numb your leg and take the pain away. I need to explore the laceration and suture the muscle back together. Then I'll glue the wound closed. You should be out of here pretty soon after," she said.

The nurse grabbed two syringes out of her pocket and uncapped the needle on one. "This is the morphexine. You'll feel it almost immediately, but it will wear off pretty quickly." She rubbed an alcohol wipe on his arm before injecting the medicine. Her other hand grazed against his leg. She handed the other syringe to Isadora.

I wasn't used to the feeling of jealousy. My first thought was to show possessiveness, to stand closer to Isaac or to say something benign like, "Isaac, do you want me to hold your hand?" something that would have shown her we weren't just friends. I realized how idiotic and immature that sounded and decided to stay put and say nothing.

"I'm going to have to cut off a portion of the leg on your jeans," Isadora told him.

"All right, just don't cut them off completely. Evie's not allowed to see that area yet," he replied, smiling.

My face immediately felt warm, which made him smile bigger. The morphexine had obviously started working. His mood was light and airy, in distinct contrast to the intensity that he usually brought to a situation.

Anastasia's sparkly eyes instantly became duller as she realized the intimacy of the conversation. The tables had quickly turned. She became the jealous one. I felt a little bit bad about relishing in her disappointment. Mostly, though, I felt giddy. I turned my attention back to Isaac.

"Hey, did you go through the bedrooms of the safe house before you left the other day? I'm missing a nightgown. It was white. Have you seen it?" I said. I bit my lip, trying to conceal my delight from Isadora and Anastasia.

"Actually, it did come into my possession. I'll be sure to get it laundered and back to you as soon as possible," he said. His eyes glimmered with mischief.

"Okay that morphexine is definitely working," Isadora said, winking at me. "I'm almost finished closing up the wound. Everything looks good. It should heal pretty swiftly. However, you need to stay off of it for a few days. Wait until tomorrow to launder that nightgown, okay?" she said, glancing at us with a knowing grin. Apparently our covert conversation was easily deciphered.

A few moments later, there was a knock at the door. Anastasia walked to the door and slipped outside. She soon came back in. "Ezra would like to come in and talk to you all about Rosa. Is that all right?" she asked.

"Yes, send him in," Isaac said.

Ezra entered and asked Anastasia if she would mind stepping out for a few minutes. He was wearing light-blue scrubs. Black eyeglasses framed his dark-blue eyes, and his hair was disheveled, but the look on his face seemed happy.

"The news is good. I just finished with her craniotomy. The bleed wasn't as bad as we initially thought. I don't think we have to worry about long-term effects from the injury, but we'll know more in twenty-four hours," he said.

"Evangeline, you can go down and visit her in the ICU. She won't be conscious. We will be keeping her in a medically induced coma for a few days. Visits are limited to fifteen minutes until tomorrow, for her sake and for your own," he said to me.

"Isaac, make sure she adheres to this advice. Despite what she may tell you, she did lose a lot of blood, and she needs rest," he told him. "Take her back to the villa this afternoon. No objections from you," he said, turning to me. "We will let you know immediately if anything changes. If you're ready, I'll lead you down to the ICU."

I was a little annoyed with Ezra.

"I'll see you in a little bit," I told Isaac. I dragged my hand along his uninjured leg as I walked out.

{19}

Nineteen

"I do object to your time limit. I'm not in that much pain today. I can handle staying with Rosa overnight," I said to Ezra as we walked down the hall.

"No, but I'll give you thirty minutes. Rosa's body needs to heal, and with her telepathy, I can't say how much stress she's going to feel with you in the room worrying. It's not just for your sake. You have been through major psychological trauma this week, and if Rosa doesn't know about Charlotte and your dad, do you think it's a good idea to let her know today? Thirty minutes is going to be hard enough for you to pull off," he said.

That was true. I hadn't thought about it from her perspective.

"Besides, you do need to rest. Nobody wants to heed my advice, and then they wonder why they have complications later. Please, just listen to me. No part of me wants you to hurt worse. I'm doing what's best for everyone involved," he said.

"All right," I agreed.

"Now when you see her, she's going to look pretty beat up. Her hair was shaved on the right side of her head, and part of her skull was removed to alleviate the pressure from the bleed. She's intubated, so you'll see the breathing tube coming out of her mouth." He pointed to the glass door, and I could see her face.

I walked through the door and sat down next to her. I grabbed her hand. "Rosa, it's me, Evangeline. Well, I'm sure you know it's me already, but your eyes are closed, and I thought I should introduce myself, just in case. I'm so happy to see you," I squeezed her hand tightly. "I can't wait to talk to you. Ezra, who, by the way, I was quite surprised to learn is your triplet brother, said it will be a few days before they take you out of the coma. I'll be here every day, as much as I can.

"Ezra has limited our visits to thirty minutes, because he doesn't know for sure how much you can take. Well, and I'm supposed to rest because of the gunshot. Oh. No. I mean, yes, I got shot, but I'm all right. Don't worry." I tried to say it reassuringly. I noticed her blood pressure was starting to rise.

"Rosa, no, I'm fine. You're fine. Isaac is fine," I said frantically.

Her blood pressure continued to go up. I couldn't get a handle on my emotions. I looked down at her frail body. I could see the area of her head where the skull was removed. Tears started to stream down my face.

"I'm crying because I'm happy and I'm sad. I'm so incredibly overwhelmed. You probably already know what I'm thinking. You don't look good; I won't lie. It's really hard to see you this way. I'm not used to being the leader. I'm failing miserably at comforting you. Mostly though, I'm just really happy that you're alive, Rosa," I said, sobbing and looking down at her frail body.

I saw Isaac out of the corner of my eye. He had changed into a pair of hospital scrubs. The glass door opened, and he walked in. He grabbed my free hand.

"Rosa, it's Isaac. If you can still hear our thoughts, you'll probably be basking in the glow of being right about Evie and I." He laughed.

I blushed.

"She's blushing right now," he said to her, smiling. "I have a cut on my leg, but Isadora just finished repairing it. I'm fine, and so is Evie, but I'm going to take her back to the villa so that she can rest. I'm sure you're the only one who knows the true amount of pain she's in, because she refuses to say anything other than she's fine. We will be back tomorrow morning—we'll see you then," he said.

"I'll see you tomorrow," I said to Rosa.

I released her hand, and we walked out. I knew that it was the right option. It would have only been a matter of time before I sabotaged the conversation further.

"I've got a car waiting for us outside. The lockdown has been lifted, but we're leaving out a side exit. Follow me," he said.

We walked down the hallway toward a white door.

Emotion flooded my mind. Anger, sadness…I felt weak. I couldn't even manage a few minutes with Rosa without breaking down. It was irrefutable that I had caused more damage than good. I was selfish. I'd failed miserably in the last few days. What was wrong with me? I focused on the yellow-colored walls, trying to will my mind into thinking about paint colors instead of the sadness my mind was experiencing.

Outside, a black BMW was waiting. I recognized the driver, Nora. Isaac walked to the car door and opened it for me. As I sat down in the black leather seats, I couldn't help but remember my dad's fondness for BMWs.

"Hi, Nora," I said.

"It's nice to see you again, Evangeline. I'm glad to see you're feeling better than the last time I saw you," she replied.

If only she knew the irony of her statement, I thought.

Isaac walked around to the other side of the car and got in. "Thank you for picking us up, Ellenora. I didn't think it would be a wise idea to drive after taking the morphexine," he said.

Nora nodded.

"If you have time later, I have some plans to discuss with you," he said.

"I'll be around later this evening," Nora replied.

"What happened to Rosa?" I asked Isaac. "Nobody will tell me anything about who took her," I said.

"That's because it's a really complicated situation, and with the sensitive nature of the intelligence, frankly nobody but Ethan and I know the specifics," he said.

"Does that mean you aren't going to tell me?" I asked.

"No, I'll tell you everything, but I'd prefer to do it once we are at the house, if that's all right with you," he replied.

"Sure. I suppose that means it will be yet another shocking story then?" I said.

"Yes. It's another rabbit hole, to say the least," he replied. "You've met my mom, Vivienne. You'll meet Ethan when we arrive back at the villa," he said, trying to change the subject.

"I like your mom. She seems extremely nice. Everyone seems nice. It's kind of peculiar," I said.

"They have their moments, but normally everyone is pretty happy. Ezra and Dori are always entertaining. I'm sure you've noticed the rivalry. Ezra is the more skilled doctor technically, but Dori is far better with people. Vivienne is usually the mediator. You'll like Ethan. He's a lot like me. A logical, more serious type," he said.

"You think you're a serious type? You tease me quite a lot for being a serious person," I replied, smiling.

He laughed. "Trust me; I'm not known for my emotion. Your ability to pull me out of that state is a rarity. I've never met anyone who had such an effect on me," he said.

"Ezra told me I'm an empath, a receiver. Well, I'm only half Veterox, so it's not as pronounced," I said.

"That actually makes a lot of sense. I'm surprised it never occurred to me. If anybody could figure you out, it's him. Did he brag to you about his osmotic-learning abilities yet?" he asked.

"Yes, he mentioned it. I may have also told him he was handsome while I was on large doses of morphexine," I admitted. I watched for his reaction, but it didn't seem to register.

"Frankly, if you said you didn't think he was attractive, I'd think you were lying. I'm not really concerned about him being competition. He hasn't seen you naked. Fuck, I suppose he has," he said.

"Yeah, he has. I told him not to look at any other parts of my body besides the bullet wound though," I replied.

His laughter echoed through the car.

"What?" I said.

"Evangeline, do you not understand how attractive you are? I assure you that there is absolutely no way that any man could resist. It would be hard to imagine he didn't notice," he said.

I rolled my eyes.

"Ellenora?" he asked.

"Evangeline, you're gorgeous. Isaac has, albeit annoyingly, chattered on about how attractive you are for years. You lived up to the hype. You're very pretty," she responded.

Isaac replied, "And just to be clear, I much prefer that you're alive. It's really lucky that Ezra was the one meeting you. Dori let me look at your medical record while you were with Rosa. I can't help but think somebody was looking out for you. If anyone else, even Dori, had met you that day, I doubt you'd be sitting here."

Charlotte's face flashed in my head.

"Of course, the entire thing could have been avoided by not taking a knife," he said. "I'm joking. I actually do understand why you brought it along. It's a logical move to want to defend yourself in what seems to be a powerless situation. Horrible weapon of choice though," he said, laughing.

"It wasn't the most well-thought-out plan, I'll admit," I replied.

I changed the subject. "Have you two dated?" There was an openness to their relationship, and it felt like there may have been more to it at one time.

"She does not beat around the bush. Yes, we dated several years ago. I'm pretty sure it was the first relationship for both of us. Right?" she asked Isaac.

"Yes," he said curtly.

She rolled her eyes. "Let me state the obvious; our relationship was a long time ago. We didn't work as a couple, but we're very, very good as a team. We've been working together for the last eight years, since we began our careers," she explained.

I couldn't deny that I felt a slight pang of jealousy, but I didn't really view Nora as competition. She didn't seem to be at all concerned about answering any of my questions. My next question was surely going to stir the waters, but I wanted to gauge Isaac's response.

"Have you had sex?" I asked, unflinching. I was sure they had. Isaac's cold response to the first question was a good indicator. I wanted to see how they reacted and watch their body language.

"Well, based on his last reaction, I think I will defer that question to Isaac." She smiled knowingly at me.

I looked over at Isaac. His face was serious, but as he looked back into my eyes, a smile appeared on his face.

"Leave it to you to ask the most absurdly inappropriate question. Some part of me thinks that you already know the answer and are trying to gauge my response. The answer is yes. That was ten years ago. Ellenora is now married, and I'm fairly confident in who I want," he replied.

I could tell that I had made him uncomfortable by asking the question, and I felt slightly bad, but sometimes going for jugular was the only way to reveal the truth. Besides, knowing that they had already hashed out that aspect of their relationship made me more confident. I dropped the subject.

The scenery started to look familiar, and I could tell we were getting close to the Crailene Villa, which was what I'd decided to call it. I recognized the winding road going up to the gate.

"Is there a hierarchy in Veterox society?" I asked.

"Yes. There aren't many families that are as well off as we are, but even the lowest socioeconomic status here is still much higher than what you find outside the VHQ. Did you know this house was designed by my mother?" he asked.

"No, but it's gorgeous. How many millions of dollars is it worth, out of curiosity?" I asked.

"Around five hundred million. It houses the entire family. It was built so it would be big enough to keep us all together when we married and had our own families, if we wanted. We can, of course, live anywhere we would like within the VHQ. However, this house is heavily secured and provides much more protection than any other place inside the VHQ," he said.

"The view is pretty hard to compete with, I imagine. I think I could lie out on the balcony all day long for the rest of my life and never tire of the view," I said.

"Do you want to move into your own place?" Isaac asked.

I wasn't expecting the question at all. "I guess I really haven't thought about it." I sighed. "No, I'm sorry; that's a lie. I'd like to stay near you."

"Good, the feeling is mutual. Would you like to stay with me in the apartment?" he asked.

"Yes, but will you be able to resist my stunning good looks?" I smiled teasingly.

"I suppose that depends on whether you want me to or not," he replied.

The vehicle came to a stop, and Isaac got out. He walked around the car and opened my door. You would never know that he had a large laceration on his leg from the way he walked.

"You'll have to go through the security scan before we enter. I'm sure lunch will be ready for us, so we'll have to oblige my parents and eat with them, but it'll give you a chance to meet my dad. After that, we can go up to the apartment and rest for the day," he said.

"How's your leg?" I asked.

"It's not pleasant. How are your abdominal wounds?" he asked.

"The same," I replied.

Isaac walked up to the door first and waited for the scanner to detect him. It wasn't long before it was my turn. I sang the song in my head as the blue light scanned me up and down.

"Go ahead," a voice said from inside the house. It took me a few seconds to recognize it was Finn.

"Thanks, Finn," I said.

"I hear you're the person to blame for the bullet wound?" Isaac said to Finn.

"I hear you're the guy to blame for sending her down with a knife?" he joked back.

"Don't you guys have the MW guns yet?" Isaac asked.

"Ironically, they were issued the next day," Finn replied.

"What are MW guns? I asked.

"Multiple-wave guns. Basically, they are designed to knock you out with sound waves. They aren't lethal like a typical gun. Well, I suppose there is the off chance that you could fall and hit your head, but the chances are pretty slim," Isaac said.

"Well, you know me. I seem to defy probability. I think I'd prefer the gunshot," I replied.

Vivienne appeared with a man whom I recognized from the picture of my mom at the banquet—Ethan. Vivienne ran over to hug Isaac.

"How's your leg?" she asked him.

"It's fine. Rosa is much worse off than I," he said.

"I'm going over there later tonight to visit," she said.

"Evangeline, I'm Ethan. You look like a duplicate copy of your mother. It's so nice to finally meet you," Ethan said to me.

"I've heard I look a lot like her. It's a little bit peculiar to finally meet the man behind all of the crazy stories I've been hearing in the last few days," I replied.

I could see the family resemblances a lot more now than earlier. Ezra looked a lot like Ethan. Isaac was a pretty equal mixture of both of his parents. He was tall, like Ethan and, of course, shared Vivienne's vibrant eye color.

"Well, I have many more stories to regale you with," Ethan said. He spoke in the same formal tone that Isaac and Ezra did.

"Lunch is waiting for us in the dining room, if you'd like to join us," Vivienne said. Isaac looked over at me.

"Sure," I said. I was eager to ask Ethan questions. I might finally get some answers. Vivienne grabbed Ethan's hand and turned to walk down the hallway.

"We're going to eat outside, if that's okay?" Vivienne said, looking back at us.

"I don't think you'll have any problem convincing Evangeline," Isaac replied.

We walked out of the back of the house, under bright ivory arches. A stone path led the way to what looked like an outdoor patio area. As we came closer, I could hear the sound of the ocean. A huge covered patio stood before us with an enormous stone table and white fabric-covered chairs. The food was already on the table. A wide variety of fruits and vegetables sat on one end. A large roasted chicken and mashed potatoes with gravy sat in white porcelain dishes on the other end of the table. Isaac sat down first, and I took the seat next to him. Vivienne and Ethan sat across from us. The conversation took on a light tone while we were eating, but I was determined to ask the hard-hitting questions once everyone was finished.

"Isaac told me you two would tell me about what happened with Rosa once you were both here," I said to Ethan.

Isaac nodded. "You can tell her. She doesn't know what she's getting herself into, but I think it will be a hard sell to convince her otherwise."

"All right. You'll have to oblige me while I explain. It's going to seem like I'm not answering your question, but I need to give you some background," Ethan said to me.

"I can do that," I replied.

"Do you have anything to prop my leg up on?" Isaac interjected. "I have a feeling this is going to take a while. Is it okay to use one of these chairs?" he said to Vivienne.

"Of course, here, I'll help you," she said as she walked over.

"Evangeline, how much do you know about theoretical physics? Are you familiar with thread theory?" Ethan asked me.

"No, I mean I know a little bit about the theory that there are small strings vibrating in several different dimensions. For example, a violin has strings. Depending on how you pluck the strings, you get different frequencies and sounds. That's essentially what the universe is made up of—tiny, vibrating strings that come together like a symphony. The multiple dimensions encompass the three dimensions we can see, the dimension of time, and many other dimensions that aren't visible to us," I said.

"Yes, you're on the right track. That's not completely how it works, but it's a good way to simplify it. Every universe has many dimensions. Now imagine that the dimensions that we cannot see are all individually floating above us. Hmm, let me think of a good analogy," he said.

"Like worms wriggling in a sky," I said, fully realizing the absurdity of the comment instantly after I'd said it.

"I mean that in the diagrams I have seen, the dimensions look like tiny worms squirming in outer space, but they don't move. They are stationary," I said, trying in vain to explain.

"Visually, you're not wrong. That is how the information is conveyed without mathematics. Well, perhaps not as worms, but it works for this example," he said. "Now what do you think happens if one of those worms accidentally crashes into another of the worms? In other words, if one dimension collides with or touches another dimension," he said.

"If two dimensions collide in our own universe? A parallel universe might be created?" I asked.

"Precisely," he said. "It's very, very rare, but it can happen. A few years ago we discovered our parallel universe."

I looked over at Isaac.

"I told you it was a rabbit hole. You're not even at the bottom yet," he said.

"How did you discover it?" I asked.

"We traveled to it," Ethan replied.

"You've been there?" I asked, dumbfounded.

"Yes, along with a few other Veterox scientists," he said.

"How?" I asked.

"It's too complicated to explain in depth right this moment. I'll get to that. The more interesting questions is what the other universe is like or, rather, how it is different from our own," he said.

I couldn't wait to hear his answer. I couldn't wait to tell Rosa that I was right about parallel universes.

"Am I alive over there?" I asked.

"We refer to it as Delacroix. Yes, you are alive," he said.

I was so excited. My mind poured over the possibilities. I was entangled in a sort of weird hyper nerd fantasy. What was I like over there? What kind of technology did they have?

Isaac started laughing. "I had a feeling you might like this area of the discussion."

"I know! I'm giddy. I've always wanted to have a parallel-universe me! Does she have the same personality? Are we interested in the same things? I have all of these questions!" I said.

"I couldn't tell you the exact similarities or differences," Ethan replied. "I don't know the specific details about who you are over there. But, remember, it would be a bit different, because she's a Veterox, not a half Veterox like you," he said.

Delacroix Evie was Veterox? How was that possible?

"Let's pan our scope out to the earth as a whole. We're going to talk about time line. While in Delacroix, we were able to see how it

216

evolved in comparison to our own universe. What we discovered was extraordinarily interesting. Imagine that up until Z3C7 our worlds were exactly the same. George Washington, Lincoln, FDR, Reagan, Clinton, and Monahan were all presidents of the United States. The Depression, World War I, World War II…anything you can think of was identical.

"On December twenty-fourth, the day of the Veterox vaccine trial at Camp Espoir, the time line took a distinct deviation from ours. Two different paths emerged. It ended up coming down to a singular decision made by your mother. Here she decided to support the decision to destroy the Veterox vaccine and hide the population. In Delacroix, she recommended to President Odelia Lincoln to release the vaccine to everyone. President Lincoln heeded her advice in both Delacroix and here. One path continued in a straight line. The other took a sharp left turn."

I was curious about which one of us had taken the left turn. A world that was full of Veterox? Now I understood what he meant by Delacroix Evangeline being a Veterox.

"Imagine being able to see what the future would have been like if we'd made the opposite decision during that meeting in Hawaii. It was fascinating. Incomprehensible, really," he said.

I wondered what that meant for Delacroix. "So were you able to come to a conclusion on which decision was better? I'm sure you had the data available to analyze. How many people did it save? What kind of negative or positive consequences did it have?" I asked.

"In the beginning, Veterox saved millions of lives. There's no question in regard to lives saved. They won that battle hands down. Technologically, at least a few years ago, they were much more advanced. Unfortunately, there were negative consequences. A series of large-scale biological-weapon attacks happened in the Middle East.

Over one million people were killed. Several nuclear bombs were dropped in different regions of the world, killing hundreds of thousands and rendering the areas unlivable.

"In my opinion, what the Veterox vaccine did to their world was take the battle of good versus bad and amplify it. It was a constant struggle back and forth. Which society made the right decision? I'd like to think we did, but I can't place a value on the human life we lost over here compared to Delacroix, which makes it a difficult question to answer. In the end, we'll probably survive longer purely because we have one-quarter of the population. Delacroix is fading away. There simply aren't enough resources to sustain it.

"The question becomes how long was the quality of life better than here? Is prolonging the human race more important? I don't know. It really depends on a complicated set of factors, which makes a conclusion very hard to come to," he said.

The way he explained the situation was captivating. I'd expected a more biased answer.

"Is my mom still alive over there?" I asked.

"She is. Actually she is the head of the Department of Medicine in the United States," he replied.

It was a peculiar thought. I again wondered whether or not Evangeline in Delacroix would be similar or very different than me. I couldn't help but think that having my mom would have shaped me differently.

"What is Delacroix like? I mean, are governments the same as here? Are houses the same? Things like that..."

"No, actually, not the same at all. I could go on and on because this topic is riveting but I'll try to summarize a bit. Delacroix didn't experience the loss that we did. They continued functioning at the same level while we really struggled. Not only did we have a good nine plus months that we were at a standstill, we lost so many people that it had a huge impact when we could get back up and running. We lagged behind for years and years. We're probably twenty years behind Delacroix in technology. Companies that no longer exist here, do over there."

"What about governments and countries? Are they the same?"

"That aspect is interesting. Simply put, no. The plague served as a reboot for us. I think a lot of people lost faith in government before Z3C7, tired of the bureaucracy. Afterwards, I think people realized how important having a good government was and they wanted to make changes. They made it better. In Delacroix that change never had to happen. Suffice it to say, it's much different. Anyway, I've gone off topic. So you may wonder how Rosa fits into all of this?"

I nodded.

"The Delacroix were behind the attack in Lincoln. They're the people who tried to take Rosa and yourself," he said.

"Why were we targeted? How do you know they were behind it?" I asked.

"We don't have the answers to those questions. We're waiting on Rosa. My guess is that either they needed you or they needed you destroyed. Both point to some motive that we don't know," he said.

Isaac interrupted, "When I told you that I thought weather modifiers were behind the attack, I had little doubt. The circumstances were too coincidental. The probability was very minute that she'd somehow be the only one who managed to escape. No sirens. Perhaps most convincingly, though, was my knowledge of the weather modifiers. They've been very successful in suppressing severe weather events for the last ten years. An EF-5-level tornado would have been noticed at the very least. It would have been halted immediately and not gone on for miles. Either something had gone terribly wrong or someone else was behind it, which left few possibilities.

"When I left to go back to the scene, Rosa was nowhere to be found, and that confirmed my suspicions. I contacted Ethan immediately to let him know about the situation and to find out if he could verify the whereabouts of all our Veterox modifiers. That's why we left so fast. If you were still a target, I needed to get you out. Once we arrived at the safe house and you were on your way to the VHQ, Ethan and I met up to discuss the situation. He was able to verify that our weather modifiers weren't responsible, which left only one possibility—that they were Delacroix," he said.

Ethan said, "I should say, that was the most realistic possibility and the one that we were most confident in. If we were right, we knew that it would be relatively easy to track down where they were headed. There are only two entry points on the earth where you are able to pass into Delacroix. One is in India, and the other is in Alaska. We ruled out the India spot as being too far away. It wouldn't be easy enough for the Delacroix to get there undetected. So we headed up to Alaska. I knew if we could make it up there before they left, we'd have a good chance of getting Rosa back. Along with there being only two points of entry into Delacroix, time also plays a significant role. Simply put, you can't just come and go whenever you'd like. I had the algorithm worked out, and I knew that their next chance to move back into Delacroix was this morning.

"We waited at the site and ambushed them. Rosa was running toward us when she tripped and hit her head. Isaac ran over to help her up, and that's when he was cut by one of the Delacroix. Neither of us got a look at who'd done it; he just grabbed Rosa, and we all teleported back to the VHQ entry point. She wasn't speaking but was conscious, albeit disorientated, when we arrived at the safe house.

Shortly after, she passed out completely. I suppose you know everything that happened from there."

"What's the next move?" I asked.

"We wait and see what Rosa knows when she wakes up, and we go from there," Ethan replied.

"Are you worried that they are still here?" I asked.

"It's doubtful. I don't think they would risk being caught. They know we are watching that area pretty intensely right now. From an intelligence standpoint, it would be most logical to return to Delacroix and plan a new attack. They could be back as soon as next week, but I think it will be longer than that. We're on high alert. They will wait until we don't expect it," Ethan said.

"That's why it is so critical that you and Rosa don't leave the VHQ. It puts us into a strategic position that creates many barriers against any intruders. You can't find someone that you can't see. They likely don't even know the VHQ exists," Isaac said.

There was a momentary lull in the conversation before Isaac asked, "Have we answered your questions sufficiently?" He smiled, knowing my answer was no, but I could tell that he wanted to be finished with the conversation. Maybe his leg was hurting him.

"Yes and no. I'd like to know more about Delacroix, but I suppose that can wait. I'm sure your leg is hurting, and I guess I'm under orders to rest," I replied.

Isaac nodded.

"If you two want to come down for dinner this evening, let me know," Vivienne said.

"Thanks for lunch. It was delicious," I replied back.

I followed Isaac as he stood up and walked down the stone path back up to the villa. "I really like your dad. I can't believe he's traveled to a parallel universe. I want to know so many things," I told

Isaac.

"I'm honestly a bit stunned that you're taking the information so well, eerily well," he said, smiling.

"Come on; don't tell me you don't want to meet Isaac from Delacroix! I want to meet Evangeline. Would we like each other? Do you wonder if she's with Isaac over there?" I asked.

"I'm pretty confident that you have managed to ensnare him in your net over there as well," he replied.

We arrived at the elevator and waited for the doors to open. We walked forward, and a few moments later, the elevator ascended to the top level and the doors opened once again.

Isaac said, "Isaac Crailene and Evangeline Rolieux."

The door to the apartment opened, and we walked in.

"I had forgotten how much I used to love this place. It's been so long," he said.

He walked toward the balcony and opened the sliding windows. "Come sit with me," he said.

I followed him out to the balcony and sat down on one of the chaises. "How's your leg doing? Can I see it?" I asked.

He sat down on the other gray chaise and pulled up the right leg of the blue scrubs he had taken from the hospital. I leaned in toward him to take a look. I touched his leg, feeling the clear bandage that sat over the top of his cut. It was starting to turn a deep shade of purple.

"Well, yours looks far worse than mine do. I only have two tiny, little scars," I said. I hesitated for a moment. "Would you like to see them?" I finally asked, smiling.

"Yes," he responded.

"Are you being serious?" I asked.

"Yes, but it's probably not a wise choice," he replied.

My skin felt tingly. I was anxious and excited. "Follow me into the bedroom. I don't want to pull off my dress out here on the balcony," I said.

"On one condition, don't try to seduce me. I have strict orders to rest." He smiled as he got up and headed for his room.

"I don't really have any good incentive not to try. I'm not going to promise anything," I said.

He glared over at me and stopped walking. I sighed. "Fine, I promise," I said.

He closed the door to the bedroom behind him.

"Can you help me unzip the back of my dress?" I asked.

He gave me a quizzical look.

"No, I really need the help. It's hard for me to reach. It hurts my abdomen."

He came closer to me and gently pulled on the zipper. His hands grazed my back as he slid it down. I pulled my arms out and pushed the dress down past my belly button, letting it hang off of me.

I turned around to face him. He gazed down at the two bandages on my side. His hands moved up to touch me, and I felt his fingers stop on each wound. He paused for a moment and removed his hands from my abdomen.

"This was a very poor decision," he said.

Then suddenly both of his hands were on my face, and he was pulling me toward his lips. Electricity buzzed through my body. Instinctively, my arms flung around his neck. He pushed me down on the bed and moved on top of me. I knew we were just a few steps away from a fully engulfing fire.

"I didn't try to seduce you; in fact, I think you're trying to seduce me," I whispered.

"I know. I'm having a difficult time following my own advice. I'm just…" He paused.

I still wasn't used to seeing the steely Isaac Crailene show emotion.

"All sense of logic fails me when I touch you. The electric current running between us is so fucking dynamic. I have no control over it. That's not a feeling that I'm accustomed to. But...you're correct, I should heed my own advice," he said.

He kissed me one last time and stood up. "I'll be back. I'm going to go take a shower. I need to cool down a little bit," he said.

He walked over to the closet and grabbed a pair of jeans and a green sweater.

I watched as he walked through the bathroom door and closed it behind him. The shower turned on a few moments later. I sat up on the bed. Fire was still pouring through my body. My mind, just like his, had been taken captive by emotion. There was certainly no logic in what I was about to do.

I heard the shower turn off. I pulled my dress down and stepped out of it. I unclasped my bra and removed my panties. I touched the pad on the bathroom door, and it opened. I knew what I wanted.

"Evie, I'm not dressed yet..." he said.

Then he saw me. His dark emerald eyes gazed up and down my body. He fell silent. I walked toward him and pushed him back against the wall with my hands. I pressed my body into his and pulled his head toward my lips. He didn't object. As he grabbed me around the waist, I kissed him. His lips burned back into mine. His hands moved up and down my body, pulling me into him.

The tempo sped up. I wanted him to touch every part of me. I felt the heat of his hands as they trailed up my body. I inhaled sharply as his fingers pressed firmly against my breasts, his palms pushing them upward. His breathing accelerated. I pulled him back to my lips and ran my fingers through his damp brown hair. Suddenly he pulled back and placed his hands firmly onto my face.

"I want you. I want to fuck you. Can I?" he asked. His eyes radiated with fervor.

My body tingled with excitement. Fuck was not a word that he used often. I grabbed his hand and guided it up between my legs to let him know the answer. "I don't know. What do you think?" I said, looking into his fiery green eyes. I bit my lip.

"Fuck, Evie. Turn around," he said.

I obeyed. His hands grazed against my backside and he slid in between my legs, pushing me forward against the wall. The question I had asked a few days ago…the answer was yes.

One of his hands reached around the front of my body. It wandered down, back in between my legs and he began touching me. My breathing quickened, and I felt the waves of pleasure burn through my body.

"I'm sorry. This is going to be faster than what I want. I don't think I can hold off much longer," he said. He placed his hands firmly on my hips, steadying himself.

"I don't want you to hold off," I whispered.

His pace increased. Within seconds, I could tell by the sounds coming out of his mouth that he was almost finished. Once he was done, he pulled me back around to face him and his lips collided with mine once again. He moved his head toward my ear. "I had high expectations. I didn't imagine we'd surpass them by so much," he whispered.

"I think we'll surpass them again later," I said, still trying to catch my breath.

Something caught my eye, and I looked down at the floor. Blood was trickling down Isaac's leg, and the clear bandage that had previously covered it was falling off.

"You're bleeding. The surgical adhesive must have come off. I'm sorry," I said.

He looked down. I grabbed a towel and placed it on his leg.

"It was well worth it. I'll have to call Dori to come fix it. Go put your dress back on. She's going to be so angry when she finds out that you seduced me." A grin appeared on his face.

"No! You're not telling Isadora," I said.

"Oh, she will find out. It's pretty hard to pull off lying to her," he replied.

Great, I thought.

I walked out of the bathroom and gathered up my clothes from the floor then placed them on the bed. My side was hurting pretty badly from all of the twisting and turning I'd just done.

Isaac appeared in the doorway, already fully clothed. "Do you need help getting your dress back on?" he asked.

"Yes, please. Actually, can you hook the back of my bra for me first?" I asked.

He took the clasp in his fingers and deftly secured it in just a few seconds. "Does your side hurt?" he asked. He looked down and checked over my bandages.

"It's not feeling great," I replied.

I pulled my dress back up and reached down to pull up the zipper. Isaac pushed my hand away and grabbed the zipper, pulling it all the way up to the top.

"Let's hold off a bit for the next few days. You need to rest. We've got plenty of time to explore later on," he said. I could see the concern on his face.

"I'm fine. You're the one bleeding," I replied.

"I never said we couldn't do anything at all," he said.

"We can try. I don't have much faith that we will succeed," I replied.

"Clearly you don't know how talented I am in that area," he said. A smile returned to his face.

"Oh really, how much practice have you had exactly?" I said.

"Enough to know," he replied.

"Isaac, I'll just tell you this now; I'm going to want to fuck you regardless of how many times you've made me orgasm beforehand," I replied.

I was awaiting his witty comeback, but he was speechless. The doorbell rang.

"In that case, don't bother putting your panties back on," he said, before turning and walking toward the door.

I followed him out of the bedroom into the kitchen. He opened the front door. Isadora was standing with a medical kit in her hand. She looked down at Isaac's leg to survey the damage.

"What happened?" she asked.

Neither of us answered. She glanced over at me, and I could feel my face turning bright red. Isaac started laughing.

"Well, I think you might have your answer," he said.

"Goodness gracious. Seriously? You two. I thought I was pretty clear earlier on your restrictions," she said.

"You were. However, I'm not sure we ever agreed with you on the issue," Isaac replied.

"By the look of your leg, you should probably have heeded my advice," she said.

"No, I would say it was well worth any pain that I'm going through right now," he said, looking over at me.

"Ugh, Isaac. No more. For the record, to be crystal clear, it's not my recommendation that you two have sex for a few days, but somehow I doubt you care very much what I think. Girl on top, that's all I'm going to say," she said. Isadora turned to me. "Are you on birth control?" she asked.

I was taken aback by her question, but I also appreciated the bluntness.

"Yes, she has an IUD," Isaac answered before I could respond.

"How did you know that?" I asked. I was absolutely sure we'd never had that conversation.

"I remember you telling Rosa about it a few years ago. Believe me; I was not pleased. I knew what that meant," he replied.

"Well, just so that you know, it wasn't for that purpose. I had heavy menstrual cycles," I said, glaring at him.

Isadora's voice interrupted us. "OK, well an IUD is a great choice for birth control, so you're covered." She swiftly changed the subject. "I think I'll be able to fix your leg here. It didn't open up all the way. I'll replace the bandage and check on it again tomorrow," she said.

She opened up her medical bag and pulled out a clear bandage. She pushed the open part of the laceration together and placed the bandage on top.

"Do you have any updates on Rosa?" I asked.

"Nope, she's stable and progressing as we expected. I would say that by tomorrow morning we'll know the answers about how much the hematoma affected her brain. She might have some amnesia but hopefully nothing too significant. The main concern with an epidural hematoma is how much pressure it was placing on the brain before surgery," she said.

"In your experience, what do you expect?" I asked.

"Well, brain injuries are tricky. I've seen people recover from very severe trauma, and I've seen long-term brain damage in people who you would think had mild trauma. It's hard to predict," she said. "Anything else? I've got to go check up on a patient. I'll see you for dinner?" she asked.

"Probably. Can you let Mom know to expect us?" Isaac replied.

She nodded back and walked out the door and toward the elevator.

{20}

Twenty

Isaac and I were alone again.

"Let's go sit down outside. I need elevate my leg," Isaac said.

We walked back out the big glass doors and sat down on the gray chaises.

"Why did you leave after my mom died?" I asked him.

"I was close to your mother, to Violet. Being a Veterox herself, she was excellent at knowing how to deal with Rosa and me. When she died…" He sighed. "I wanted to be around people who could relate to who I was," he said.

"Why didn't Rosa go with you?" I asked.

"Because of you. Even at ten years old, she felt an enormous sense of responsibility. I think she wanted, maybe needed, to be there for you after Violet died. It was an easy decision for her. She never seemed to regret staying," he said.

"What was my mom like?" I asked.

"Calming. She could control emotions very well. That was her Veterox ability. She was also kind, just like you," he said.

"Everyone tells me how similar we are. What was the biggest difference?" I asked.

"Your ability to communicate. Violet was cautious with her words. She was methodical. With you, I never have to worry about wondering what you're thinking. You will tell me the truth, even if it's unpleasant. Earlier today, you freely admitted that you had told Ezra he was handsome. I admire that about you. You're confident. You're very intelligent and kind—perhaps gorgeous. Those characteristics are hard to find altogether," he said, smiling.

It was probably the nicest thing anyone besides Charlotte had ever said about me. Beyond those adjectives, there was only one more thing that I wanted to be—brave.

"How long have you liked me?" I asked. I felt a little bit juvenile asking the question, but I wanted to know. The answer was more important to me than any worry of sounding immature.

"A few years. What about you?" he asked.

"Longer than a few years," I replied.

"Well, it's a good thing I didn't know that. The last two years were hard enough," he said, smiling.

"How many girlfriends have you had?" I asked.

"Is this a roundabout way of asking how many girls I've slept with? I'll just tell you. Seven. Don't worry. I assure you you've blown the competition out of the water."

Seven? A pang of jealousy jolted through me, but the last sentence made up for it a little bit.

"How did my mom become a Veterox?" I asked.

"She took a dose of the vaccine before anyone else on the day of the trials. She explained to me that she wanted to test it on herself before the kids. Nobody knew, not even your dad. Her powers didn't show up until she boarded the flight to Hawaii with your dad," he said.

"Then what?" I asked.

"Well, in part, that's the reason why she wanted to leave the meeting with the president so fast. Your dad found out she was a Veterox soon after the Hawaii meeting. He didn't get to tell you about it—the conversation was supposed to take place after your birthday dinner. Your mom and dad managed to keep her secret hidden for months, but Ethan inevitably figured it out. He agreed to keep it a secret and, in exchange, asked her to take in Rosa and me. Your mom agreed and also requested that they take Dori in as their own. Your dad had no knowledge about any of that; he just knew that we were Veterox twins and needed a home," he said.

"So did my dad ever find out who you two were?" I asked.

"No, he had no interest in knowing. I think he knew that it would be more dangerous for everyone if he did."

"Since you were a homicide detective back home, what happens now? What will you do? I mean, what will I do? Will we ever go back?" I asked.

"Probably not. You can return to school here; the programs are the same as back in Lincoln. With Ezra and Dori, you'll have plenty of opportunity. We'll be able to return eventually. I mean, we can't go back to Lincoln, but if you wanted to go back outside the VHQ, I'm sure we could manage," he said.

I liked how he spoke of us as "we."

"My family has several houses around the world that would be good candidates. Venice, Mumbai, Copenhagen, Sydney, Florence, London, Havana, Fiji, Costa Rica, Greece, Bangkok, Buenos Aires, Tokyo…you have a variety of options to choose from," he said.

My jaw dropped open. "How is that possible? Do all Veterox get to travel around freely?"

"I, myself, can travel freely. My family has permission from the government but they have to submit their plans in advance. As far as other Veterox, it's kind of a case by case basis."

"Who owns homes in all of those countries?" I asked.

"It's a collective. Ezra owns the Venice, Bangkok, and Copenhagen properties. Dori owns the Fiji and Mumbai houses. I own the Havana, London, Florence, and Greek properties, and my parents own the rest," he said.

Considering the $200,000 Bentley sitting in the driveway, it shouldn't have been so staggering. I couldn't imagine the amount of money that those properties equated too. Billions? Billions upon billions? But how did Isaac afford four houses?

"I'm not a homicide detective," Isaac replied, as if he already knew the question that I was about to ask.

A female voice suddenly interrupted our conversation. "Dinner will be served outside in five minutes. Please join us."

It was Vivienne, but she wasn't in the apartment. I realized it was coming from the same speaker that had announced the code orange this morning.

"We can talk about this later. It's a long conversation. There's only one mistake that you can make with my mom, and that's being late. Believe me; I've tested that limit many times," he said.

The word "mom" sounded unnatural coming out of his mouth. It was odd to hear him refer to anyone so informally. "Mom" was so plebeian, so normal.

He grabbed my hand, and we walked out the door.

"What are your mom's Veterox powers?" I asked as we entered the elevator. I knew he hated the word "powers," but it just sounded weird to put it any other way.

"She has the same abilities that I do. Of course, until a few days ago, I didn't know that I could also teleport like her. She doesn't use her abilities—she hasn't in years," he said.

I wondered what had made her stop, if there was a story behind it. I made a mental note to ask her later.

We exited the elevator on the ground floor and walked the familiar path toward the outdoor patio. The sun was still glimmering in the sky, but it was starting to fall down toward the horizon. Ezra, Isadora, Ethan, and Vivienne were all sitting down in their chairs talking to each other as we walked up. There were two open spots at the table, one between Isadora and Vivienne and the other between Ethan and Ezra. Vivienne and Isadora were smiling at me, and I assumed that they wanted me to sit next to them, so I walked toward their end, leaving Isaac to sit by Ezra and Ethan.

The food was already on the table. It was all Italian. I dished up some farfalle pasta with red sauce and picked a few pieces of bread out of the large bowl. A huge platter of fresh fruit was passed from person to person. I grabbed some raspberries, blackberries, and watermelon. Two bottles of wine were passed around, one a Chianti and the other a Sangiovese. I picked the Chianti, solely on the reason it was handed to me first. Everyone was too busy eating to have much conversation for the first few minutes, but once we were mostly finished, Isadora was the first to speak.

"How was the rest of your day?" she asked, slyly smiling at me.

"Um...it was good. Uneventful," I replied. I tried very hard not to look her in the eyes for fear that I wouldn't be able to stop myself from smiling.

"Yes, Isaac, how is your leg doing?" Vivienne asked. "I heard that Dori had to come up and rebandage it a little while ago."

No, don't ask about that, I thought.

"Yes, she did." He glared at Dori. "I suppose she needs to work a little harder on her wound-gluing skills so that doesn't happen again."

Dori glared back across the table at him, and then a smile crept across her face.

Oh no. I knew what she was about to say. I looked over at Isaac in horror. He instantly realized what was about to happen.

"Perhaps did you do something against doctor's orders that might have caused the wound to open back up? If I recall correctly, you were participating in a vigorous activity when it tore back open," she said.

My face burned. I felt the blood rush into my cheeks. I tried to look around in various directions so that nobody would make eye contact with me. It was too late. Ezra looked over at me. He immediately started laughing.

"What Ezra?" Vivienne asked.

"I was just thinking about how many evil glances Evangeline will receive from all of the women here when they find out Isaac has been taken off the market. I predict that I will gain some new admirers, which will be quite fun," he said, smiling.

I couldn't breathe a sigh of relief out loud, but I was certainly doing so in my head. I smiled at Ezra, grateful for the change in subject. He winked back.

Wait.

"What do you mean by 'all of the women'?" I asked.

"Oh, Isaac has been quite a hit with the ladies for a very long time. He's always stolen Ezra's thunder. I guess women find the international spy more attractive than the brilliant surgeon. Be prepared for a lot of mean looks," Isadora said.

Spy? He was a spy? He was a spy!

"Well, thank you, Dori. We haven't had that conversation yet. I'd hoped to do it a bit more privately." Isaac turned to me and mouthed, "I'm sorry." I looked away, ignoring him.

Ezra's voice broke through the silence. "Well to be clear, he's very good at his job. When you sign on to being an intelligence agent, one acknowledges that certain lies will have to be told in order to maintain cover. You don't go out and proclaim you're a spy." A wry smile crossed his face. "Also, in no way did he steal my thunder. I have no problem in the lady department."

"I wasn't referring to your difficulty in attracting women. It just seems like all of the ladies you really want end up with Isaac," Isadora said. Her face was beaming. She knew just how to twist the knife with her words. She was cunning.

Ezra countered back, "Shall I count out all of your relationships? There was Ava, Viola, and then Marchesa while you were with Adela. I think my point is made, so I won't go on with the entire list. You seem to be quite the romancer yourself, yet I don't see a ring on your finger."

Huh? Did that mean Isadora was a lesbian?

Sensing a war of words was about to occur, Isaac quickly changed the subject. "I couldn't tell you about being an intelligence agent, Evie. I was there to protect you and Rosa and to gather intel outside of the VHQ. It was my job. I didn't anticipate falling for you, which made the situation intensely more complicated. Honestly, I don't want to talk about it anymore here. It's a private conversation between you and me." He looked at me, trying to convey how uncomfortable he was with the situation.

"Don't be offended; Isaac operates sub rosa. He's not particularly partial to being open with his thoughts or feelings in public," Ezra said.

"But rumor has it he is quite the lover," Isadora said.

Jealousy was successfully engaged. The knife had been twisted.

"Oh really?" I said, glaring at Isaac.

"Dori, that was extremely inappropriate," Vivienne said angrily.

I forgot that Vivienne and Ethan were sitting at the table. While Vivienne appeared annoyed, Ethan seemed distant. I recognized the look in his eyes. His mind was in another place, and in this particular situation, I was grateful.

"Oh goodness, it's not like she has anything to worry about. The man's been in love with her for years. I told Evangeline earlier that I've never seen Isaac so passionate about anybody else. All you have to do is be in the same room with them for a few seconds to see the heat between those two. It's full-on sickening, soap-opera-y passion. I might also be slightly jealous," she said.

I grinned with delight. My whole face was smiling. Passion. I thought back to a few hours ago. I bit my lip and looked over at Isaac. His eyes were sparkling with excitement. I very seriously considered taking a bathroom break. I legitimately didn't know where the bathroom was. Isaac would be forced to come with me. I was glad that nobody had mind-reading powers at the table. Actually, I didn't know; maybe someone did.

Isaac interrupted my thoughts. "Have you sufficiently embarrassed us for the night, Dori? Can we move on to some other topics now?" he asked, in a joking yet serious voice.

She nodded and shrugged her shoulders.

"I'm sure you have a list of questions about the VHQ. Four of the most powerful Veterox on Earth are sitting here, at your disposal. Take advantage of this situation. Is there anything you'd like to ask us about?" Vivienne asked.

"Well I can't guarantee my questions will be interesting, but I do have a few. To start, why is the weather always so sunny and warm here? I'm guessing the answer has to do with weather modifiers. I've always assumed this area was one of the cloudier and rainier climates in the United States."

"Yes, it's weather modification," Vivienne said. "Once you've been here a bit longer, you'll notice the rain. There isn't any way to keep the vegetation this green without water, but we've calibrated it to occur at the most efficient times of the day. I suppose that's a bit of an oxymoron, because it almost never occurs during the day. Anytime between when the sun goes down around eight and the first few hours of light in the morning, it will rain.

"It's interesting to note that the timing is intentionally scrambled as to when it will occur between those hours. Early on in weather modification, the WMs set up the schedule so that rain would fall at four in the morning, for two hours, every single day. Nobody liked it. It didn't seem natural, and in an already-surreal world, normalcy turned out to be essential. They ended up changing it. Now it's set up to occur randomly throughout the night and early hours of the morning. It seems like such a trivial change, but it made a world of difference."

It didn't really seem that odd to me. Variation was what made life interesting. I didn't think anyone would want to live in a perfectly controlled bubble, or at the least, nobody would want to feel like they were.

"It seems as if VHQ technology would be advanced enough so that you could fly everywhere instead of driving. If that medevac plane was any indication, it looks like you can take off and land without much space. Why isn't everyone flying?" I asked.

Ethan responded, "It's a fairly straightforward answer. We do have the tech, but frankly, it's still much more efficient to take the rail or drive. It's expensive to waste the fuel on such a small distance. We also want to keep the air space open for emergencies, such as yours or Rosa's. With the population booming here, it's just not feasible for everyone to travel via air. There isn't enough space."

"Speaking of population, how many Veterox are there now? The original number was fourteen hundred and ninety-seven, right? How much of a boom have you seen in the past twenty-five years?" I asked.

"We've seen a dramatic increase in the past few years actually," Ezra said. "Many of the children, like Isaac, Rosa, and me, who were born during and after Z3C7 are starting to settle down and have their own children. As you may have guessed, Veterox couples have multiple children at a time. In fact, it is very uncommon to see a singleton. Consequently, we are seeing an explosion in population. Space is becoming more of a problem. As far as an actual number, it's hovering around eight thousand," he said.

"Do you know what the life expectancy is of a Veterox? Has anyone died?" I asked.

"Nobody has died naturally of old age. Although, that's to be expected, because the oldest Veterox are just now starting to hit their sixties," Isadora said.

"The short answer is that we don't know the life expectancy, but we suspect it's longer than a normal human. As a physician, I'm not seeing the normal breakdown that a human body goes through as one ages. At the least, it's happening at a far slower rate," Ezra replied.

"I'm wondering what the plan is for the future here? If the population is swiftly rising and the number of deaths is close to zero, will there be a point where you can't expand anymore?" I asked.

"You've hit the nail on the head," Isaac said. "That's precisely the biggest problem we are currently encountering. We are quickly running out of resources, and as the population shifts, the possibility that our 'secret' will be revealed to the general population increases. We've been planning the solution for the past few years, and we're on the precipice of an announcement. It's set to take place in a few months. Well, it was. With the current situation, we're wondering if it should be pushed further back—"

Ethan's voice interrupted, "Yes, the last few days have put us in a rather precarious situation. The threat from Delacroix is still being evaluated, but it's certainly thrown a storm our way. We don't want to take any chance of being perceived negatively among the world's population. Actually, we've taken painstakingly careful steps to ensure that we won't be viewed as threatening. That's the worst possible scenario," he said.

"I'm curious; how do you go about introducing a genetically superior race of humans to the rest of the world? It's really hard for me to imagine that there won't be negative backlash," I said.

"Well, we are trying to attack the issues from multiple angles," Ethan said. "Is it an ideal situation? No, but we're attempting to manage a controlled burn. It's inevitable that we'll be uncovered in the future. We're just trying to enter the world as a wave instead of a tsunami."

"There are four main issues we want to address," Ezra said. "First, we want to ensure that people feel safe. We will be playing up the fact that we've been alive for twenty-five years without any negative consequences. Secondly, we will introduce technology that makes the world irrefutably better, like the S-Sphere that encompasses VHQ, our advances in medicine, and more superficial things that just make life a little easier. The third issue is transparency, ensuring that we have nothing to hide. Some of the Veterox population will be moving out of the VHQ into secure areas of the US mainland. We will also be allowing people in to visit the VHQ."

"It's a large endeavor," Vivienne said. "You can imagine how stressful the last few days have been for all of us here. Everything we've worked for in the past three years could disappear."

"What's the fourth issue? You only listed three, right?" I asked.

"The fourth issue is a bit trickier; it involves reproduction," Isaac replied. "We can prove that a Veterox couple can successfully make a child, rather children, just as a human couple can. I, among many others, am an example of that. However, the most important component of integration between a Veterox and a human is the ability to reproduce. In other words, if we can't have children with humans, it would be a deal breaker, a huge red flag."

He paused. I could hear the sound of waves crashing on the beach nearby. I stared up at the bright stars shining in the dark black sky, waiting for Isaac to finish the answer. I could feel the mood shift.

"You are the link, Evie, and that's why you're being protected so fiercely. As the sole half Veterox on the planet, you're one of our biggest security concerns. I know this will sound arrogant, but it's nevertheless true. I'm the best agent in the field. I went back to Lincoln because I was assigned to ensure your safety. Well, also Rosa's. She's one of the most talented Veterox alive," he said.

"Rosa has such a strong connection with you. She would never have left to come live in the VHQ, even though it was infinitely safer for her," Vivienne said.

"Your dad was vehemently opposed to taking you out of society and into the VHQ. He wanted you to grow up in a normal environment," Isaac said. "He agreed to my return strictly on the grounds of safety, and he was entirely against telling you about the Veterox up until a few days ago. I told him about the upcoming announcement, which prompted him to change his mind. I wasn't expecting the decision to come so soon, and, as you know, I wasn't on board. Besides the safety risk, I had my own personal reasons. I'm sure you can wager a good guess as to why," he said, smiling at me.

Jesus. I felt like I was doing a one-thousand-piece puzzle but didn't have the box to see what the picture looked like. I had the edge pieces connected to make the border, and my brain could manage to find what looked like tiny kitten eyes, but the body pieces and background were a jumbled mess. Patiently, I sat, trying piece after piece to make a match, and slowly, the picture was emerging. My puzzle wasn't complete, but I knew that I was only a few steps away from being able to tell what the image was.

"So now what? What's the plan for me?" I asked.

"I don't know, Evie. Five years ago, I wanted you to be the public face for Veterox-humans. You are a twenty-one-year-old, forty-nine percent Veterox who is beautiful, intelligent, and kind. You are the quintessential human, and you descended from a Veterox-and-human marriage. It's the perfect unification. It's logical," he said.

His tone seemed angry or upset; I couldn't tell which one.

"But you've destroyed the logic behind it for me," he said. "My mind is conflicted. I don't want you exposed. If things were to go badly, you'd be one of the first targets. It's not worth wagering your life. I don't feel like I could adequately protect you."

He sighed. "I've spent the last few years carefully holding myself back from you. Somehow along the way, the switch flipped on, and I didn't realize it until it was too late. I can't turn it off. I've tried," he said.

He looked at his family. "I'm sorry. You know I never want anything. I want her."

The air was eerily silent. I glanced around the table. Everyone's eyes were transfixed on Isaac. I looked back at Isaac then pushed my chair out and stood up. I wanted to run, but I thought that might be a bit dramatic. Instead I walked steadily toward him, touched his arm, and bent down. "I want you too," I whispered into his ear, making sure nobody else could hear my hushed voice.

243

Isaac turned his head to meet mine. His fingers touched my hair, and he tugged on it, pulling me toward his mouth. Neither of us cared about the audience we had sitting a few feet away.

"Holy fuck. You weren't exaggerating, Dori. I never thought..." Ezra said.

I pulled away from Isaac. He placed his hands on my waist and pulled me onto his lap.

"I know! I told you!" Isadora said. "And the irony. The one girl he shouldn't be with."

"Isaac," Vivienne said, "there is nothing to be sorry about. I, well...I am a little bit speechless. In a wonderful way."

"What she means is that nobody at this table expected...that. We're just taken aback. Such a display of affection from the always-even-keeled Isaac Crailene? That's about as rare as a patient coming into the ER with a broken leg and not being in pain," Isadora said, laughing.

Ezra nodded his head in agreement.

Ethan interrupted, "Evangeline doesn't have to be involved. That was the easiest solution to the problem, but it's not the only one. We will come up with an alternative. There's a meeting tomorrow afternoon. We'll discuss it then."

"Not to detract from this glorious spectacle, but I need to leave for the hospital in about ten minutes. Evangeline, are there any other questions you want to ask?" Ezra said. He had a keen ability to change the subject at just the right time.

"What is the most interesting Veterox talent that you've seen?" I asked.

"Tellers," Isadora said, "and maybe healers."

"I would agree. Tellers are pretty remarkable," Ethan said.

Vivienne said, "Readers, like Rosa."

"I think tellers are the most interesting, but Ezra's abilities rank up there," Isaac said.

"I agree with Isaac," Ezra said, smiling.

"What are tellers and healers?" I asked.

Vivienne explained, "Healers are, as their name implies, able to heal. Some are only capable of regenerating themselves; others are able to heal different types of ailments. Not a very common talent. I think there are only five. Two of them are doctors at Violet Hope."

Ezra spoke, "A teller is a future teller. It's a pretty spectacular talent. These are the people who are able to see the future or, rather, futures. It's a rare ability as well. One, in particular, is the most accurate. Her name is Isla Brooke. She's both a teller and an empath, which is probably why she is so successful. All tellers are able to see every possible outcome that could occur in the future. Think about every choice you make in a lifetime. They are able to see the results of each choice, which number into the hundreds of thousands, but it's very hard to accurately predict which future is the most likely. Isla has a knack for understanding how people will choose."

"Will I get to meet her?" I asked.

"If you'd like, but don't expect her to tell you anything about your future. She only consults on important decisions, but regardless, she is captivating to speak with," Ezra replied.

He stood up and set his napkin down on his plate. "I'll update you all on Rosa if anything changes through the night. Thank you for dinner, Mom," he said.

"You're welcome. I'll walk you out," Vivienne replied. She stood up and accompanied Ezra down the path back toward the house.

"I have a meeting with Ellenora. You can stay here with Dori and my parents if you want, or I can walk you back up to the apartment," Isaac said.

"I think I'll head back up with you. I'm going to lie down. It's been an eventful day," I replied. I stood up, and Isaac followed behind me. "Thanks for dinner!" I said to Ethan. "Hopefully I won't be seeing you later, Isadora," I said, smiling.

"G...O...T," she replied, smiling.

Once we reached the elevator entrance, Isaac touched the pad, and the doors opened. We walked through, and the doors closed behind us. Isaac pushed me up against the wall. Our lips rushed together, and his hands ran up my body.

"Is anyone watching us?" I asked.

"Yes, but clearly I don't give a fuck," he replied. He ran his left hand up my leg, underneath my dress. "I wasn't serious," he said, referring to my lack of undergarments. "If I had known you weren't wearing any panties earlier...dinner would have been more interesting."

"That would have been very much welcomed," I replied.

The doors to the elevator opened. He grabbed my hand and pulled me out. "Isaac Crailene, Orchid," he spoke.

We crossed into the apartment and abruptly continued where we'd left off in the elevator.

He pulled back for a moment. "I have to go. I really do have a meeting with Nora," he said.

"Seriously?"

"Yes, she needs to update me on the Delacroix situation," he replied.

My disappointment must have been apparent.

"I'm sorry," he said, and a smile washed across his face. "I assure you I'd rather be here." He grabbed my hand and pulled it toward the zipper of his pants. My hand grazed against him.

"Isaac Crailene, did you just let me touch your penis?" I said.

"Maybe. By the way, was the answer to your question in the car sufficiently answered?" he replied. His smile turned into a grin.

"I don't know if I want to give you the satisfaction of my first impression," I replied.

"You just did."

My cheeks flushed.

He laughed, clearly satisfied with the reaction.

"How long are you going to be?" I asked.

"I'm not sure. We have a lot to cover, so it might be a while. Don't wait up. Actually, I insist that you go to sleep. You're going to be expending a lot of energy when I return," he said.

His mood turned a bit somber. "I have something for you." He walked over to a backpack sitting on the table and removed a small, rectangular object. It looked like some sort of memory card. "Hold on; I'm going to go grab the tablet so that I can show you how to use it," he said.

He returned to the entryway with the tablet. "This is a tablet and remote. It controls all of the electronics in the apartment. This disk goes into here." He shoved the disk into the matching spot on the side of the tablet.

"What is it?" I asked.

"As you now know, I'm an intelligence agent. I work with the US government; actually I'm an agent in the clandestine service for the CIA. It affords me certain liberties other citizens do not get. Let me just get down to it. This is a video of Charlotte's funeral. I wanted to make sure you were able to see it, and so I sent an agent to obtain the footage from a drone. On this memory card, you will also find pictures of the scene where your dad and Charlotte's bodies were recovered. They are very graphic. Obviously, it's up to your discretion on whether or not to view them. I want you to have closure. Some families need to see the body. Whenever you'd like to view it, it's here. I'll watch it with you, if you'd like, or you can view it by yourself," he said.

I felt sick. My natural reaction was to push the thoughts out of my mind, like I had been doing for the last few days.

"Thank you," I replied. Despite my somber feelings, it meant a great deal. I needed to understand every detail about their deaths, even the most morbid. Isaac knew that, and he didn't judge me for it. I smiled at him, trying to pull off looking as if I wasn't about to cry.

He pulled me to his lips and then let go of me. He glanced down at his watch.

"Go. Tell Nora hi for me. I'll see you later," I said.

The door opened, and he exited into the elevator.

{21}

Twenty-one

I held the tablet in my hands and walked into the bedroom. My white nightgown was lying on the bed, folded up nicely. A small slip of paper was lying on top of it.

Wear it for me?—I

I stripped all of my clothes off and carried the nightgown into the bathroom. The Japanese soaking tub looked appealing. I turned on the faucet and let the hot water fill the tub. I walked over to the window, looking out over the star-strewn sky. It was beautiful, but I couldn't keep my thoughts from wandering to my dad and Charlotte.

I still didn't understand why my dad and Charlotte died. If the Delacroix only wanted Rosa, why did they have to needlessly kill hordes of people to accomplish their goal?

I turned off the faucet and slipped into the tub. As much as I loved the feeling of the warm water, I wasn't enjoying sitting alone with my thoughts. I wanted to watch the funeral. I hadn't yet decided whether to view the pictures. I got out and grabbed a towel to dry off. The tub started draining automatically. I took the white nightgown off of the sink and pulled it over my head. Then I walked out of the door into the bedroom.

I pulled the covers back on the bed and slid in. After propping up a pillow, I grabbed the tablet and turned it on.

The pictures were the first files on the card, and I decided in that moment to view them. I clicked "view" on the folder, and the first picture popped up. It looked like a scene from a movie. The brick walls of the restaurant were collapsed, and tables were strewn about, some lying in the street. Plates and silverware were shattered everywhere. I noticed a red pool of blood in the bottom left corner and quickly saw the body it was coming from. It looked to be a young man. His body was lying in an abnormal position, and it was clear that several of his bones had been broken. The blood was pouring out of his thigh, where you could see a bone protruding. I felt sick. I clicked on the next one.

I immediately saw Charlotte and my dad. Just as Isaac had said, Charlotte was lying on the floor of the restaurant, and my dad was on top of her. His hands were placed above his head, shielding Charlotte's head. The wall had hit him just below his neck, and his head was propped up unnaturally. I could see one of his legs sticking out, and it was crushed halfway up the calf. Blood was pooled everywhere. Besides Charlotte's face, which was turned to the side, I couldn't see any of her body. Her eyes were closed, but her head looked swollen and purple.

It was too much for me, too real. I felt like I had been punched in the heart. I clicked the tablet off and placed it on the nightstand. I turned the lights off and pulled the covers up, and I cried for a long time. I didn't remember falling asleep.

I slept so deeply that I didn't wake up until Ezra's voice boomed across the room. "Evangeline."

I sat straight up.

"Evangeline," he said.

"What is it?" I asked. I could hear a shrieking voice in the background. "Where are you?"

"Evangeline, you and Isaac need to get to the hospital right now. Rosa woke up, and she's screaming for you two. She wants you here."

"Okay, I'll get dressed and head over there. Isaac isn't here. He had a meeting, and he said it might run late. I don't know how to contact him," I said.

"Hold on." I could hear him speaking in the background. "Dori, Isaac's not there. Ev said he was going to a meeting."

I couldn't hear her answer; the line was quiet.

"Evangeline, I'm contacting Vivienne. Meet her at the door in a few minutes," he said, sounding frantic.

"What's going on?" I said. The connection went silent. I rushed over to the closet and opened it to look for my suitcase. A huge white room with white drawers and racks full of clothes lining the wall stood before me. I didn't see my bag anywhere, so I just pulled a white dress from the wall. The hanger clunked to the floor as I changed out of my nightgown and into the white dress. I grabbed my flats and headed to the bathroom. I threw my hair up into a ponytail and walked to the door. I was surprised to find Vivienne standing a few inches in front of me.

"Geez, how did you get here so fast?" I asked.

"I teleported. We're teleporting over to the hospital," She said. Her voice was somber. She grabbed my hand delicately.

We arrived near the side doors Isaac and I had departed from the day before. "I can't teleport into the hospital. It's not allowed. Please follow me," she said, her tone deviating from her normal cheery, happy self.

I followed along as we swiftly walked through the side entrance of the hospital and down the halls. I could hear the piercing screams of Rosa's voice as we neared the ICU. I started running toward the sound. Something was horribly wrong.

When I was right around the corner from her room, I could finally make out what she was saying. "I was trying to tell you! Where is she?!" she screamed.

As I entered the room, I could see Ezra standing beside her. He looked over at me eerily, his face devoid of any expression. I looked past him to Rosa. She was sitting up. Medical equipment was strewn about the room. The breathing tube was still sitting on her bed, bloody. Clearly she had pulled it out herself. The look on her face conveyed the hysteria of the situation.

"Rosa, what's wrong?! I'm right here," I said. I grabbed her hand.

She calmed down almost instantly. Despite her waveless facade, I could feel the undercurrent of emotion. She was trying to ease the situation, and that's when I knew something bad had happened.

"Tell her," she said to Ezra.

"We can't find Isaac," he said. His blue eyes gazed into mine.

"What do you mean? He's with Nora. He left around ten thirty. What time is it?" I asked. I looked around frantically for a clock.

"It's five in the morning," Ezra replied.

It had been six hours. My brain finally started to connect the dots. I felt my stomach lurch forward, and the acid rose in my throat. Bits of red-and-white pieces flew out of my mouth, covering part of the bed and a little area of the wood floor beneath it.

Ezra grabbed a paper towel and handed it to me. He walked out of the room and asked a nurse to call a health assistant into the room to clean up the mess.

Tears fell down Rosa's face. She sobbed as she spoke, "I tried to tell you yesterday when you were here. I was trapped. I couldn't speak. I couldn't move."

Her blood pressure! She was trying to get our attention. That's why it was so high yesterday, I thought. My ears were ringing. I felt numb.

"What happened?" I asked.

"I wasn't the target. It was Isaac and you all along," she replied.

"How do you know?" I asked, my voice cracking.

"Just before the tornado hit, I could hear their voices. They had watched us all come into the restaurant—"

"Who?" I asked, interrupting her.

She explained, "What caught my attention initially were these voices. I couldn't place them—nobody around us was in close enough proximity to create them. I also heard Isaac's voice, and I knew that he'd gone to the restrooms with you. He was beyond my range. I listened in closely, and I realized what they were saying. A few other voices that I didn't recognize were talking to him. I couldn't hear them very clearly, but it sounded like they were speaking about taking you and Isaac back to Delacroix. I heard the other group of voices speaking about the tornado and how much destruction it was going to cause. I literally had just a few seconds to put it together, and that's when I yelled to Isaac as you were coming out of the bathroom."

I remembered back to the horrific sound of her voice that day.

"You two disappeared before they could reach him. I tried to tell Dad and Charlotte to run. I watched them get up. I heard the sound of dishes crashing to the ground, and then I was pulled away. Everything went silent," she said.

Isadora, Vivienne, and Ethan appeared in the doorway of the hospital room. Their faces conveyed distress. Isadora walked over to me and placed her hand on my shoulder. I could feel sadness radiating from her body.

Ethan looked over at me. "He's not here. Isaac was supposed to meet with Nora outside the VHQ after he left you at around ten thirty. We have verified that he did make it to the safe house, the one you two stayed at a few nights ago. After that we don't know what took place."

"I do," Rosa said. "He's in Delacroix."

"Why? What would they want with him?" I asked.

"He's the head of intelligence. They want everything," she said.

I sat there in shock.

"How did they do it?" Ethan asked.

Rosa took a deep breath and answered:

"After everything went silent, the first thing I remember is feeling cold. I could tell I was in a bedroom of a cabin because two of the walls were made of wooden logs. A small bed sat in the middle of the room, against the far back wall, and there was one window up high in the ceiling. It was dark, but I could see tiny white snowflakes falling onto it. A tall man I didn't recognize was in the room with me. He was wearing an odd type of armor. He didn't speak to me, but I could hear his thoughts. He was there to guard me. I could faintly hear other voices. One of them was Isaac, but, of course, it wasn't our Isaac. The other two voices I didn't know, but they were all conversing together.

A male voice asked if he thought I could hear what they were saying. A female voice answered back that it didn't matter, that it wouldn't be a problem.

"What are we going to do now?" the male voice asked.

"We will get Isaac. He'll come for her, and once he does, we'll follow him back to wherever Evangeline is hiding and capture her as well," she replied.

"How?" the male asked.

"Isaac will be here when it's time to cross the threshold to go back home. We'll use Rosa as bait. Once they have her, they'll transport back, and we'll follow. I'll be able to track him once I see him," said the male who sounded like Isaac. I was certain by that point that they were Delacroix.

"We don't need to kill Rosa; we can just render her unconscious until we have Isaac and Evangeline. I'll take care of that," said the female voice.

"If we can't get the girl?" the male voice said.

"Then we'll just take Isaac. He's the most important," she said.

"For the next thirty hours, they kept watch on me. I was fed and given water, but they wouldn't speak to me. They were very guarded with their thoughts or were out of range; I couldn't tell. Then about fifteen minutes before Isaac and Ethan got there, I heard commotion. The female came into the room, and for the first time, I saw what she looked like. She was in her twenties, with long black hair and dark skin, and she was wearing a very tight white dress. Without speaking a word, she walked toward me. She stopped a few feet in front of me and touched my head. I felt dizzy.

"Then I heard Ethan's mind, and I knew he was close. I was forced out of the cabin and onto the cold ground. I saw Isaac, the real one, running toward me, and I ran. Everything started to go blurry. I felt a tug at my ankle, and I fell down. It must have been Delacroix Isaac, as he also gashed the real Isaac's leg. Isaac pulled me up, and we ran back toward Ethan and a few other people I didn't know. The next thing I can remember is being outside of the VHQ."

"They must have followed us back to the VHQ, and when they couldn't get in, they waited. When Isaac left last night, they pounced. It's far too late to get to them. They've already crossed over into Delacroix. They had at least a six-hour head start. I'm sending a team up to Alaska right now, but I doubt they are over here," Ethan said.

"What do you think they will do with him?" I asked. My mind immediately thought of the horrible possibilities.

"I don't know. They'll keep him alive until they get what they need. I have absolutely no idea why they would need him," Ethan replied. I could tell he was angry. He quickly walked out of the room. Vivienne followed closely behind.

"I'm so sorry, Evangeline. I'm so sorry," Rosa said, crying.

"It's OK—" I said, but I didn't get to finish my reply. Rosa's eyes rolled back into her head, and she fell back onto the bed. Her body started shaking, and then she went limp.

"Stand back. Call a code! I need the crash cart. NOW!" Ezra screamed.

Isadora ran out the door.

Ezra climbed on top of Rosa and started CPR. He pushed down on her chest over and over again, giving rescue breaths in between.

"What can I do? What do you need?" I asked frantically.

"I need an intubation kit. I think there's one in the second drawer down," he replied.

I knew what to look for from working at Haven. I flung open the drawer and grabbed the endotracheal tube, a laryngoscope, and a packet of lubricating jelly. I quickly handed them to him and then went back for the airbag.

I could see Isadora running with a crash cart and several doctors rushing toward the room. I knew that I needed to leave.

I walked out of the ICU and down the hall. I could hear Ezra's voice, "I need epinephrine!"

I followed the exit signs toward the entrance of the hospital. My pace increased. The lobby was full of people. I wanted out. I walked faster. I saw the large glass doors to the hospital and headed straight for them. The humid, warm air swept past my face as I exited the building.

My legs started to run. My head obliged. Faster. I was sprinting. I followed the sidewalk leading away from the hospital. A small swath of tulips lined the concrete path. I trampled as many as I could, making sure to push my foot down into the dark brown dirt underneath. I resumed my sprinting pace. The blurry world passed by. My lungs ached, unable to keep up with my body, but I didn't care. I wanted to be in pain.

The path curved to the right, and as I rounded the corner, I immediately felt a sharp pain radiate up through my leg. My ankle gave out. I tripped and tumbled onto the grass.

Anger poured out of my body. I sat up and pounded the cement with my clenched hands. I pulled them across the rough concrete, intentionally trying to scrape my knuckles so that they would bleed. I was silently screaming. I reached underneath my dress and ripped the bandage off of my bullet wound as hard as I could manage. I wanted the physical pain to match the feelings in my mind.

I laid down in the grass and looked up at the blue sky above me. The pain I had inflicted on myself still didn't compare to the anguish in my mind. Tears cascaded down the side of my face into my hair. The sadness of my heart was too much for me to quell. I turned onto my side and pulled my legs up. My hands rested underneath my head, catching the tears as they dropped from my face toward the grass below. The sky turned dark. The clouds hung heavily in the air, casting a distinctive dark-gray color that I knew meant rain was on the way. A few drops splattered onto my face.

Splat...splat...splat...splat...splat...I felt the pounding of each drop as they fell onto my skin. It started as a sprinkle and turned into a downpour. I closed my eyes. Everything went silent.

{22}

Twenty-two

The distinct scent of perfume permeated the air. It was light and citrusy. A happy smell.

"Evangeline," a voice called out.

Immediately, I recognized it as Charlotte's. I looked around. A dirty, pothole-ridden road sat across from me. Cars passed by, but I noticed the drivers were sitting on the right side of the car, not the left side as was normal here.

A very old and dingy stone building was behind me. A metal sign read "The Blue Nile Restaurant." Hundreds of motorcycles were parked in a long line a few feet away from me. The sound of nonstop honking rang through the air. I was sitting on a stone bench. I looked beside me and saw Charlotte.

"Charlotte?" I said.

I reached over to touch her hand. My fingers pressed down into the soft skin of her palm. She felt real, but I knew it wasn't possible that she actually was.

"You're dreaming, but I'm real. I know that doesn't make sense. I wish I had time to answer all of the questions running through your mind. You'll wake up soon," Charlotte said.

Her voice was serious, and I knew that I needed to listen, not talk.

"The world is falling down around you, but you can't fall with it. You have to fight to keep yourself upright. It's going to seem like you're not winning. The earth will try to knock you off balance many times in the coming future. Fight with all that you have, Evangeline. Look at me," she said.

My red, tearstained eyes gazed back.

"You possess the strength. You possess the kindness. You'll need both."

"Charlotte, I don't know anything. I don't know what to fight for…" I was struggling to find the words to convey the sadness and defeat in my heart.

"Evangeline, you can't change the past. We're gone. Until the day you die, you'll be without us. You can't let that affect you," she said.

"I can't forget the people who make up all of my memories, Charlotte."

"You don't have to forget us, but don't fear the future because of the past," she said.

Her words resonated inside my head. For the past few days, it'd felt like I was riding a horrifying roller coaster, and I wanted off. I didn't want to go forward. The engineer was clearly a poor one and especially cruel. Everyone riding along with me had been picked off, one by one. I just wanted to release my seat belt and jump off instead of being subjected to whatever sadistic turn was next.

"Isaac isn't gone. Rosa is still hanging on. That's why you need to stay on this ride," she said.

"What about you and Dad? Why…" I said.

"Don't waste time looking for the reason why we died. Nothing you find will ever justify our death," she said.

I couldn't hear the horns anymore. Silence hung in the air for a moment.

"You've lost a lot in the last few days, but you're going to lose more if you fail to take action. Run. Sprint as fast as you can. Don't look back until you see me again," she said.

"Will I see you again?" I asked.

"We'll be here waiting when you reach the end," she said.

I knew the end meant my death.

"*Jeg elsker dig,*" she said.

"*Jeg elsker ogsaa dig,*" I replied.

I woke up. The rain was still falling from the sky. My dress was soaked, and the blood from my knuckles had run down my hands. I stood up. Fire raged in my heart. Euphoria rushed through my veins— a feeling that I had only ever experienced when a particular song struck the right notes and made me feel invincible or when a violin was strummed at just the perfect pitch so that it sent chills down my spine. I felt as if I could do anything. It propelled me. I took off, sprinting back toward the hospital.

The pavement curved around, winding its way back toward Violet Hope. I could see sun peeking through the dark-gray clouds, and it illuminated the massive complex as it rose up through the sky.

Ezra appeared several hundred feet in front of me. He was running toward me. His dark-brown hair was dripping with water. The light-blue scrubs he was wearing had turned a shade or two darker from the rain. He was visibly distraught. He stopped. I continued running and grabbed his arm as I passed by, pulling him along for a few moments until he caught up to my pace.

"You're bleeding. Are you all right?" He took in a deep breath. "What happened?"

"No, I'm not all right," I said. "Would you actually believe me if I claimed otherwise? I might be on the borderline of insanity. I just spoke with Charlotte. We are going to Delacroix."

ABOUT THE AUTHOR
A CROUCH

I grew up in rural Nebraska—in a town so small that it was considered a village. Although it only encompassed one square mile, in my imagination, the space was infinite. On any given day the town transformed into the setting for a spy club, a scavenger hunt, a hotel, or a trip back to the pioneer days. I spent summer nights with a huge group of "town" friends, playing four-hour-long games of Capture the Flag or Hide and Go Seek. Sometimes I would go on hikes, disappearing into the massive cornfields behind my house. Eventually, I grew up and moved away. I had a baby, got married, had another baby, and yet another. In comparison to others, my life has been very fortunate. I hope I never need to be reminded of that.